Breaking Faith

ALSO BY ANNA BLUNDY

Vodka Neat

Breaking Faith

ANNA BLUNDY

Minotaur Books

New York

A THOMAS DUNNE BOOK FOR MINOTAUR BOOKS.
An imprint of St. Martin's Publishing Group.

BREAKING FAITH. Copyright © 2008 by Anna Blundy. All rights reserved. Printed in the United States of America. For information, address St. Martin's Press, 175 Fifth Avenue, New York, N.Y. 10010.

www.thomasdunnebooks.com
www.minotaurbooks.com

Library of Congress Cataloging-in-Publication Data

Blundy, Anna, 1970–
    Breaking faith / Anna Blundy. — 1st U.S. ed.
        p. cm.
    "Thomas Dunne books" —T.p. verso.
    ISBN-13: 978-0-312-36865-4
    ISBN-10: 0-312-36865-8
    1. War correspondents—Fiction. 2. Women journalists—Fiction. I. Title.
PR6102.L86B74 2009
823'.92—dc22

                                                    2009010726

First published as *Double Shot* Great Britain by Sphere, an imprint of Little, Brown Book Group

First U.S. Edition: July 2009

10 9 8 7 6 5 4 3 2 1

For Shash

Breaking Faith

Prologue

We are in a cellar that smells as though it's full of wine-making equipment. Before the door shut I thought I saw some of those big glass globes that people used to keep wine in around here. Or is it olive oil? Anyway, there is a reek of alcohol. There's no floor though. I can feel soil under my hands and I can hear things rustling about. I have decided to think of them as lizards rather than snakes since, let's face it, there is nothing I can do about it either way.

I want to reach forward to touch his forehead or stroke his arm but, obviously, I can't because my hands are tied behind my back. I'm sure there's some trick and I wish I'd learned it. Isn't there some way of wriggling that makes the ropes just magically pop off? Though actually this is electrical flex, not rope, and, in any case, I seem to remember that the trick is to hold your wrists in a certain way, muscles tensed, while they are tying them. Too late now.

He was unconscious before they hauled us down here, but I can hear him breathing so he should be all right. I mean, clearly he's not all right. He's dying. But it's unrelated to this deeply unfortunate kidnap experience and they didn't hurt

1

him, I don't think. Punched me in the bloody jaw though. Bastards. I remember when I was very little and my mother's father had had a stroke, though I didn't know what that was at the time. Anyway, he was enormously tall and there was something particularly sad about how incapacitated he was, this huge man who kept falling. Such a long way to fall.

And now this big old man too. Dying. Dying like the rest of us with none of the heroics. Radiotherapy. Another six months. Chemo. Maybe a month or two. And eventually (assuming I can get us the hell out of here), a morphine drip and a gradual lapse into eternity. God, no, don't cry now. There are more important things to do.

My feet are cold, which is strange since it's so incredibly hot outside. The oranges were heavy on the trees and even the sea breeze, sitting out last night, was thick, salty and warm. They took my boots off after I kicked the one with the goatee in the face and broke his nose. A couple of the others laughed though so they probably hated him too. Sibling rivalry, I expect. Aren't they all brothers these types? Morons is what they really are. They must know who and what they're dealing with. How hopeless this is and how suicidal.

So, either I try and get my hands free and effect some kind of escape, or we are waiting for rescue. Will they ask for a ransom? From whom? From Eden maybe? From the *Chronicle*? Will someone pay it? And are we at least safe here from the others? Or have they realised now that he's dying? That it's all over, at last?

I just shuffled across in the dirt towards the sound of his breathing and leaned my back up against the wall next to him. Feeling me there, he seemed to wake a bit and to sit up. 'Hey,' I said and he rested his head down on my shoulder, his breathing shallow and rasping. I kissed him and sighed. There were crickets singing by the big wooden doors and, round the edges of them, I could see the blue, blue sky.

For the things we hope in the secret of our hearts. If they were realised, would they really be the answer we'd prayed for?

All this time I had wanted to rest my head like that, to close my eyes. And there was a dream in which it was real, my head on a broad shoulder, and everything all right. But, I think, I won't be assigned that role. Not in this lifetime. In this lifetime it will always be the other way round. I understand that now.

And so, that knowledge in mind, I grit my teeth and I start to scrape the flex round my wrists up and down against a sharp ridge on the damp wall. And the boys outside are shouting now and there is gunfire from up in the hills. Something is happening. Christ, I thought. We're going to walk into a hail of bullets like Butch Cassidy and the Sundance Kid if we ever get out of here. And I think I must have said it aloud.

'Like Butch Cassidy and the Sundance Kid.' Because he whispered from my shoulder, almost a croak now, but sense of humour intact, a smirk in his voice, 'Which one am I?'

I laughed, despite myself, and my eyes filled with tears.

'You're Sundance, of course. Just like Robert Redford.'

Chapter One

It seems as if the whole entire bloody world has changed since Tamsin dragged me into her office to start going on about Cairnbridge. Office being a bit of an overstatement since the whole place is really just lots of pieces of chipboard compartmentalising everything and, if you're really important, which she is, some Perspex and a door holding your bits of chipboard up. Not exactly a walnut desk and a view down the Hudson or anything.

'Zanetti! Get your arse in here,' she shouted, chewing the end of her pen. She thinks this lends her gravitas. It doesn't. The fact that her skin is entirely grey, having spent less than ten minutes in natural light over the past ten years, probably does though. That and her Charles and Camilla scoop. She got sent the Camillagate tapes. Not that this involved any actual intrepidness on her part, but it guaranteed her a lifetime of employment in newspapers and the respect of her peers. She lives with one of the subs and thinks nobody knows. They drive in together and then ignore each other all day in one of these office absurdities I wish I didn't know about. Anyway, in I went.

Since I had Ben (hacked out at the last minute when his heart started failing, and mine too) I've been 'helping' on the foreign desk. A fat lot of help I am. I have to phone up friends in the field and ask for five hundred words by four o'clock.

'Hi. Blitz? Can you file on the news of the day? Who's doing what. Who's dead. What are we doing about it.' I sigh and look at my bitten nails.

'Zanetti? Is that you? Fuck are you doing on the desk? Christ, it's a mess here. They've forgotten who the hell they're supposed to be fighting, the treaty's not holding and . . . Shit! OK. Got to go. Talk later.'

My stomach twists and writhes in an agony of jealousy and then I haul my cowboy boots up on to the desk in an effort to seem more in control. Anyway, they're all as sick of me here as I am of them. I can't smoke at home so I spend most of the time out on the metal stairwell calling the nanny and holding a cold espresso in a plastic cup.

So, anyway, I assumed I was about to get sacked.

''S up?' I asked.

'The Editor's got a thing . . .' she said.

'I always imagined he must have,' I nodded, sitting down.

Tamsin rolled her eyes back in her head. Hey, if you don't laugh and all that.

'The Editor's got a thing about Cairnbridge,' she said, trying not to look at me.

I groaned and threw my head down on to her desk with my arms over my head.

'Now, Faith. I knew you'd be like that . . .' Tamsin sang.

I sat up. 'Yeah. Well I am like this. What is WRONG with him? We have been the only paper printing these nutty conspiracy theories since it bloody happened and that Libyan JUST got sent down AGAIN in the Hague, as if he needed retrying when about a thousand people SAW him put a case

6

that said "BOMB" on it on the plane!!!' Not pinpoint accurate, but the basic deal. Plus which, it really was an awfully long time ago now.

It's true I wasn't handling the situation that brilliantly but, man alive, the editor's preoccupations were tedious. Everyone knows, of course, that you have to be clinically insane to be a newspaper editor. It's no secret. I mean, look at Andrew Neil. It's like being the Prime Minister or something. If you really really want to be it then it's a sure sign that you shouldn't be allowed to be it. But, obviously, nobody nice and sane and normal wants the job so . . . Well, the psychos just have it in the bag.

Our editor is obsessed with Princess Diana and is convinced she was murdered by Christian fundamentalists to stop any Muslim ever becoming formally connected to the Royal Family. Basically, he met her once at a thing and decided, despite a mountain of evidence to the contrary, that she was thenceforward his best friend. He lost about four stone when she died. Don't get me wrong. He could have afforded to lose ten.

His other obsession is Cairnbridge. He has put the 'Under Scrutiny' team on the story about fifteen times and given page after page of space to all the madmen who claim they worked for the CIA and know what happened and it wasn't these Libyan blokes and the reason that the US government and CIA and everybody else claims not to know who on earth they are and dismisses them as random loonies is because they 'know too much'. Yuh-huh. Well, let me tell you, I know too much. FAR too much.

'Zanetti!' Tamsin shouted.

I had accidentally lit a cigarette. The smoke alarm started

wailing and before I could even dunk it in Tamsin's coffee cup, this security guard leapt in with his hand on what I could swear was a gun.

'Oh my God! You are ARMED!' I said to him.

'Since July,' he nodded. 'I'll just switch that off for you. Naughty naughty,' he tutted, climbing on to Tamsin's desk in his black boots.

'That's me,' I said.

Tamsin leaned her head round his legs and tried to maintain some level of dignity. 'As you indubitably know, it is the twenty-fifth anniversary this year . . .'

Oh, Lord save me. 'Indisputable,' I said.

'And The Editor . . .' she went on. It's not me putting the capital letters on The Editor. She did it with her voice. Why she couldn't just call him Sam like a normal person I have no idea. 'The Editor is keen to put together a special commemorative issue of the paper . . .'

'Jesus, Tams! I thought we were trying to attract a new generation of readers. I thought we were supposed to be sucking in those poor fools who weren't even born when this happened. Seriously, I'm going in to talk to him!' I said, standing up and turning to go.

'Faith. Luvvy. Sit down,' Tamsin whispered. The security man with his big gun had gone and she had her desk back to herself. She wiped away imaginary boot prints with the palm of her hand. Her fingers are pale and bony and made death white by the black suits she wears. 'Faith. Do you honestly think I didn't try to talk him out of this? Do you think I didn't say everything you've just said.'

I sighed and took another cigarette out of the packet and put it back in again.

'No. I think you nodded and said, "Oooh, Sam. What a superb idea. Let's do it!"'

It's hard to tell in the green sepulchral flicker of a dim fluorescent strip light, but I think that Tamsin actually blushed. She bloody well ought to have done. 'Well. Your views aside,' she said, making new piles of paper unnecessarily in front of her. Hell, we hardly even use paper any more. She'd probably emptied out her recipe drawer or something. 'We are putting together a commemorative issue which, yes, will include some of the various theories about the bombing that The Editor has espoused over the years. However, he would also like a hard news scoop for the front.

'This is where you come in. Under Scrutiny has consistently failed to identify various of the actual people involved . . .'

'Yuh. Because, right, it was these TWO LIBYAN BLOKES who nobody was allowed to interview because they are IN PRISON!'

People were peering in at us and my hair had frizzed out of its bobble and was looking a bit wild. I have a blonde afro and Ben is always sucking coils of it like I used to do when I was little.

'Under Scrutiny has consistently failed to identify various of the . . . well, the drug mules who were using flights to the US with government permission and, most importantly in The Editor's eyes, the person who issued the Reykjavik warning. I'm sure you know about the warning . . .'

I banged a fist dramatically on Tamsin's desk. She didn't flinch. 'Nah. I've worked half my life on this paper but I've never bothered to read a word. The Reykjavik what?'

Actually, it was true that I didn't always manage to get through the whole entire paper cover to cover every day, but there was no need for my boss to know this and, anyway, obviously I knew about the Reykjavik warning. Basically, two billion years ago when this thing happened, somebody phoned the US Embassy in Reykjavik to tell everyone it was going to happen and the notice was posted on embassy bulletin boards all round the world but nobody bothered to tell the security people in Frankfurt, even though the warning specifically mentioned Frankfurt as the conduit for this bomb. Yes, conduit.

'Faith? Find the guy who gave the warning, get him to say he made the warning, write the piece and then pick up your pay cheque as usual. A picture would be nice. Bye.'

Ooooh, no way. No way. No way. Passport to failure assignment. Now it's not that I hold the Under Scrutiny team in reverent awe (they do that for themselves) but I'm sure they made every effort and all that.

'I'm not doing it.'

'Fine. Tell Sam that. And good luck finding another job where they'll send you anywhere with a baby, an alcohol problem and an attitude,' she said, tapping send on the email that had been preoccupying her throughout our little meeting.

'Ahh. Tams. It's almost sweet how you take out the emptiness and futility of your life on your staff.'

I blew her a kiss on my way out, slomped down at my desk and wrote 'Cairnbridge' in Google. That's about how intrepid I was feeling that afternoon. Interestingly, even this word is a contentious point. The Americans call the disaster TAA 67.

Anyway, I don't have an alcohol problem so she can fuck off. I started going to meetings when I was pregnant in Moscow and it turned out to be quite fun because people get up and talk about all the terrible things they did when they were drinking, like sleeping with their husband's best friend and stuff that they would almost definitely have done sober but then wouldn't have had the dream excuse of seventeen gin and tonics. I didn't imbibe a single drop of anything for nine months and now it's not as if I'm rolling around drunk the whole time, so I don't see why she thinks she can make a big deal out of it.

Christ, it wasn't long ago that it was basically obligatory to be pissed in the office after lunch. Down El Vinos for ten bottles of claret and a tongue sandwich and sober again by the time the paper's put to bed. That was, admittedly, in the old days when the print unions were king and Docklands was still a swamp. Eden's on my case now too, as if he's sober as a judge. He's had this epiphany which basically means living in a huge house up a mountain in Tuscany while he works on his China book and writes a column about Tuscan life for the *New Yorker*. No, honestly. I mean, if that isn't money for old rope I don't know what is. 'As the evening sun goes down over my small olive grove and the lizards dart into the last spots of dappled light . . .' You know the type of thing. Anyway, like all epiphanies it was a huge great big steaming heap of selfishness and meant that I was lumbered with the sodding baby. Not that he's a sodding baby. He is a little slice of heaven and squashy enough to make the whole festering world worthwhile. But still. I'm lumbered with him while Eden makes friends with the local signorinas and learns where to pick mushrooms after the rain and all that stuff that Russians are so good at. He had Don and Ira to stay from Moscow last time I took Ben over and you could hardly drag Ira out of the forest, so mad was she for the porcini or whatever they are. Don, who was once an award-winning war photographer, says that domestic life in suburban Moscow has turned him into a bloody mushroom.

Anyway, Eden claims that he now drinks like an Italian. A glass at lunch and one or two at dinner and bed before ten. Well, congratulations.

'Let me tell you, Jones. If you were schlogging into Tower sodding Bridge every day and staying awake with a baby, no, YOUR baby, all the livelong night you'd be drinking a whole load more than that. I mean, I could probably survive on a sip of spring water and a truffle if I had your life,' I said to him. Or maybe I just say it to him in my head a lot. Whatever. I liked the old Eden who I could count on at a midnight check-point when dope-crazed teenagers were pointing Kalashnikovs at our heads. May his book's lone reader perish. Actually, that'll probably be me in the end. The reading it and the perishing. I mean, if there is someone alive who wants to plough through Eden Jones's research on Chinese economic development over the last forty years. You? Surely not . . .

So, I called him after my 'meeting' with Tamsin.

'Jones,' I said.

'Oh God! Is Ben OK?' he choked.

'Bloody hell. I don't know. I'm at the office. Call the nanny. Jones, listen. Do you know anything about Cairnbridge?'

He laughed. I could imagine him at his desk, looking out over his fruit orchard.

'Is that seriously actually birdsong I can hear?' I asked, lighting my fag.

He laughed again. It was, though. 'That man is a lunatic. Hasn't anyone told him that the Hague upheld the ruling against the Libyan? You should mention it Eff Zed.'

'Yeah, well I would, but he'd sack me. We're doing a twenty-fifth anniversary edition . . .'

That got his attention.

'A quarter of a century. Makes a girl think,' I nodded.

'Holy shit. Is it really twenty-five years? I can't be that old. I still haven't decided what to be when I grow up.'

'A tosser?'

'Oh yes. That was it. No, honestly though. God.'

'All right. All right. We're old. Anyway, we're doing this anniversary edition thing . . .'

'Whooooh! That should send circulation through the roof!'

'Oh my God! Eden! Seriously. You've got to help me. Didn't you go to Cyprus?'

'Yeah. I did a whole investigation for the tenth bloody anniversary. The thing for the *Telegraph*. Big budget. I went all over the place. But Faithy, let me tell you. It was that Libyan bloke . . .'

'OK. OK. I know. It's not him I've got to find. Where is he, anyway? Scotland? Did they extradite him to Libya? I've got to find whoever made the Reykjavik call thingy.'

'No chance.'

'Great. Thanks. Bye then.'

'Look. Get the next flight to Pisa. I'll pick you up. You're welcome to all my notes. Bring the nanny though, will you? I've got a lot of work to do.'

'Sure. If you pay for her flight.'

'Faith . . .'

'Eden . . .'

'OK. No nanny.'

'OK.'

Chapter Two

Now you might think that having a baby together would have clarified things between Eden and me. That is, if you've never had a baby. Everybody who's got one knows it makes things a billion times less fathomable than they already were. When two parties can't sort it out, does adding a third help? It does not.

I did tell Eden I was having our baby in the end, of course. Well, it seemed churlish not to. There was a certain point at which it became hard to disguise from the rest of the world, so, obviously, he was going to need to know. It was when I'd come back from Moscow to have lunch with a publisher. She took me to Orso where we ate mini pizzas with goat's cheese and asparagus on top.

She kept these black sunglasses on and talked to me in a thin voice about writing my memoirs. Well, that's got to make you feel old. 'What am I, about to die or something?' I thought. She had heard, she told me, fishing some photocopies out of her bag on the floor, that a senior British television executive working for an American network had called his colleagues into a meeting to tell them that they needed 'more tarts in the trenches.' This, she thought, would be a good title for a book. *Tarts in the Trenches.*

'Is somebody supposed to be a tart in this scenario?' I laughed, fiddling with the foil on my packet of Nicorettes – a neurotic pregnant woman in a restaurant. I was joking but she looked embarrassed.

'No, I didn't mean . . .' she said, and we both had a sip of our mineral water.

'It's OK,' I smiled at her. Anyway, then somebody recognised me and was staring incredulously at my stomach. I winked at him.

'Zanetti?' he asked loudly, nearly knocking his bottle of claret off the edge of the table. I think he works for Associated Press. Derek. Derek or Craig. Won something for writing about a schoolful of tiny corpses he found in Rwanda. I remember his face when he turned up at the Mille Collines, took us all out on these Toyota pick-ups into the dust, guarded by red-eyed teenagers with missile launchers over their shoulders. Don McCaughrean was sick. Well, Derek or whoever you are. You deserve the claret. I patted myself.

'Yup. Turns out I am biologically female, after all. What do you know,' I said.

And after that I called Eden to tell him the news. Don't know what I'd been waiting for really. Did I think it was still not technically true if I hadn't told the baby's father? Probably.

'Resign from Moscow, immediately,' he said.

'No,' I told him, though in fact I came back to London in the next reshuffle (i.e. spate of sackings) anyway.

And I said I'd do the book even though it feels like writing my own obituary. Someone once told me that the key to making good decisions about your life is to write your own

15

obituary every now and then and see if you are pleased with the sound of it. He didn't have much to say about what to do if you are not pleased with the sound of it though. Come to think of it he died of an enormous cocaine overdose a couple of years ago. Eloquent enough.

Eden did an 'oh darling, let's move in together and be a family' schtick for a while. He loves to pretend he means it – hey, maybe he even thinks he does, but it is a mad fantasy. The suggestion is, basically, 'Let's try and be somebody else.' I mean, who are we trying to kid? His mountain-top epiphany won't last another six months and he'll be back at war again before his olive harvest's in. And as for me . . . Well. It hardly takes a genius to see that I'm not going to be pruning roses and making jam. Not in this lifetime.

You get to an age, I suppose, when all the angst about what you're going to be like is over and you're left with whatever you're left with. I can't pretend I don't get butter-flies in my stomach when I get off a plane into a blanket of heat to have some moustachioed official's gun pointed at my head. I want to drive out to the front line in my flak jacket and a sandstorm and find out what's happening from the boys who are lying in the dirt with a grenade in their fist. I don't have to. I want to.

So, Ben lives with me and I would die for him without a second thought. I have never smiled like I smile at him, never felt how I do when he says, 'Mama.' Dying becomes a frightening thing only because he would be left motherless, not for all the big black abyss-like existential reasons that pre-child hangovers accentuate.

Die for him, of course. But I won't live a living death for him. I've seen people do it. Atrophying in mind and body as they sit in a grey tarmac playground weeping with loneliness and boredom. Starved of physical and mental stimulation and, mistaking this for actual hunger, getting fat. Not that there is much danger of that in my case. In fact, I should put some weight on. You don't get too many calories in an espresso.

I think, I hope, he will agree one day that he would rather have a happy (hell, it's all relative) mother who might not be there every second of every day, than a bitter rag of a person whose despair would surely take him down with her. That's the choice I made. Sadly, however, until now Tamsin wouldn't listen to my pleas to be sent on assignment again. It's true I had a bit of a rocky patch after Baghdad (went mad) and then when she finally put me out in the field again (well, only Moscow but what can you do?) I went and got knocked up. So this stupid pointless Cairnbridge thing is actually quite a big deal. If I find this bloke, assuming it is a bloke and assuming he is alive and assuming that if both those things are the case he will speak to me, then I might be in a position to pick my assignments again.

I thought I might just shrivel away and die when bloody Alessandra Biagi got sent to Jerusalem after the Israelis went into Lebanon. I had to talk to her on the phone and edit her copy (can't string a fucking sentence together) and know that she was sitting under a lemon tree by the fountain at the American Colony, which is my favourite hotel in the known universe, even though my friend Shiv killed herself in it. 'Yeah, I was just out in Ramallah,' she'd say, and I'd picture the dusty road and the palm trees and the big piles of water melons for sale and the sunset over the desert and the concrete hell that is a Palestinian city and . . . Well, Docklands just doesn't really do it for me in the same way.

I went home that afternoon when Tamsin officially gave me 'The Reykjavik Job' and gave Kristy, the nanny, the week off.

17

(She gets paid anyway so she's always elated – she has the word 'serendipity' tattooed on her shoulder and an earring in the bit of skin between her inside top lip and her teeth. Why? Who can say.) Ben cried when she said goodbye and I tried not to be pissed off. That's the price you pay, of course. The price I pay, rather. Anyway, I read him *Hairy Maclary* on the Gatwick Express and he did all the woofs. I told him we were going to see Daddy and he bounced up and down on my lap. The first call only hours away now – strange to look at life that way round, to think about how you'd feel if you'd known.

So perhaps it's only retrospectively that the airport seemed different. Normally I'm travelling on my own, running late, getting the flight nobody else is getting – the one with all the extra security and the tense people. I've always thought of airports as full of adrenalin, everyone doing vodka shots at the bar, smoking in the 'smoking area', running for the plane.

But now all I could see was families, women with pushchairs and fathers queuing for the bureaux de change. People going off to their holiday homes; 'Don't forget that thousand euros for Stefano and the roof.'

I know it's weird, I do watch the news and all that (stranded people, strikes, cancelled flights), but I've never personally associated airports with holidays. Come to think of it, I'm not sure if I've ever actually been on a holiday as an adult. It would make me nervous. Stuff going on while I had to sit by the sea and dig my toes into the sand. But here they were, thousands and thousands of people doing exactly that, already wearing the weird clothes they were going to be wearing on the beach. And here I was, still in my leather jacket, jeans and cowboy boots, but pushing a pushchair. When I sat down at that champagne bar a young guy with hair shaved like a marine looked up at me, interested. I smiled. A bit young, but nice not to be ruled out on grounds of age and haggardness. There is a brilliant bit in the Disney *Beauty and the Beast* where the narrator tells of a woman coming to the door and the prince being 'repulsed by her haggard appearance'. Hey, she'd probably just had a few too many bevs the night before.

Speaking of which, the stewardess gave me two bottles of Sauvignon Blanc with a one eyebrow raise because I stopped a drunk man insulting her. 'Thank God we're going to a civilised country!' he shouted. He wasn't allowed to keep talking to his agent on his mobile. 'Sorry, Danny. This trolley dolly is making me switch off.' He was about to start yelling at her.

I reached across the aisle to shake hands. 'Hi, I'm Faith,' I said. 'Tell me about your book.'

He seemed pleased. There was a rough patch just after Ben was born when my approach stopped working, but it's all better now. I hadn't realised I cared until I didn't have it any more. I just thought all men looked pleased when a woman sat down next to them. It turned out not to be true. I'm not proud of caring. But I do. Anyway, his book was about someone with a tumour on his head that took over his mind. Or maybe I misunderstood.

Eden met us at the other end dressed in this ridiculous outfit that is somehow connected to his whole Tuscan thing. He, who normally wears jeans and a white shirt, strode towards us in a pair of mustard-coloured trousers, a coral shirt and a green cashmere jumper slung round his shoulders.

'Ciao. Ciao. Benvenuti,' he said, grabbing Ben off me and covering his face with kisses. An Italian woman with a lap dog on a thin pink lead looked on approvingly. She would. Men get points for liking their own children. Women don't.

'What's with the outfit?' I asked, lighting a cigarette.

Eden spun round sending out wafts of aftershave. 'I've gone Italian,' he said, bumping into a bloke holding a sign up. 'Andiamo.'

The whole airport at Pisa smells of coffee and pizza and there are shops everywhere selling things you actually want. I saw the guy from the champagne bar in the airport. Funny because I hadn't noticed him being on the plane. Then again, why would I?

On the way 'home' (and it was here that he was imagining we'd be setting up this life of pastoral idyll in which I would presumably be buxom and kneading bread dough – I was tempted, but only by the fantasy) Eden wanted to stop and get some trout. 'You'll love Enrico,' he told me. I felt a lesson in Tuscan life coming on. In a minute he would start telling me unexpected things about Italian vocabulary. 'Did you know Vespa means wasp? You see? It looks like a wasp, Faithy.' Uh huh. 'Guess what ciabatta means. No, go on! Guess! What does a ciabatta loaf look like? Any ideas? Slipper!' Right.

'Who are you?' I asked him. He thought I was joking. People always think I'm joking. It's a problem I have.

We drove up alongside what looked like an abandoned warehouse by the tumbling river. There was a wooden sign on which someone had scrawled 'Trote Vive'. Eden got out of the car, beckoning to me and rang a bell signposted 'campanello' with an arrow. The bell wiring looked as if it might electrocute him. Ben, lucky for him, was asleep in the baby seat in the back of the Cinquecento (another piece of Eden's strange dream). We waited by the big metal doors in the cold dark and after a couple of minutes a bloke pulled up in an Ape, one of those 60cc three-wheeler cars. (FYI, ape, pronounced ahpeh, means bee.)

'The bell rings at his house up the hill,' Eden explained.
'Right,' I nodded, stamping my boots and smoking.

Enrico, who was smoking too, but without taking the cigarette out of his mouth at any point, unlocked the chain on the door and we went inside. It was even colder in here, a vast vast empty space with one flickering bulb hanging from a dusty wire, the river diverted into the building (which, apparently, used to be a paper mill) and into large vats of squirming fish, all the tanks haemorrhaging water in frightening spurts. There were bits of old furniture scattered about – a chest of drawers, a jug and bowl, a Singer sewing machine that you'd have worked with your foot – covered in a thin layer of cold fishy slime. I know this because I ran my finger along the top of a dresser and regretted it.

So, Enrico puts a huge net into the water and catches six or ten glittering fish, all of them trying to leap from his clutches. He took the two biggest ones out with his hands and bashed them quickly on the head with a wooden stick ('The Irish call it a "priest",' Eden helpfully informed me. 'They would,' I said), weighed them on a set of scales that I imagine the village store might have had in the 1800s, gutted them and handed them to Eden in a plastic bag. We got back into the car, Eden deeply satisfied by the fishdeathhorror experience, where Ben was still fast asleep, sucking the blanket he came home from hospital in. And it was still a twenty-minute drive up the winding one-track road to the house. We saw a porcupine dashing for the bushes.

Bitch about the symbolism of it though I might want to (and will), Eden's house is really lovely. It's miles up this mountain in a place that doesn't look like the Tuscany on postcards at all. It's lush and green and remote and his village is a dead end at high altitude with a population of about

21

thirty very old people (half of them bedridden) and a lot of wild boar. Tonight the whole place was in a cloud and the air smelled of the chestnuts people burn on their fires. The house is pink and crumbling with a wrought-iron balcony at the front and a fountain in the front garden. It's got terra-cotta floors ('cooked earth, it means. Well, it makes sense. Panna cotta means cooked cream.' Unsolicited information is one of the things I hate most in the world. I mean, if you wanted to know you'd ask or you'd look it up, now wouldn't you?) and beamed ceilings and huge fireplaces that you could roast a hog in. In fact, it is basically obligatory to roast a hog in them.

'Welcome home,' he said, kicking the front door open, Ben in his arms, a smell of last night's garlicky supper warming the house up. I flicked a light on.

'So where's the Cairnbridge stuff?' I asked, dumping my bag and the folded up pushchair. 'And wine.'

Eden disapproved of my not settling in first, doing family things. I can't. It makes me twitch. He put Ben on his hip and opened a bottle of wine out of his big blue fridge that looks like a 1950s Chevrolet.

'Glasses up there,' he nodded. I hauled the glasses off a green shelf and took them into the kitchen.

'I put the Cairnbridge stuff out on my desk,' he said and reached out to touch my hair. I considered softening for a second but decided against it.

'Great,' I smiled, took my wine and skipped up the stone stairs to the study. There was a whole heap of paper on the desk – typed stuff, official documents, trial transcripts, notes Eden had made himself. I pulled the chair out with my foot, scraping it across the flagging, and sat down, not expecting to find any of it remotely affecting. I could hear the boys gurgling downstairs and it was all I could do to stifle the warm cosy feeling that my stomach was trying to have. Must have been the wine.

All systems in a 747, including communication and navigation systems, are located in a control centre two floors below the cockpit. The explosion would have smashed through the wall separating this vital centre from the forward cargo hold, violently shaking the flight-control cables. Crash investigations revealed it was this blast that caused a roll, pitch and yaw motion in the forward section of the fuselage.

God. That vocabulary. Fuselage. Bulkhead. Roll. Pitch. Yaw. Cables. The only time you read the word 'cable' in the press is when one has snapped, its two ends flying backwards, twisting, flailing. Was it cold in here or was it this stuff that was making me shiver? My dreams have plummeting lifts in them sometimes.

Eden had underlined the sentence: 'A section of the 747's roof several feet above the point of detonation peeled away.' Something was tapping at the inside of my skull. I lit a cigarette. A memory? People say things are on the tip of their tongues but I don't have a problem with the vocalising. It's the fishing out that's laborious.

The 231 passengers and 14 crew were all killed. When the cockpit tore off, a tornado-force wind must have rushed through the fuselage, ripping clothes off passengers and making service trolleys and other items into lethal shards of shrapnel. Loss of air pressure meant the gases inside people on the plane expanded to around four times the normal volume, making their lungs swell and then collapse. Anything not fixed down was blown out of the aircraft into an air temperature of minus 50 degrees Fahrenheit. Their six-mile fall lasted no less than two minutes. Some passengers were still attached by their seatbelts to the fuselage, and landed still buckled into their seats. Though they must have lost consciousness through lack of oxygen, forensic examiners think some passengers regained consciousness as they fell into the oxygen-rich lower altitudes. Dr Graham W. Cheam, director of the International Center of Forensic Sciences at North Carolina State University, examined the autopsy evidence and believes the cockpit crew, some of the stewards and 147 passengers survived the bomb blast and the depressurization of the plane and were probably alive on impact with the ground. Dr Cheam informed police that unmistakable marks on the pilot's thumb revealed that he had been hanging on to the yoke of the aircraft as he came down to earth and may well have been alive and conscious when he landed. Captain MacDonald, the first officer, the flight engineer, a flight steward and some of the first-class passengers were discovered still buckled into their seats in the nose section where it landed in a field. The inquest heard that the flight attendant was still breathing when found by a farmer's wife, but she died before help arrived. A male passenger was also found alive and doctors think he may have lived had he been found more quickly.

Was I tired? I found it impossible to distance myself from this story, sitting upstairs while the trout fried. I fell through the cold sky with that flight attendant as if in a dream, feeling the coarse nylon of her uniform against her neck and her sensible fat-heeled shoes flying off her feet, the impact of her skull on the ground and the blood that would have rushed into her nose and mouth, the relief – perhaps even relief? – of feeling the solid earth holding her and smelling the grass and the dirt before she died, her head singing with the rushing wind and the deafening suck of the explosion, the scraping metal. And I thought about the captain and his thumb. How tight can you hold this? Go on. How tight, MacDonald?

Why is it that some things grab you more than others? I mean, Christ, the number of bodies I've seen, the terrible things that have happened to so many people since this one thing. Rwanda and Yugoslavia, Afghanistan, Iraq. The murder, rape and torture that never end, however many people scrunch up their eyes and squeeze prayers out of themselves that any compassionate god would surely answer, their hands pressed together as tightly as that poor thumb on the throttle. That little pink thumb that his mother had once kissed, delighted by its mere presence in her rose petal life. I suppose this stuck because it is the stuff of nightmares, carnage out of nowhere wreaked on the unsuspecting. Or I wonder, if on some level, I knew. Perhaps truth fills the air like invisible cobwebs, wrapping itself around those who are searching and even, sometimes, those who aren't.

Fucking hell, but I was almost crying. I think I was. And it was then that my mobile phone rang. It plays 'Love Me Tender'. No, it does.

'Your phone's ringing, Zanetti!' Eden shouted up. It was right next to me. It annoys him that I don't always answer it. And that, in its turn, annoys me. It's not his bloody phone. He was attaching himself like an alien with sucking tentacles to every bit of my life, gradually taking me over so that, one day, I wouldn't be me any more, but a part of him. I had uncovered his evil scheme. Ha!

Chapter Three

Obviously, my mobile phone rings a fair amount. It is in the nature of these things. So it wasn't the ringing itself that was surprising. I rested my cigarette on the side of Eden's desk (which is in fact a mirrored door balanced on two rusting bits of farm machinery that he found in the cellar or, as he prefers to call it, 'the snake pit') and answered it.

'Salaam u Alekum?' I said. I like to pick the phone up in different languages. Hey, I've got to entertain myself somehow.

Somebody cleared their throat. No, I knew it was a him. He cleared his throat.

'Faithy?' he said.

My heart lurched up towards my neck, throbbing wildly, trying to get out through my mouth, choking me. I leapt on to my feet sending the chair crashing to the floor behind me, and my wine glass smashing down with it, the liquid seeping straight into the cotta in a spreading stain. I spun round to see if someone was hiding by the door and I could feel the colour drain from my face like those pens where if you hold them upright the girl's bikini falls off.

'Dad?' I whispered. Then I clamped my hand over my mouth and threw the phone at the floor where the battery snapped off the back and went skidding behind the computer where it upset a lizard that skittered wildly into the room.

'All right up there?' Eden shouted.

'Yup. Yup. Fine. Sorry. Dropped my glass,' I shouted back, trying to sound normal as I crouched down with my head in my hands concentrating on not fainting. Is it English, this need to seem 'normal' at all times? What would be wrong with sounding abnormal, agitated . . . emotional? Well, everything, of course.

You see, my dad is dead. Has been dead for a long long time. He died in Northern Ireland covering the troubles when I was little. I was already living with him and Evie (a Coco-Chanel-style model from Pittsburgh) though really just with Evie because he was always away. I remember it coming on the news as the last item and how Evie suddenly looked old, just that instant (though she can't have been more than thirty-five). She didn't cry. She just bit her lip until it bled and tried to hold my hand but I wouldn't let her. I was wearing a yellow dress with multi-coloured teapots on it that my dad had liked and I understood immediately that I was on my own now.

They sent us his clothes in a big plastic bag. Some of them had blood on them. His watch, his big trainers, his jacket, the one I still wear, and his jeans. 'Where are his pants?' I wanted to know, but nobody would tell me. The funeral was packed and everyone said how young he was though he had seemed old enough to me. His hair had started to grey and his face was weathered by wars in hot places (where they do so go in for them). I refuse to acknowledge that Eden's is weathered in a similar way and that Eden must be about the height Dad was too. Though it is true, I suppose. I hate this Freudian business. Catches me out every time.

There were lots of women who cried and I had to throw earth on to the grave. We sang 'The Lord's My Shepherd', though He of the capital H most certainly wasn't my shepherd or Dad's and it seemed absurd beyond belief (my secret comfort prayer, I decided, wasn't incongruous with atheism since it was secret). The arrogance of childhood. I'm not as certain any more. Not about anything. Certainly not now, after all this. And, crouched there on the Tuscan floor at Eden's house, I pulled my wallet out of the back pocket of my jeans and took out the ragged photo of my father which has changed over the years. It has transformed slowly, but before my eyes, from a photograph of an older man, a father with a career, into a picture of a very young man, younger than I am now, someone for whom it might not have been too late to start again. Nobody mentions this. How pictures change – the opposite of Dorian Gray – but they do. Dead people get younger.

'Do you need a hand?'

It was Eden again. I smiled. God, yes, I thought.

'No, it's fine,' I shouted down, standing up again now, slotting the photo back in its place. I could hear Ben singing like he does. 'Badoombadoombadoomba.'

I had a shrink after my thing in Baghdad and I tried to think now what he would say. I tried to piece together the things that were going on that might make me believe – psychotically – that my father was calling me from the grave. Thinking about it rationally, I had no way of even recognising his voice. I couldn't remember what he sounded like and could only barely remember what he was like – my own memories embellished by everyone else's anecdotes, by Evie's grief. It was a mad sort of instinct that had made me say what I did just then . . .

And I was immediately embarrassed because it was probably somebody from the office and I'd gone crazy on them. Ugh. I needed more wine. I picked up the bigger bits of glass and went back downstairs to where Eden had made a fire and was wrapping potatoes up in foil and putting them round the edge of it.

'Sorry,' I said. 'I'm an idiot.'

'It's not news, Zanetti. Here, have another glass. D'you find anything?'

'What? Some incredible proof that all the conspiracy theories are true but you just failed to spot it ten years ago? Yeah. Gottit.'

'Good.' He turned away, back to the stove where the fish were smelling of rosemary and sage, and he sang to Ben, 'You shall have a fishy, in a silver dishy. You shall have a fishy when the boat comes in.'

That feeling (surely not . . . happiness?) tried to creep back into my stomach but I wouldn't let it. I drank a bottle of wine and ate my fish.

'It tastes like that stuff . . .' I said, pushing it around my mouth trying to remember.

'What stuff?'

'Oh, you know . . .'

It came to me. 'That chewy drug the Fijian soldiers had in Iraq. Remember? We chewed it with them that night before the thing.'

Eden laughed.

'Oh yeah. Kava. It does a bit. He got killed, didn't he? The one that had it? Big guy with the scar. Must be the fennel seeds.'

That was pretty much my effort at the chatting and I went to bed, too freaked out by my behaviour to inflict myself on people any longer than necessary. A good night's sleep. That was what I was after. It was probably just the pressure of this sure-to-fail assignment that was doing it. And the 'family' pressure from Eden.

'Put him in with me when you come up, won't you?' I said, kissing the top of Ben's head and, in a fit of affection or at least the knowledge that I ought to show some, I ruffled Eden's hair too. We hadn't slept in the same bed together since Ben was conceived, basically. Strange how sleeping together now would be a far bigger deal than it had ever been before. It would be the final tentacle round my neck.

But it wasn't over. How could it have been? Things that I try to clamp down always come for me at night. Which is why I usually try to stay up. Because that was the night I had my terrible dream. I dreamt that I was sitting in Evie's kitchen with Dad and a few other people and we were all talking. And I was feeling left out and upset that I didn't even know which paper he worked for, let alone where he'd been all this time and he didn't seem that interested in me or what I was up to. Then I noticed that he'd bleached his teeth.

'Oh my God! When did you do that?' I asked him, wondering why he hadn't told me he was planning to bleach them, why we hadn't chatted for so long, didn't seem to be friends any more. 'Let's have a look.'

I went over to him and he opened his mouth which was full of bright white even teeth but also of black ooze. I suppose I thought it might be squid ink or something and we all set off to a wedding or a funeral, walking together.

I told my cousin how pissed off I was and she looked at me sadly, putting her arm round my shoulders. Just then we stopped walking because there was something on fire on the pavement. It was a piece of fuselage. A piece of burning plane.

'Oh, Faith,' my cousin said. 'Didn't you know? Everybody knows. He's dead.'

I put the light on and sat up, getting my bearings. Ben was asleep next to me in pyjamas that we'd left here last time and that were sweetly too small for him. Soft with rabbits on them. The village church bells were clanging four in the morning and a pale blue stripe was outlining the mountains in the distance. I crept out of bed and padded across the cold floor into the study where Eden had put the pieces of my phone on the desk. I tried to put it back together, to see if a number had come up with that call, if there was someone I could call back to apologise to . . . Well, just to check. I smoked a cigarette staring at the computer screen in front of me. It was switched off. Then I called Evie.

'Hey, where are you, pumpkin? It's late,' she murmured. She'd married a guy in finance who's never around. Even their kids were grown up and gone now, so long ago was all that, the time when Dad used to come through the door with his suitcase and his tan and presents from the other side of the world.

'I'm in Italy. At Eden's. How are you?'

'Sleepy, baby. Kinda sleepy. How's that little sugar lump doing?'

'He's fine. Fine. Listen, Evie. Did you . . . Did you see Dad's body?'

That woke her up. I heard her rustling around in the bed-clothes and switching a light on.

'Did I WHAT, honey?'

'Did you see it? I was . . . I was just wondering.'

'Sure I did. You have to go and . . . You know what? I don't really want to talk about this in the middle of the night.'

31

'No. Sorry. But you did see it? Him, I mean?'

She sighed deeply. 'Faith. Are you OK?'

'Not sure. Yes! Yup. Fine. Great. Bad dream. Back to sleep like a normal person.'

'OK then. You sure?'

'Utterly. Night then.'

'Night, pumpkin.'

I imagined her pushing her black silk mask back over her eyes, plumping up her pillows and flicking the light off. I wish I could be more like that.

I opened the windows and leaned out. It was absolutely silent and still mostly black out here. Eden told me that during the war the Germans came into the village in tanks over from Boveglia on the track that now would barely take a sheep. Hard to imagine war coming to a place like this. But it does. All the time.

Chapter Four

Eden burst into the bedroom letting in an explosion of light.

'Look what we found!' he said, putting a basket down on the bed next to me. I hauled myself up on to one elbow and peered into it. Mushrooms on a bed of ferns.

Don't get me wrong. I've got nothing against the mushroom per se. Mushroom risotto is not unpleasant and I'm sure there are all sorts of other things you can do with them. But, I ask you. They're not exciting enough to warrant all this fuss. There are signs all over the forest forbidding people from picking them without a permit, vietatissimo. There are mushroom weigh-ins at the local bar and everyone's competing to tell you how many kilos they picked in how little time.

'Ooooh,' I said, getting one out and smelling it. I wrinkled up my nose and Ben laughed. 'Yummy.'

'I'm teaching him to be a real little funghaiolo,' Eden told me. 'Actually, I feel a bit of a column coming on.'

'As the pungent smell of damp forest overtook me and the morning dew dripped glistening from the fern fronds, my son and I . . .'

Eden hit me over the head with a pillow. 'Fuck you, Zanetti,' he laughed, and he took the boy and the basket out of the door.

'We're going for lunch at the Irvings,' he shouted over his shoulder.

I considered this, collapsing back into the warm duvet and the taste of sleep, tangled dreams still pulling me towards them. I shut my eyes.

I sat up.

'The Irvings!?' I said, leaping out of bed in my pants and T-shirt and running out on to the landing. Eden, halfway downstairs, stared up at me.

'Yes. They live less than an hour away. He's publishing a book you might want to hear about.'

The air outside was buzzing loudly with insects.

'Walter Irving?'

'And Phoebe.'

'Why? Why? Why are you doing this? What would make you imagine I would want to have lunch with these people?'

I held on to the banister and jumped up and down.

'Ummm. Earth to Zanetti. What is the problem exactly? Just a spot of lunch. You know. Bruschetta, salad, figs and what have you. Pretty innocuous stuff, Faith.'

'Oh, come ON, Eden! You know Walt Irving was a friend of . . . Oh, fine. Never mind. Lunch. Figs. Fine. I'll look out a clean T-shirt.'

'Don't overdo it, Faith. We don't want to dazzle them now.'

I had thought I would spend the day reading all the Cairnbridge stuff and searching on the computer but, after last night, it didn't seem like an altogether bad idea to go out for lunch instead, even if it was with the Irvings. So we drank

coffee out in the garden and Eden greeted every single vil-
lager and mushroom picker who walked past the garden wall
(all five of them) and Ben watched the lizards on the wall
and reached up for the grapes and plums, stuffing them
straight into his mouth and sending me diving towards him
to fish the pips out with my fingers. It's supposed to be relaxing all this sitting out in the sunshine and easing into the
serenity of the surroundings but, well, it isn't. I was rapping
my fingers on the marble table top, pacing up and down
under the vines and glancing periodically over my shoulder
in a way that doesn't look so weird in downtown Grozny.

Cradled by tempests. I know, I know. But it's true. It is
comforting when the outside world matches your inner state.
I think war correspondents and Médecins Sans Frontières
and all the people who go to these places where the immediate crisis of continued survival distracts you from whatever
else might be happening, they probably all spent years looking for an external match for their psychological symptoms.
We all pretend we were sent mad, or developed mild post
traumatic stress because of the awful things we've seen, but
I bet you that most of us were like that beforehand. It's just
nice to have an excuse.

In any case, I know my behaviour doesn't go very well
with normal life. Eden tells me I'm 'coiled' like a snake
about to pounce. Do they pounce? Whatever. Actually, I
think here they drop out of trees on to your head. Not very
often, but they do. Adders or vipers. You don't die if you
keep still. I imagine though that it's hard to keep still if a
snake's just bitten you. I met someone once who was bitten
by a cobra or a rattlesnake or some killer thing in India. He
had the antidote but you can only take it once and he lived
there so there was a chance he'd get bitten again. So, rather
than inject himself with this serum, he went through the

pain, like acid running through your veins, he said. And then paralysis.

'Hup'ma,' Ben called. Off we go. I got into the car feeling like a teenager being taken to see her grandparents. Stroppy, tense and wishing I was somewhere else. It was miles away, the Irvings' house, and it was, Eden informed me, 'toad season' near the river, which we drove alongside. In fact, the whole entire way the road was blocked by hundreds and hundreds of big enormous ugly toads. Well, I say blocked, but that would suggest that people stopped for them. Nuh uh. We just ploughed right on through them and they burst under the tyres, dying next to the flattened corpses of their friends, festering in the hot sun. It made me gag.

'Oh, come on, Faith. There are a lot of them,' Eden said, laughing at me.

'That's what Stalin thought about people,' I reminded him.

'Am I Stalin here?' he wanted to know, squinting slightly at the road even though he was wearing sunglasses, big old 1970s Ray-Bans with gold frames.

'You are he,' I nodded, putting my hand over my nose and mouth to try and block out the smell of roast road toad.

It seems appropriate now, looking back, that the way to the Irvings' house smelt of death, though at the time it was just funny really. I don't mean to sound cruel. Poor toads, of course. But when you've seen teenaged soldiers with their legs blown off crying for their mothers the odd dead amphibian doesn't raise an emotional response. Everything, I suppose, is relative.

I feel I ought to say something about the countryside on the way to the house, but that's more Eden's area. His columns are full of the gently swaying fields of sunflowers raising their faces to the rich golden light, the cool shade of the deep green chestnut forests where the wild boar roam, and the emerald green of the river that gives a luminous glow to the cool white bellies of the swallows that dive down towards it, saving themselves with an upwards swoop at the last second . . . Oh, well, you've probably been there, after all. And you've certainly read his column, unless you've been hiding under a rock for a year (it's syndicated all over the bloody place).

We turned off the road, swerving into the sheltered lane and just avoiding a huge death crash with someone who had radically misjudged their overtaking and would have killed us head on if we hadn't been going right. They drive like the Lebanese. The lane wasn't surfaced and we bumped and lurched for miles along this thing, stopping for ages for a herd of goats with bells round their necks. The noise made Ben cry and it was getting too hot to be in a car just for recreational purposes. Except that it seemed worth it when we got to the house.

There were giant statues of heads in granite and marble, all the height of a very tall person and all over the front lawn, and a terrace on the edge of the house shaded with wisteria. A trampoline stood in a kind of cypress grove and there were glass lanterns in different colours hanging from all the trees, and from the balcony above the front door, which was overflowing with pink and red wild roses.

A woman in a long white kaftan and bare feet, her greying hair tied back in a ponytail and a cigar in her left hand, came rushing towards the car as Eden killed the engine.

'Oh, thank goodness! Here you are!' she cried, hugging me in an inappropriately intimate manner. She left her hands on my shoulders and pulled back to have a proper look at my face. 'Was the journey a complete incubo?' she asked. 'Ugh.

You must be stanchissima! Come in and have some prosecco immediately.'

Eden emerged from the car holding the baby, his sunglasses pushed back on his head.

'Ah! A bambino!' Phoebe exclaimed, as though she'd never seen a real one before. 'Isn't he heavenly. As handsome as his babbo!'

She swooshed off into the house, waving her cigar at us to follow and muttering 'ecco' to herself with pretty much every exhalation. She was clearly completely crazed but managing to pitch it as eccentric English ex-pat and just about getting away with it.

She sat us down on the terrace at a bright green marble table with two bottles on it and a lot of antique champagne boats that were being filled by a thin, grey-haired bloke in a blue and white striped shirt that could have looked smart in different circumstances but was hanging out and mostly unbuttoned today. He looked up at me and smiled.

'Hey, Eff Zed,' he said, holding out a glass.

I reached forward and took it and then I nearly dropped it when I recognised him. 'Fuck me. Pip Deakin. God, you look terrible. What happened?'

As I said it I vaguely remembered what had, in fact, happened. Always the BBC's Mr War with dyed orange Paul McCartney hair, standing on a balcony in his flak jacket being shot by a video phone even when the crew were equipped and available, he'd had a nervous breakdown or something and eventually been sacked for refusing to fly. He used to fancy me even though I was always mean to him. Or rather, because I was always mean to him.

'Yeah, thanks, Zanetti. Nice to see you too.'

'What's with the grey hair?'

He laughed and ran his fingers through it. 'The Beeb made me dye it. Young gun thing, you know. It's a relief to have let it go, to be honest.'

'Oh, you don't have to be honest with me,' I said, taking a sip of the sharp gold fizz. 'I much prefer hypocrisy.'

Honesty. Always overrated. People only ever say 'to be honest' when they're lying. I mean, wouldn't we otherwise assume that you were being honest? If you have to qualify then there must be a reason for it. And usually 'honesty' just means unburdening yourself by admitting to affairs or how much you fancy somebody you shouldn't or some other thing that you really ought to be keeping to yourself.

'You are so full of shit, Zanetti. Anyway, you didn't think I dyed it out of choice, did you?'

'I just assumed you did it because you were a tosser, Deakin.'

He nodded. 'Well, that too. That too,' he said and we both laughed. His teeth were badly stained (were mine?) and the skin around his eyes was translucent, the blue veins throbbing.

When Eden came outside from changing Ben's nappy the atmosphere prickled. They had always been rivals in various ways. Eden is famous for being a devastatingly handsome womaniser and brilliant journalist. Pip is famous for faking a piece to camera in which he pretends someone is sniping at him. They had to film it twice and they forgot to edit the first take out before it got sent back to London. And, well, it was me who accidentally told a gossip columnist about it. Except, as Eden and my shrink and anyone who's read any Freud will tell you, nothing is an accident.

They shook hands and we all wondered what to say.

Eden coughed.

'You working at the minute, Philip?' he asked.

'Nope. No. Not right now. Bit of a . . . sabbatical . . .' Pip explained.

'Right.'

'How do you know the Irvings?'

'He published my last book actually. They invited me to . . . you know . . .'

'Right. Yes, he's doing mine too.'

'Right.'

There are very few journalists in the world who are not writing a book. It is a sorry state of affairs.

It was Phoebe who rescued us.

'Ah, you've found each other. Meraviglioso! I've never had quite so many war veterans at table together. Walt's coming down in uno secondo. Just finishing something up in the ufficio.' She pronounced all the Italian words with no change whatever to her posh English accent. Teenaged girls in tight off the shoulder tops, mini skirts and flip flops started bringing big bowls of salad out to the table. I assumed they were hired locals rather than members of the family. I imagined that the scene was every man's dream, though one can never tell with men and dreams.

One of them, shaking first her hair and then the Prosecco bottles and finding them empty, went back inside to open some more but, when she popped the first cork, Pip whimpered and threw himself to the slate tiled floor with his arms over his head.

Eden and I met each other's gaze and Ben said, 'Oh no!' which he always says when anyone falls over, including himself.

I nodded.

'Oh no,' I echoed and knelt down next to Pip. Phoebe, who I now realised was completely drunk, seemed not to have noticed.

I touched his hand and he opened an eye to look at me mistrustfully. There was an ant crawling across his shirt back.

'Hey, Deakin. It's OK. Everything's OK. Don't worry,' I told him, my hair bouncing in front of his face, my skin glowing in the heat.

'Really?' he asked, not at all sure if he believed me.

'Honest. It was a champagne cork. You know . . . the prosecco. Come on. Hop up,' I whispered and helped him up by the elbow.

He brushed himself off and looked around, shuffling and sheepish. 'Yup. OK. Just a little . . . you know. Bit hairy in Baghdad. Well, you remember. You were there. . .' he coughed.

'I do. I was none too sane afterwards either.'

'Really?'

'Really. Mad as a fish.'

Incident over, we sat down at the table, Ben on Eden's lap, Phoebe at one end and Pip and I facing each other across the salads. The sleepy-eyed girls were bringing cold roast meat now and then, just when I'd forgotten all about him, Walter emerged from the cool shadows to confront us.

'And here IS Walt Irving,' I said, quietly. It was a joke my dad had had with Walter and he had always said it whenever Walt walked into a room. Not that I really remembered him ever walking into a room in my presence, but I remembered the joke. You know, as if you were just talking about him and he's embarrassingly interrupted you. He laughed, an old man now really, but grand and still handsome, with bright blue eyes and thick dark grey hair. He had the air of wearing a three-piece suit and walking into the Harvard Club in New York, when actually he was in a creased linen shirt and trousers with leather sandals on and bi-focals which he had perhaps forgotten to take off.

'And here is Faith Zanetti,' he said softly, walking over to kiss me on both cheeks. 'I knew you'd grow up to be beautiful.'

He sat down and started ladling food on to his plate, eating slices of salami with his fingers at the same time. 'God, what do you think, Faith? I've got this agent trying to sell me a novel set in Jerusalem and it's wonderful but it's not going to play in America. Should I take it? Do you know Jerusalem? I expect you know just about everywhere. I read your articles. Very good. Really jolly good. You should do a collection. I would publish a collection of your articles. *Between the Lines.*'

He raised his hands up to suggest a billboard with the title on it. Phoebe rolled her eyes and sloshed some more booze into her glass.

'Here we go,' she muttered. Her cigar was balanced, still burning, next to her plate while she ate. 'Andi-fucking-amo.'

I noticed that Pip reached out and put his hand over hers with a little supportive smile.

'No! No! That's wrong!' Walter almost shouted, the garden baking behind him now and Lucca glinting in the distance. '*War and Peace.* No. Been done.' He winked at me. '*Battle Babe.* Huh? What do you think? *Battle Babe?* Don't you love it? I love it! Let's do it! Who's your agent?'

I still hadn't actually spoken though he'd fixed me with his slightly ironic gaze as soon as he'd come outside.

'Allegra Pearce,' I said. 'But, actually, I'm writing a kind of—'

'Allegra! I know Allegra. We love Allegra, don't we, honey?' He glanced over to Phoebe who raised half her upper lip in a kind of snarl.

'Phoebs just adores her. Allegra. Allegra,' he sang, waving one hand as though conducting, presumably a piece of music to be played 'allegro'.

'So, tell me, tell me, Faith. Tell me about Jerusalem. Should I do this book? God, I want to take this book. What do you think? You know Jerusalem, right? Of course you do. Like the back of your hand. Huh? Like the back of your hand? Right?'

He had taken hold of my hand and was scrutinising the back of it, chewing his food open mouthed. He let go and tipped some wine in to follow the food.

'Well,' I said. 'I haven't read the novel, but it's a wonderful setting, an amazing city. I mean, Pip and Eden and I have all spent a lot of time in the American Colony hotel and going out to Gaza City and—'

'Ah! The American Colony. Did you know it was founded by a couple named Anna and Horatio from Pennsylvania? All their kids died on the way and you know what they did? They just had some more. Anna and Horatio.' He shook his head. 'I mean, who is named Horatio? Hey! Have you read *Anna Karenina*?'

I was beginning to relax into his lunacy. There was something familiar, comforting about it. Something I understood in there.

'Have you?' I asked him back. He grinned, enjoying a confrontation, someone engaging with him.

'Sure. Sure. *Anna Karenina*. Sure. What? I should read it again? Read it again, right? This Jerusalem novel, kind of reminds me. The plot. Come to think of it the guy lifted the plot. From under Tolstoy's nose. Can you believe that? Can you believe that, Faith Zanetti? I'm not gonna publish that crap. Good. Good. Thank you. I feel much better now you've helped me make the decision. Much better. You

43

should be in publishing. Can you believe that? You should be in publishing. I don't know what I'm doing with myself. Dead in the water. We all will be sooner or later.' He looked genuinely stricken, his eyes wandering to a point beyond the horizon where we would one day meet our maker. 'The great equaliser. Kings and vagabonds.'

He looked as though he might need comfort but I had none to offer.

'Yes,' I nodded. 'Sooner or later.'

Strangely, he decided to take this as comfort and visibly rallied.

'Here. Drink this.' He took an empty glass, filled it and handed it to me though I still had a full one right in front of me.

'Thanks,' I said, and drank it, smiling.

'Cheers. Salute.'

Ben was asleep on Eden's shoulder and wasps were buzzing their last in big globular honey traps that hung from the potted olive trees. Pip and Eden were talking about Bosnia and telling, again, between them and sort of to each other, a battle of machismo, the story about how they tried to wash their pants and trousers on a tank but they froze solid and they had to put them back on anyway, cracking the ice on their Y-fronts.

'God, those were the iciest plums I've ever had. Shrank to the size of raisins,' Pip said.

Phoebe picked up her empty glass and tried to drink out of it.

'Cavolo!' she exclaimed. 'Bring out another bottle won't you, cara mia!' she said to one of the girls.

I heard Eden start giving one of his Tuscan culture lessons to Pip. 'Cavolo means cabbage, you know. Quite a common exclamation, oddly,' he said.

Pip was too gracious to say, 'Yes, I know,' or, 'I don't care.' He just nodded.

'So, Faith Zanetti, tell me about Sam Fischer,' Walter went on as though he'd never paused. It was unimaginable that these two men were so much as remotely acquainted with each other. But, as would be proved to me if it needed proving, it is a small world. All the little bits of it are small anyway. And you can only inhabit one bit at a time. 'Can you believe he got to be editor of the *Chronicle*? Worst damn spy I ever laid eyes on. None of the old spooks will even talk to him, will they? I bet you knew that though. You know a lot that you're not telling, I can see that in you. Well, your old man's proud. Very very proud. Kids? Oh, of course. That one right there. Grandfather? Hmm. I don't suppose he'd have liked that very much. Well, he'd have been a great granddad, as long as you didn't call him that in public. Huh? What do you think? Wouldn't he have been a great granddad?'

'You know, I can hardly really remember what he was like most of the time,' I said. 'To be honest.'

I knew he'd bring my father up and had pre-glazed myself to any assault on this subject. I was more interested in what he'd said about Sam Fischer. I had dimly known that my esteemed editor had once been a spy, but so had lots of people. Everyone knows spying is one of the staggeringly boring things that posh people do after university. You just have to read lots of boring documents and condense them for your boss. A strangely glamour-free profession that I could imagine Sam Fischer doing badly.

'Honest? Honest? Don't you dare be honest with me. God. What is this talk? Honest? You're gonna tell me you just slept with my best friend, is that it? Honest. Please.'

He shook his head in despair. Despite the fact that he hadn't stopped talking for a single second, he had polished off a whole plate packed with food and half a bottle of prosecco while I hadn't taken a bite of anything.

'What?' he asked, looking at his plate. 'Am I right? Honesty is just another word for cruelty. Freedom's just another word for nothing left to lose . . .' he sang.

'Yes. You're right,' I said.

'Faith. Faith. Faith.' He was off again. Phoebe had started another cigar and had put some music on, a compilation of Bob Dylan, Joni Mitchell and Leonard Cohen. Not many laughs, but the sky was dusting over with pink and it seemed to fit the late afternoon blaze. 'You know anything about Cairnbridge? You know? TAA 67? Do you? I bet you do? Your husband here – not husband? Boyfriend? No? Well, that man over there holding your son, he tells me you've got a commission and guess what I've got? I've got a guy says he 'knows'. Says he was involved. Wants to talk. Well, wants to write, but what can you do? Everybody wants to write a book. What can you do to stop them? I'll tell you. Nothing. You think anyone still cares? I mean, do we? Do we give a shit any more? It was a long time ago. That's what you're thinking. Prehistory, right? You were, what? Nine? Ten? Better things on your mind. What do you think? Should I do the book?'

I put my glass down and felt suddenly cold. Coincidence, of course, and obviously with the anniversary coming there would probably be lots of books. But it was uncanny that this had come up today, or was this why Eden had suggested we come? Yes, I think it was. And anyway, I've no idea why I was being so bloody edgy about it. Perhaps he knew Walter had this book proposal up his sleeve. He babbled like a maniac but he seemed to almost read my mind. It was as though he was just doing both halves of the conversation, leaning forward into my face, his eyes boring through my head, glittering and sparkling, a huge firework display of a person seeming to absorb my personality into his as though it belonged there. I was dissolving into him, an aspirin, bobbing and fizzing in his giant glass of water.

'Well, I've actually been asked to do a big thing about Cairnbridge for the anniversary. Sam Fischer is obsessed with it. I'm sure he'd pay a fortune to serialise the book if it was out in time. And, in fact, I'd love to interview the author, if you could put me in touch.'

'Sam Fischer! God, what an idiot. Of course he's obsessed with it. He would be. Doesn't know shit about shit, does he? What do you think? Doesn't know shit about shit. I know what you think. Hmm. Well, sure. Sure. Put you in touch? Sure. Why not? He's coming over to talk turkey. Don't you hate that expression. Talk turkey. Who would say that? Why would I say that? You must hate me. I would.'

'He's coming here, is he?'

'Who? Oh! Sure. Sure. Well, not to the house. He is a very nervous guy. I mean nervous. Like, breakdown nervous. Worse than Philip here. He is a wreck. A total wreck. You know the line? You know the joke? What shivers at the bottom of the sea? A nervous wreck. Right? The guy's a wreck. But you can meet him. Sure. Sure. He's already in the country. Using a pseudonym. All the crap. I have to go to . . .' He paused and leaned back rolling his eyes and tongue like Tigger tasting extract of malt for the first time. 'Honey. Where am I going to see the Cairnbridge guy?'

'Frascati. As you know perfectly well, mio angelo.'

'Right. Frascati.'

'Well, if it were possible . . .'

'Oooh. Faith Zanetti and the subjunctive. Were possible. Can you imagine? Being foreign? English is the worst language in the world. If there were to have been any beautiful women they would have had to have been blonde. Right? Huh? Translate that into Latin, huh? So, are we going to Frascati tomorrow?'

I supposed we were.

Chapter Five

Dear God, please keep everyone in the whole wide world perfectly perfectly safe in the whole of this evening, the whole of tonight and the whole of tomorrow. Thank you, dear God. And please do not let death fall upon anyone in the whole of this evening, the whole of tonight and the whole of tomorrow (unless they truly want death to fall upon them). Thank you, dear God. Please do not let there be any fires, murders, killings, robberies, rapings, kidnappings, wars, war declarations, bomb explosions, shootings, sinkings, crashings, drownings, fights, hurtings, frights, shocks, horrors, weeing or pooing in awkward places (for people over five earth years old), embarrassments, upsetness, disappointedness, crossness, aggravatedness, frustratedness, boredness, much too hotness, much too coldness, unhappiness, sadness, anything scientific (like the coming of too much gravity or the losing of gravity or the sun coming too near the earth), landslides, whirlwinds, hurricanes, tornados or anything of that sort anywhere in the whole of this world in the whole of this evening the whole of tonight and the whole of tomorrow. Thank you, dear God. And please, dear God, put in anything that I have missed out of this prayer that I normally put in and please let me have a good night's sleep and help me through tomorrow. Thank you, dear God. Amen.

I just woke up muttering this to myself, the end of a terrible nightmare that I couldn't grasp hold of. There was a bat in my room, flapping its leathery wings, desperately looking for the way back out. I switched the light on, breathless and sweating. I looked for Ben but Eden must have taken him in with him. Then I remembered that bats can't see, that they have some sort of sonar system and I switched the light back off again, lying down with every muscle in my body rigid, until it flew out, clumsy, skittering, wild and confused.

I made that prayer up when I was little. When I still lived with Mum, before they moved me in with Dad and Evie. A superstitious thing rather than an act of any kind of devotion. I wasn't religious, obviously. Mum sneered at God and at anyone who believed in Him. But I wonder what she thought about eternity when she died.

My dream, the one the bat woke me up from, wouldn't go away, wrapping its smoky tendrils round my brain even though I was awake. I'm not even sure if it was exactly a dream. More of a memory.

I was on this boat in Paris with Mum, wearing (was I?) a white frilly dress, the kind people wear for their first communion. Not that I would have known that then. Or was there another little girl wearing a dress like that? A little French girl with ribbons in her hair and black patent leather shoes like someone in a book. Little rosy-cheeked Françoise or sparkly-eyed Jeanne-Marie. Yes. More likely. I was probably wearing something much more ordinary. Though when I shut my eyes again to fish the dream back out of the black gloop (as I'm doing a lot at the moment because I'm really drinking too much. Must stop. Must go to a meeting.) I can almost feel the ruffles on the white dress brushing against my bare knees, can almost look down at the white lace frills round the top of my socks. But I know they're not mine.

It was dark on the river that night, the water oily black and the sky smoky after the fireworks, dense with heat, strings of multi-coloured lights, green and red, strung across the river or maybe just decorating the old painted boat. It was a big party, grown-ups drunk and crashing around, their legs climbing up wooden ladders, missing a step, a high heel catching as a woman squealed, red wine slopping over the side of her paper cup. God knows now, if I'm not making it up, cutting and pasting scenes from romantic comedies I've half seen on planes, rumbling towards some action.

In the dream I'd been asleep. Someone found me a room, a pile of coats, a low bed on the floor, batik curtains nailed over the port-hole, the noise of the party more distant, dream-like. I was lying there, rocking with the slight, sickening movement of the Seine, a full glass ashtray on a table by my head. And I hadn't even started smoking yet. Well, I wouldn't have done. I was six. I woke up, suddenly, scared. I did this a lot. Still do. Maybe I'd wet the bed, woken in a warm, stinging wet patch, my dress, if it was a dress, soaked. I can't have known the French, so I must have shouted 'Mummy!', running round the boat, wanting to get off but knowing, surely, that the darkness that already surrounded me would then engulf me entirely.

People were kind, bending down all concerned, asking each other about me, putting their hands on my head. 'Qui est la maman de la petite?' a man with a moustache might have said, blowing his smoke, politely, out of the side of his mouth. 'Je ne sais pas,' his girlfriend, in her twenties, holding a lighter and a purse, might have replied. And then

51

somebody spoke a word that made me sick with terror. I think it still would if I'd ever heard it since. It might have meant 'dead', 'gone', 'horrifically disfigured'. I was quiet, blank-faced, waiting for the news.

'La polichinelle.'

Someone took my hand. The little girl in the communion dress? Françoise in the patent leather shoes? She repeated 'la polichinelle' over and over again, leading me up stairs and down dark corridors, the boat rocking, the music pounding, the fireworks blasting into the sky, the people swaying and laughing, mad and inaccessible, to where Mum was having sex with a clown.

He gave me his red rubber nose. And, lying there listening to the crickets singing, I opened my hand as if it might be in there now, that nose, squashed and sweaty in my fist.

Really, really ought to get a grip, I thought, rearranging the pillow, cold side up. I have no idea how I knew about God enough to pray. Or even how I knew people said prayers at all. I feel as if I had 'Liar!' etched across my forehead at birth. I had been taught – nothing, nobody, never. But perhaps we'd been taught something different at school. Something, somebody, always. Maybe. And perhaps I'd already put my hands together to pray, nails ragged and bitten, bottom on overvarnished parquet, warm sickly bottles of milk with blue straws waiting for us in the corner. That must be it, I suppose.

At that age I could only look as far as tomorrow. It seemed unrealistic to ask for anything except to survive until morning. For my God (or at any rate my subconscious – are they the same thing? Ugh. I'll think about it when I'm sober – in the morning) was cunning and cruel, looking for any loophole through which to slip his twisting nightmares.

Some parts of that prayer I didn't say that night on the

boat though. The landslides came later, on a holiday to Malibu where we were staying in some very seventies beach house and there had just been a huge landslide. I saw signs and watched the news (Dad was glued to the news) and was sure I was about to be drowned in a sea of fast flowing mud. At night, of course.

And it was Dad (who else?) who taught me the names of so many horrors. If he wasn't watching the news he was participating in it. Like father like daughter, I thought, trying to release the madness muscle by muscle in the dark. The telly showed burning cars, boys throwing bottles which exploded where they landed, people bleeding in the middle of an ordinary looking street, like the street where I still lived with Mum. Before. That, where the bullets were flying, was where Dad was. Sometimes I saw him, running with a notebook in his hand. Or maybe I was imagining that. Maybe I just expected to see him. Perhaps he described it so vividly later that I thought I'd seen him, shambling into the shot, his sleeve on fire, a photographer running behind him, screaming, 'Duck! Duck!'

Dad's battle-scarred friends, now dribbling their last glass of claret on the desk in London where I'd just left them, gazing at the screens where the wars we all long for rage on, were atheists. Are atheists. You can't do this job, I don't think, and still hold out hope that there's some order, some purpose, let alone some goodness. The people I grew up with had seen the unspeakable things men and women (but mostly men) do to each other, had looked at the bodies of children raped, tortured, set on fire in the name of some sort of freedom. But do they hope in the darkness? Now that it's not their turn any more? Secretly, when there's nowhere else left to turn? When their wives have left for better men, their children become shy and polite and the world still screaming and running, the sky burning? Doesn't everyone?

It was something Walter had said but now I couldn't remember what. I shivered, trying to shake off the feeling of these dreams that close in with their gunmen climbing the stairs, their cancers creeping into my lungs and breasts, their falling buildings, plummeting planes, toxic gases released by madmen, poisonous snakes, failing light switches leaving me flailing blind, faces at a fifth-floor window and a heart that might not take the strain. But if I can just make it to morning.

Something Walter had said. A turn of phrase, a little smile. Something had sent me spinning and whatever it was I wasn't allowing myself to face it. Eden would tell me that this was typical of someone as repressed as myself, facing childhood fears as though they were present, as though something could still be salvaged. All his Freudian drivel.

I switched the light on again and lit a cigarette.

'Christ, Zanetti. You are a grown woman. This is ludicrous,' I said to myself, out loud, staring up at a spider on the beamed ceiling. 'Ludicrous.'

Chapter Six

Eden and Ben found me downstairs at dawn. I made myself an espresso and went outside to watch the sun come up. The garden at the front of the house (there is a huge old pizza oven and an orchard round the side with a shed big enough to inhabit) has been covered over with concrete. Weeds grow up through the cracks and there are strange shapes – a heart, a liver, some circles – full of soil with trees growing in them or rose bushes. The fountain doesn't work any more but looks almost more romantic for it. There is a low wall around it all which has fallen down in some places and a bank of lavender bushes near a creaking metal gate, painted pale green half a century ago. The old lady next door grows geraniums in pots and has dark ivy shutters that she swings open at 5.45 a.m. Straight ahead of me, as I sat in pants and T-shirt, smoking a cigarette and squinting at them, were the mountains, covered in chestnut trees and wreathed with clouds. The sunrise was gentle, like pink lemonade being poured into the sky.

'I'm going mad here. I've got to get back to work,' I told him, wriggling my toes.

'You are at work,' he pointed out, plonking Ben down into my lap.

'No, I know. But I mean proper work. This stuff . . . it's soul destroying.'

'You want to go and watch people dying, do you? And then describe it?'

'Well . . . yes. Don't you? No, I mean, I just want to feel some sense of urgency.'

Eden laughed. 'It is urgent. You've got to finish by the time they put the anniversary edition together. Come on, I introduced you to Walter, you've got a lead . . . This guy in Frascati. Sounds interesting. I've never heard of him so at least it's new. And anyway, why do you want to go back to all that stuff? Look at Pip, for God's sake. He's an embarrassment.'

'A nervous wreck.' I smiled to myself at Walter's joke. 'Anyway, he's not. He's just a bit . . . He was always very sensitive.'

'Puh,' Eden choked. 'As Lady Castlemaine said to Charles the Second. I'll make some more coffee.' I didn't bother to ask why this lady whatserface was making coffee for Charles the Second. Or was it the Puh?

'No. I'm going. I'm going. Don't forget to make him have a nap at eleven. Otherwise he's from hell.'

Walter had, in fact, offered to come and pick me up but it was out of his way and, anyway, I hate being driven. Not being able to leave whenever the urge takes me makes me panic. One of my life rules is: never go anywhere or do anything with anyone. I'd had to pull Eden away from the grappa the day before and I don't like the role that puts me in. That's the trouble with relationships. You get assigned a role and it's usually a crap one. So, I took the Cinquecento and trundled off down the mountain towards Rome. Frascati is near Rome. That's what the map says.

Much though the cute Fellini image of the tiny weeny little car annoys me – or at least Eden's aspirations do – it's fun to drive one in Italy. All the other Cinquecentos beeped at me and waved and I beeped and waved back as though I'd see them soon at the next Cinquecento rally where I was thinking of replacing the original chrome bumpers. Oh, buongiorno, buongiorno, I thought to myself.

Or, I did for the first three hours. Because Rome, it turns out, is a very very long way from northern Tuscany and by the time I got there it must have been 100 degrees in the shade. And then I had to find Frascati, which is a hill-top retreat where Romans have villas with pools. So, when I eventually crunched up on to the gravel outside this terra-cotta-coloured house with a gleaming fish pond in front of it and a pot-holed dirt track running for five miles behind me, I was soaked in sweat and my hair was plastered to my head. I had smoked my last cigarette an hour earlier and I had bitten the inside of my cheek until it bled.

The shutters were down and it was in no way obvious which door of many was the front door, and all of them were open. There was a low buzz of insects and fat lizards basked on the walls. I decided to shout. 'Hello! Hello?'

I heard movement inside but nobody came out. I shouted again.

'Oh, salve!'

'That you, Faith Zanetti?' Walter yelled back. 'Come on in.'

Now he appeared on the balcony, beaming into the sunlight, holding his mobile phone in one hand. 'That one in the middle.'

It was cold inside the house and it smelt musty, as though

nobody had lived there for a very long time. I crept up some wooden stairs, past some painted canvases stacked on a landing and a collection of patterned plates that had been displayed but were now thick with dust. I collected some on my finger as I passed. Walter blocked my way at the top of the stairs, silhouetted by the open balcony door behind him. I squinted.

'Hi. Fuck of a long way,' I said, having almost to push past him to avoid . . . what? Kissing him hello? Perhaps.

'Oh, not for you, Faith. Well travelled war correspondent like you. No kind of distance at all. Now, listen. I've got this guy here. Talking. A bit edgy. Don't . . . well, don't do anything to startle him. He's . . . I've got to tell you, he seems a bit volatile. But you know all about volatile people, am I right? You can handle him. If anyone can handle him you can handle him? I think so. What do you say?'

He touched me on the shoulder to reassure me, not that I was in any way worried. I flinched away and he looked embarrassed. Being touched is not my thing. At least, not unless the parameters are very clear. Anyway, I wasn't nervous. At least, not about the author. I've met these kind of conspiracy theory nutters before. That bloke who's always on about the Holocaust not having happened. Got put in prison somewhere. Austria, I think. I interviewed him years ago. Pitiful really, if he weren't so vile. That people like him believe the Holocaust didn't happen would be proof enough on its own that it did happen, quite without the heaps of corpses and enough personal testimony to make you weep until the end of time.

Peregrine Boyd was huddled into, or rather engulfed by, a big old sofa against one end of the room. It was almost completely dark apart from the stripes of light that made it through the shutters, but, even so, he had sunglasses on. He was thin and so pale he almost glowed, with a shabby dark suit on and brogues with the laces undone, thin socks, the kind that all posh blokes wear, pulled up high on his shins. His trouser legs had ridden up over them and it was the look of someone who might have worn those terrible gartery braces to keep his socks up, though actually he didn't. Red and white stripy shirt, signet ring, fag in his hand with the burning tip long and the filter pinched by the desperate force of his huge inhalations. He was in his late sixties, I thought, and had a nervous tic so that half his face convulsed every few seconds. His hands shook – perhaps he needed a drink – and he jiggled one leg incessantly.

Walter presented me. 'Perry. This is my dear friend, Faith Zanetti. We're old friends, aren't we, Faith?' he lowered his voice to me. 'I think we can safely say that. And we do need to be safe, don't we, Faith Zanetti? Or do you prefer dangerous? I think you do. I think that's what Faith prefers. Well, OK, let's dangerously say we're old friends. How about that?'

I smiled at him. I found his babble comforting. It was a way, perhaps quite a clever way, of making you feel, of making me feel, like the very centre of his attention. As though he would never stop talking, never waver, never disappear. In the way that I keep talking to Ben when I put him down to answer the phone or cook or have a bath, that kind of comforting talk to show that I'm still there.

'Walter? Shush,' I said and he smiled at me.

I walked towards 'Perry' (for the Lord's sake) and shook his hand. It was cold, thin and filmed with a light sweat. He seemed seriously unwell.

'Hi. I'm Faith Zanetti. I work for the *Chronicle*. You probably know that our editor suffers from an unhealthy obsession with Cairnbridge. With TAA 67. I've been given an absurd assignment. To find out who gave the Reykjavik warning and why. Where the intelligence came from. This can be on or off the record.' I sat down on an armchair that threw up a cloud of dust particles that glittered in the slatted light.

Walter stood by the door, as though guarding us.

'Well,' Perry said, in an unexpectedly feminine voice, 'you'll know as well as anybody that Al Nasir and Musa had absolutely nothing to do with it. The Dumfries and Galloway constabulary had the wool pulled over their eyes something proper. But then that wasn't difficult. The FBI knew what they were doing.'

'And what exactly was your involvement here?'

Perry coughed up thirty years of phlegm from deep down in his lungs and lit another cigarette with a little Bic lighter. I would have had one myself but the look of this guy put me off somehow. Amazing how people do eventually sort of turn into cigarettes. 'I was working in Cyprus at the time. Ended up passing on a few little bits of info to the DEA, that's the Drug Enforcement Administration to you, my dear, and the Defense Intelligence Agency – contradiction in terms is for sure. Who is that? Woody Allen?'

Walter piped up from his post over by the door.

'Groucho Marx. Military Intelligence.'

'Ah. Yes,' Perry coughed again. It was unpleasant. They should use people like this in anti-smoking campaigns. Just pictures of people who've smoked for more than a decade having a fag. They could write 'smokers' under it. I'm sure it would do the trick. It was certainly working on me.

'Anyway, it was common knowledge that the Americans were letting suitcases chock full of heroin on to planes heading for the US. The poor bugger who took the case on, Syrian chappie . . .'

'Karim Mohammed,' I said.

'That's the fellow. He probably had no idea it had been swapped for a bomb. But the CIA knew – or, at least, the chaps who had set up this quid pro quo in order to get information about terror groups in Lebanon and Palestine. Amazing, isn't it? It was all going on back then too. Just with a lot less fuss.'

I sighed and let myself sink back into the armchair. This was not a new theory. This was the old 'protected suitcase' chestnut that had been touted around by various different lunatics (none of them any too different from old Perry here) over the past twenty-five years. It was cute, it might even be true, but I suspected that proof was going to be pretty thin on the ground.

'Right,' I said.

'Thing is, they were about to be grassed up. The whole scam had been uncovered by their superiors . . .'

I was losing track. Or, rather, interest.

'The CIA chaps. It was, the drugs deal I mean, a bit on the unofficial side to say the least. In any case, they got rumbled and the men, their own colleagues, who were going to report to HQ were sitting in twenty-one A and twenty-one B.'

OK. Now I perked up a bit. I looked back at Walter and he smiled, nodded and raised his eyebrows. 'Whoah,' I said. 'So they knew there was a bomb in the suitcase and not drugs? And they let their superiors be murdered so that their undercover drugs-for-information thing wouldn't get reported?'

Perry dropped his cigarette on the floor and leaned forward to pick it up, burning his fingertips and swearing. His hair seemed to shift as he bent over and I realised he was wearing a toupee. It is astonishing how vile a person can look even when he obviously cares so deeply about his appearance. And where do you get a grey toupee? No, don't tell me. I don't want to know.

'Any booze in this place?' he asked. I had been wondering the same myself. This was the first sign though, that the house had nothing to do with him. Walter had apparently brought him here. Or someone had.

Walter stepped out into the hall and came back a second later with three glasses of whisky and ice on a tray. I rather thought he hadn't poured them himself. Someone else was here seeing to our needs. Perry had kept his gaze averted from mine while our keeper was out of the room, but now he perked up and the three of us clinked glasses in the cool gloom before Walter took his own drink back to his post. Perry swilled his down in one. No surprise there.

'Ah. No.'

'No, what?' I asked.

He had stopped shaking.

'They didn't let them be murdered. They murdered them.'

Ooh. OK. Now I wish I'd been a bit clearer about whether or not we were on the record. Nor was I sure whether he'd already written his book and would embargo publicity until publication or whether it was just a project that might never happen, especially if he'd already unburdened himself in a big newspaper interview. 'Clever, really,' he sighed. 'They used all the same stuff as Jibril's people were all plotting to use in Germany. Pretty much framed them at the same time. Nobody really thought about the Libyans at all. I never understood quite where that came from.'

I tried to seem calm. Not that interested. This is very important if you want someone to keep talking. If you gasp and squeal and start scrabbling for your tape recorder they take fright. And, let's face it, Perry here was already quite frightened.

'But one of the men . . . one of the men on the plane . . .' and now his chin started to wrinkle and wobble and it took me a second to see that this wasn't his tic. He was going to cry.

'One of the men on the plane . . .' he steadied himself and sat up very straight, holding his head up high, defiant. 'Rhett Summerman, in twenty-one A, was my lover. He'd been in Beirut trying to deal with Hezbollah, poor angel. On his way home for Christmas. But I knew what they were up to and I wasn't going to let them get away with it, Miss Zanetti. Oh no.'

That was about the most effort he could manage and he immediately collapsed again into his slumped twitching position.

'And so you . . .' I prompted him.

'And so I made a call to the US Embassy in Reykjavik and I warned them. I gave them a warning so that no US government officials would be allowed to travel TAA. That is what I did.'

Right. Well. This was frankly quite odd.

'Bullshit,' I said. To myself really, but it sort of came out in a mumble that I tried to disguise as a cough. I took a sip of my whisky. So, I'd told him what I wanted and he'd given it to me. Just like that. This was bullshit.

But he'd heard me.

'If you don't believe me,' he said, lurching out of his seat and looking angry but, staggering, falling back to sitting, 'I can tell you the very words I spoke. I can give you the names of the men who did this. I can—'

I interrupted him. 'Everybody knows the exact words of the warning.' Actually, I had no idea whether or not this was true but I was pretty sure I'd read a transcript in Eden's stuff the night I got here. Just before that phone call. God, the phone call. The nothing to do with Reykjavik call. I shuddered with shame.

How could I have said that? I forced myself back into the room.

'And I'd rather know what you were doing out there to get so involved. You were giving tip-offs left right and centre, apparently, but you weren't actually employed by anyone? Who the fuck moves to Cyprus and just happens to end up selling stories to the DEA? It's insane. You must already have had a job with the British or, God knows, the Russians. Or were you supplying the stuff – the heroin? What?'

Boiling while I was speaking, Perry now raised his empty glass and hurled it at the wall. It hit the floor but didn't shatter. It just rolled under a dusty wooden chair, making the whole thing pathetic, as if it needed to be made more pathetic. He put his head in his hands and started sobbing.

Quite pissed off now, I stood up. 'Well, it was nice to meet you,' I said, and walked towards the door. Walter stood aside to let me pass and shrugged apologetically.

'What can you do? They often break down like this. Give me two seconds and I'll see you outside. Just wait for me by the fountain and we'll talk about this, about what you think about this. What do you think? Well, you'll tell me in a minute, Faith. Let me just deal with . . . you know. I'll deal with this and see you downstairs. You won't go anywhere? You won't go anywhere.'

Outside it was still hot and I found shade under a heavy purple wisteria where I'd have lit a cigarette if I'd had one. Now, why in the name of God would somebody lie about something like that? And some of it had rung so true. I believed the guy, one of the guys, had been his boyfriend.

Nothing fake about the grief. But I didn't believe he'd known anything about it beforehand. He could have stopped his own boyfriend getting on a plane with a bomb on it, couldn't he? He would surely have told him himself about the swap for the bomb. Or was he maybe supplying the drugs?

Anyway, he certainly wasn't the Reykjavik caller and it was surreal that he would want me to believe that he was. Unless . . .

Walter skipped down the stairs and out into the sunshine. He walked over to me with his head cocked to one side. His eyes questioning.

'You gave him a hard time. Why d'you give him such a hard time. You don't think he's for real? No book? Tell me. Give me the Faith Zanetti line. Come on. She speaks. She speaks. She's searching for the truth. Did you find it? I got him here just for you. He's been calling, calling. Says he's in danger. Says they're out to get him. You know. The men in white coats. Wants to talk before they find him. On the run for twenty years. Argentina, Sicily, wherever. Like those old Nazis, you know. Dig them out in Panama. Don't cry for me . . .'

Even in the short time I'd known him I'd learned to filter what he said, to pick out the detail, to realise what it was he wanted to say, what he wanted to know. It sounded so round about but it wasn't. It was direct.

I scraped out a semicircle in the gravel with my boot and a lizard darted for cover. 'It's not him. He's speaking for someone else. Someone else is feeding him. I think he was there. In Cyprus. I believe the bloke was his lover, though I'll have to make sure he exists and was CIA and all that. We know there were a few on the flight, some from Frankfurt, some joined at Heathrow. But he's standing in front of somebody else. Presumably someone more powerful.'

65

I looked into Walter's face, half in the sunlight, showing the lines, and half in the shade. He was downcast. Disappointed. As though he'd wanted to provide me with an impressive scoop and had failed. Though I'd thought this was really his project, nothing to do with me, his possible book deal.

'So, you should find out who's behind him and get them to write it. This "Perry", and I assume that's not his name, is all washed up. No good to anyone,' I said, resurrecting the pretence that I was here to advise Walter on the book deal, to take the preliminary interview.

'No good to anyone,' Walter repeated. 'No good to anyone.'

He shook his head and I laughed. It was something Dad used to say. If you chose the less expensive thing, only ordered the one slice of cake, wanted the bike without the streamers in the handles.

'Where did you find him? Why now? And it's so strange that I told him who I was looking for and he just immediately claimed to be him. It's not credible.'

'Ever hear of coincidence, Faith?'

'No,' I laughed. 'Never.'

'He's been on at me for years. Every now and then I'll get a call to see if I'm ready yet, and I'm not interested. He won't go to anyone else, wants me. Me alone, Faith! But now, well, now because the anniversary's coming up. There'll be coverage – free publicity. It might sell. What do you think? Money in or money out? Money out, right? I knew it.'

'Strange though.'

'Well,' Walter said, and sort of guided me over to the car, sending me on my way, getting rid of me. I was surprised to find my heart sink. I didn't want to go. I dug my heels in, literally, like a mule on a rope, and he looked into my face questioning. I smiled in answer. The sun went behind a cloud. He moved slightly closer and I thought I might fall backwards or, worse, forwards.

'Let me show you something,' he said and took my hand, leading me round to a path at the back of the house and then down some steps that ran on both sides of a small stream that seemed to start at the mouths of two stone lions at the top of the hill. His hand was dry and firm. It was cool back here, the water and the shade of the tall trees making it a private stairway down to a terrace of golden stone.

Stepping out, we were standing above Rome, the whole city shimmering beneath us and, nearer, the hydrangea gardens of a vast stately home.

'The Villa Aldobrandini,' Walter said with a nod. 'The Prince is a good friend of mine. Very close. We were at University together. Wonderful man. You'd love him. Always helps me out in a jam. Lent me the cottage today. Guy refused to go to a hotel, refused to go to a restaurant. Spooked. But kind of interesting. Don't you think?'

The sun's colours were seeping into the sky as it slipped, huge, below the horizon. Suddenly, as we stood there, all the fountains of the villa spurted into life, fish standing on their tails, cherubs spitting water from their mouths, dolphins leaping and fawns piping. We smiled at each other but didn't comment.

'Yes, he's interesting. But it's more interesting that he's lying. I never thought this Cairnbridge thing would have a flicker of anything in it. But I like the murder thing. I've never heard that before. The suitcase yes. Planted by the Iranians as revenge for that passenger plane the Americans shot down . . . Made in Germany by Jibril's people, Abu Nidal, the whole business. Kind of old-fashioned somehow.'

'Shot down by accident. The Iranian plane.'

'Whatever. Maybe. Maybe not. Or the other Cairnbridge theory, you know? Because of the UN Commissioner to Namibia who was on the plane too and the South Africans . . . or . . . well. Whatever. But as a murder . . . Well. Dramatic. I mean, that's a lot of people to murder just to get your man.'

'Just to get your man,' Walter muttered under his breath. 'Just to get your man.'

He turned to face me, serious as cancer.

'There were a lot of children on that plane. A lot of kids. People's kids. Do you know? Do you know about the Gulhanes? Five of them coming from New Delhi. They were meant for Flight twenty-nine but the little boy had an asthma attack. The pilot, God help him, took the plane back to the stand before take-off and let them off. He got better. Sure he did. And there they were on TAA67. Soraya, the little girl. She was three. Three years old. In a red dress. A kurta and salwar in fact. "To the little girl in the red dress who made my flight from Frankfurt such fun. You didn't deserve this." Remember? The note? Do you, Faith? Do you? What's your son's name? Ben? Ben, right? Was one of them Ben's age? Was his mother holding on to him when they went down? The children. Who gives a shit about the others? Though they were kids once too. Right? Faith?'

I had tears in my eyes and he smiled, victorious. Well, I was tired and frayed. He knew he'd got me. I was on assignment now. Properly.

'Dinner?' he asked.

'Famished,' I agreed, blinking the emotion away. Well, I was. There's only so long a person can last on a fig and a mushroom. It was not, however, to be.

I think it was when we were climbing the stream, but Walter later said he thought it was as we were coming up to the door. Anyway, I've heard gunshots before and this was one. Just one. 'Oh, holy shit,' I said.

'You don't want to see this,' Walter called out over his shoulder, running into the house and up the wooden stairs, sending a plate shattering on the floor as he went.

'I do,' I said, and should probably have been ashamed, running after him, even darker in here now that the sun was gone.

The smell was so familiar. Blood is sweet and it makes the air thick.

Walter was leaning over him by the time I got there, but the body was still convulsing, the head and face pretty much gone, the whole wooden floor sticky and warm, blood still flowing on to it. The gun, a Berretta, was in his right hand though the grip had slackened and his finger had bent back under the trigger as he'd fallen on to the floor.

Looking back I can almost hear the gravel crunch under the hurried wheels of a car. But perhaps I'm inventing that with hindsight.

Probably not. Unimaginable that at that point I didn't know who I was dealing with. I feel like an idiot. As though it was so obvious, even then. But I suppose one always feels like an idiot in retrospect. In the before life.

Chapter Seven

'I don't get it,' I said, forking some tagliatelle into my mouth. Eden, Ben and I were sitting at Villa Aurora, a restaurant down the mountain and up another mountain from his house, a place where the bloke who owns it, Marco, makes rose petal and hazelnut pasta sauce from his own roses. Horses were wandering sleepily round the fields and his dogs were barking. The dark mountains were silhouetted all around by the beginnings of night against a pale blue sky. Ben was in a high chair feeding himself fusilli in tomato sauce with his hands. There was a young bloke on his own, reading the paper, with short hair like a . . . Hey! I could have sworn that was the marine-type bloke from the airport. AirportS, rather. Hmm. Small world.

Marco approached our table to shake hands with Eden and kiss the baby on the cheek.

'Bellissima,' he said, when I was introduced. Yeah, yeah.

'Anche Lei bellissima,' I said. 'You too.' I speak enough Italian to flirt. In fact, I hope I speak enough of most languages to flirt. Ahlan habibi – kief halek? You know.

'That should have been bellissimO,' Eden said when he'd

gone. 'He would be bellissimO. As a man. You're bellissimA. Anyway, what don't you get?' Eden asked, sloshing wine into our glasses. They do this thing where they leave the bottle on the table and you pay for what you drink. Uh huh. We were already on our second. Brilliant policy.

'Why he would just claim to be exactly who I was looking for. I was like, "I need to find whoever gave the Reykjavik warning," and he was like, "That's me." He didn't even do much of a preamble or anything. Apart from the boyfriend thing. Twenty-one A and B were Rhett Summerman and another more junior CIA guy. Biff someone. Nobody ever knew what their report from Cyprus was actually going to say.'

'What are they doing with Boyd's body? I can't believe he never cropped up when I was doing this story.'

'You always have been the world's worst investigative reporter. Fuck knows what they'll do with him though. We were there for hours, waiting for an ambulance, police, the whole deal. The bureaucracy was Soviet. I told you – I was back in the car the second they let me go. I mean, not exactly the most complicated case in the world. Very depressed, probably fatally ill old man kills himself. Though I imagine his identity might be hard to prove. Relatives hard to find.'

'Or did he kill himself? Maybe "they" were out for him. Maybe they got him.' Eden smiled, raising his eyebrows in a 'spooky, isn't it?' face and wiping Ben's mouth with a paper napkin.

'Well. Funny bloody time to get him. Just AFTER he told his story.'

'But you said he was lying. Maybe his story was some other story.'

'Yes. Good point. Possible.' And as I said it the memory of

71

the sound of a car slid into the back of my skull and disappeared again.

The swallows that had been diving around us had turned imperceptibly into bats. An amazing metamorphosis.

I wiped my plate with a piece of bread and glanced round to find some of the shrubbery flashing at me. No, not like that, for God's sake. I watched it for a bit before my brain processed the information enough for it to stun me, so alien a thing was it.

'Oh my God! What IS that?' I asked, pointing. The whole thing was alight with little moving glowing things.

'Fireflies,' Eden said. 'What glow worms turn into.'

'Wow! That's amazing!'

I dragged Ben out of his high chair and carried him over to have a look.

'Fairies!' I said. He laughed, gratifyingly.

Marco came out with two glasses of limoncello which he told us were on the house. Well, they'd better be because nobody in their right mind would pay for this crap. It is thick viscous yellow alcohol that tastes dimly of lemons and very strongly of sugar.

'I suppose,' Eden said, putting his elbows on the table and his hands in his hair like he does when he's thinking. 'I suppose he's being used.'

'Who? Oh! Perry. What do you mean?'

'Well, I suppose that whoever is frightening him . . .'

'Was frightening him.'

'Was frightening him . . . told him to give you whatever story you were looking for so that . . .'

He paused and we froze, staring at each other, like the moment of recognition in a Shakespearean comedy. You know, when one of them takes their hat off and turns out to be the hero's sister in disguise.

'So that I would stop looking! Oh my God. So that I would stop looking! Shit!'

'Exactly.'

My whole skin prickled with goose bumps. I often think about how skin is an organ, is one thing that gets infected as a whole, that ages as a whole, like a liver (oh God) or a heart. And when it prickles it prickles on your ankles, back, head, everywhere.

So that I would stop looking.

'Walter! But why would he want me to stop looking? He's a fucking publisher. And anyway, he talked about the children. He told me to keep looking. As good as. Encouraged me, anyway. He told me that Ben could have died on the plane, that someone like Ben who would have grown up and had a twentieth birthday with a cake and a present from his girlfriend . . .'

'Did he?'

'Well, not quite.'

I looked down and noticed that I had drunk the limonsoddingcello. 'Yuk,' I said, at the sudden realisation of the taste.

Eden leaned back and fished Ben out to sit on his knee. They looked just like each other these boys, face next to face. Funny boys.

'No, not Walter,' he said. 'He's not setting you up. That's just . . . I remembered from when I was doing my own Cairnbridge thing . . . I sat next to him at a book awards and he said he had someone on his case wanting to spill something but when I called him about it the guy had disappeared again. And then when they heard I was living here and invited me over I brought it up because you'd said you were doing your anniversary piece. And he said oh come over because his source was on the scene again and maybe the book would work for the anniversary. So, I don't think he's . . . Well, I'm pretty sure he doesn't know anything.'

'Hmm. Well, he's funny with me.'

'He probably fancies you.'

'Please.'

'Well?'

'Please.' I shook my head. What I thought was, Fancy is not the right word. But I wasn't about to get into all that bollocks with Eden now.

'Anyway, Zanetti. You seem to be missing something.'

'Like what?'

'I don't know. Something huge. A soul. A heart. Something like that.'

'Shalom?' Oh here we go, I thought. A gripping moral lecture from the father of my child. Some psychoanalysis, I shouldn't wonder. I twisted my red paper napkin.

'Seriously. I mean, the bloke killed himself. You are the angel of death. Remember in Jerusalem? Everyone you met just dropped dead the second you left the room.'

'Sometimes before.'

'Right.'

'Look, Jones. Honestly. People die all the time. People a lot nicer than Perry whatsisface. People who are a much greater loss to mankind. It's a sad and beautiful world. And, anyway, since when did you become Christ himself?'

Eden sighed deeply and we drove home down and up the deep dark mountains in virtual silence. He always manages, somehow, to end the evening like this.

Not, as it turned out, that the evening was over. When we got back up to the house, Eden taking the corners like an Italian to show he was cross with me, as if I didn't know (though I like him better cross than righteous), there was an

Alfa Romeo hatchback thingy outside with its headlights on. It is funny to be somewhere where this is something that you would notice. Can't really imagine it in Beirut or Moscow. Oooh, look! A car! Wonder who's in it?

We got out into the still of the night (apart from a few forest rustlings) and Eden, carrying the baby, leaned into the window of the mysterious car.

'Fuck,' he whispered.

'What?' I said, coming round to where he was standing, my boots loud on the road.

'It's Phoebe,' he said.

It was. Her eyes were shut and her mouth open, her head hanging back and one hand still resting on the wheel. The old lady in the house next door to Eden's banged her shutter shut. She had obviously been wondering who was in the car too. A cautionary thought – this is what happens to you if you stay up a mountain too long.

'Is she dead?' I whispered, knocking on the window before Eden's arm could stop me.

She was not dead. Lurching to her senses, taking a startled second to recognise us, she drew her hand across her mouth and put her public face on, brightening her eyes, turning the edges of her mouth up and patting her hair. She got out, stumbling slightly as she turned to shut her car door.

'Phoebe, hi,' Eden said, craning over the top of Ben's head to kiss her on both cheeks. I followed him quickly, holding my breath between kisses so as not to breathe my supper all over her.

'Come in. Come in,' I said, picking my way towards the front door across the black dark of the front garden. The big iron key was always left in the lock. I realised that my 'come in' could easily be read by Eden as proprietorial, as a Freudian slip of an admission that I considered this my

75

house too. Would have to be careful with that. Those tentacles were coming for me, I could feel them slithering around at my feet.

Obviously we'd looked confused about her presence – and who wouldn't be? – because she immediately started explaining herself. Or, rather, failing to. 'It was so lovely to see you all the other day. What a nice afternoon and how assolutamente meraviglioso that Walter was able to help you with your work, Faith. He's so good at having the right people up his sleeve at exactly the right momento. I thought I'd just pop up and see if you were about for a drink. So we could carry on with our lovely chat.'

We were inside now and Eden had stepped over some letters and switched the lights on. Lovely chat? What on earth was she on about? She'd hardly spoken to either of us, not least because she was totally arseholed before we even arrived and she certainly hadn't seemed that pleased that Walter was helping me at the time. Plus which, you don't 'pop up' to Brandeglio, let me tell you. It is a good couple of hours from her house and, in any case, you would have to have a very very good reason indeed to be up here in the middle of the night.

Which, as it happened, she did have.

She sat down at the wooden kitchen table under a bright spotty lamp that Eden bought himself in Moscow that time, and clasped her hands together, her old gold rings a reflection of a very specific kind of status. This was inherited jewellery, not bought. When the gold goes deep and rosy and the stones seem to fit less well in their settings. A life spent warming herself against Agas in freezing cold kitchens, going for long walks in the drizzle with dogs, amongst people who give themselves almost moral points simply for being outside. A grand house her dad should have inherited but by some tragedy didn't, a title lost a couple of hundred years ago, friends in the House of Lords. And the quiet knowledge (or, at least, belief) that, in the grand scheme of things, she mattered.

Eden poured some grappa into fat shot glasses shaped like upside-down geese that rest on the tips of their wings – also from Russia. From Stalin's Goose Factory. Eden specialises in Soviet kitsch. 'Well,' he said. 'It's very nice to see you.'

'Fabulous glasses,' she said, sipping her drink.

She paused with an important intake of breath that made us stand very very still for an instant. 'Actually,' she said. 'I came to have a word with Faith.'

Okey dokey. What she meant, of course, was that she wanted Eden to bugger off. With the extremely good excuse of putting the sleeping child on to his cloud of dreams upstairs, Eden buggered.

I sat down. It was cold in the kitchen even though it was still warm outside. Eden had put posters of crumbling paintings from Pompei on the doors and they looked as though they'd been painted on when the house was built. All awfully authentic, or, as Phoebe would probably say, artigianale. I speak more Italian than I will let Eden know. I don't want him to think I'm settling in.

I sighed myself now. I've been in this situation so many bloody times before. It bores the crap out of me. 'Phoebe,' I said, looking her right in the eye, 'I'm sorry. I really am. I don't do it on purpose. I think I just have a flirtatious nature, or an intense one, perhaps. I do tend to get into big-dealy conversations with people, especially men. It doesn't mean anything. It's just the only way I have of talking, of interacting. And, perhaps, I've developed it a bit for work, so that people tell me things they maybe shouldn't and help me out when I need something set up – a bit like the introduction your . . . the introduction Walter set up for me the other day. He probably told you it was all a bit more exciting than planned. In any case, I'd hate you to think . . .'

Phoebe held her hand up in front of her, palm out, to stop me. How! I stopped and put my hands on the table. She rested one of hers on top of mine. It was strangely comforting. She was wearing a floor-length shapeless cotton dress with bright patterns of flowers and exotic birds all over it, long flowing sleeves and a high neck. Red beads bobbed at her bosom and her nails were dirty from gardening, perhaps. 'Faith,' she said. 'Do you honestly think I came up here because I was worried about my husband? Dio mio, he has been sleeping with everything that moves for the last twenty years. Knocked me for six the first time, I admit. But now . . . Well . . .'

She stared at her grappa. Now I've got this little friend, she seemed to be saying. Yes, well, scant consolation, I thought. Why do women put up with this? No, really. It's weird. This is what Eden wants to me do. Get so locked into some nightmare relationship with all the 'tie-ins' (awful word) that I can't get out even when I find him fucking the au pair. It will seem like too much upheaval to leave and, after all, what about the children? Please.

'Oh, Phoebe, no! We haven't even . . . not even close!' I squeaked. Pathetic. Cornered. And we hadn't either.

'I know, cara. I know. I'm good at reading the signs by now, darling.' She smiled. Kind of smiled. You know those smiles with no hint of amusement or joy in them? There ought to be another name for them. More of a twitch really. Or a twist of sadness and resignation, bitterness and loss.

'But it's not Walter's liaisons I've come here to talk to you about,' she said, breaking my stream of criticism. 'It's mine. You see, I was first. I do believe he was faithful until then. I mean, not that he ever knew. But something shifts in the relationship, never gets mentioned . . . and there you are . . .'

Where? I wondered. But I didn't interrupt.

'When I saw your face at lunch . . . those eyes . . . the way you hold your cigarette. Faith, you look just like him!' she said, her own eyes filling with tears. She was looking at me sort of plaintively, her cheeks flushed.

Oh, Jesus. I had got it wrong when she said she wanted to talk to me privately, or however she put it. But that doesn't mean that this was any less familiar a deal. I feel as if I spend my whole life sitting next to someone at dinner who turns out to have slept with my father. What do they want? Congratulations? Why do they feel the need to tell me, of all people? One of them once even wanted to rate his performance but I put my fingers in my ears. A lover, sure. Why not. But what kind of lover precisely? No thanks. This wet-eyed forgive me/accept me look is one that I've seen a lot of times. I snatched my hand away.

'Oh! I see!' I said, suddenly feeling a lot less sympathetic. Or, rather, no longer feeling the need to make any pretence at sympathy or empathy. Hell, what's the difference?

'It was many many years ago, Faith, and I've never told a soul. Walter never found out. Never suspected. Or, perhaps, he just never wanted to know. You know how it is? When you know but you don't know. Perhaps that's how it was.'

She twisted one of her rings round her finger. Well, she had obviously been beautiful. The only qualification for the role she had come up here to describe. I found myself wondering if it had been before or after Evie, whether Evie too had been someone who had to choose not to know this stuff. But I banished the sliver of thought. I do not get involved in this. Censure. Life is complicated. People take what comfort they can get. It is not for anybody to judge.

79

'Well . . .' I said, and stood up. 'It's sweet of you to come. But I must be getting to bed . . .'

But Phoebe didn't seem to have noticed my getting up. She just carried on. 'You see, Jessie was born less than a year after . . . and . . . well . . . I thought I should . . . I wanted to tell you.'

I sat back down again. Floored. Or, I suppose, chaired. I didn't need to mull over, to digest the implications of what she was saying. I'd often thought about the likelihood of this. It had floated around in my consciousness always. A possible half-sister. Or brother.

'Jessie?'

'Jessica.'

Sister. You see, I knew I must have one or two. Probably more. But there would never be any way of finding them and so I never wanted to try. I grew up on my own and I knew I'd remain on my own, however many half-siblings were scattered around the world. I don't like hope. It destroys people.

And would I have asked her questions? Does she look like him too? How old is she? Maybe. But maybe not. Maybe I would have left it hanging, not wanting to plunge into it all. I have never had a family. I have Ben, but that's different. I'm sure Jessica has her life and, God knows, I have mine. Or, at least, I'm trying to have mine.

Anyway, I never had the choice about whether or not to let Jessie under my skin because Phoebe at this point bit her lip. Her chin started to tremble and the tears spilled out of her bright blue eyes. I leaned forward to touch her (a tiny weeny bit against my will) and that seemed to make her cry more. This always happens to me. I end up comforting people who have unburdened themselves on to me. How does this happen? I'm the one who just had the unsettling news. And she'd gone and put her head down on the table, really sobbing now. Like someone who has got through a tragedy and is now letting it all out in one choking go. I have seen this a lot. People keep it together while the crisis lasts and, when it's over, they double up in screaming pain. Actually, I have done it myself, but we don't need to go into that. She refused all comfort, and eventually, still clutching her stomach and whimpering, she pretty much ran out of the front door towards her car, saying, 'Sorry. I'm so sorry. Sorry.'

I called after her, offered her a room for the night (ah! Proprietorial again!), tea, wine, more grappa, and I genuinely hoped she'd stay. I didn't at all think she should be driving for hours on these roads with these other drivers. Never mind the fact that she was completely pissed. On the other hand, when I leaned against the door, my feet sliding on the tiles, moths crowding round the outside lamp, I was glad she'd gone. With her news and her hysterics.

I leaned down to pick up the letters Eden had walked over, at last lighting the cigarette I'd been longing for while Phoebe was here. She didn't seem to leave enough pause. I sighed and looked up at the photos Eden had framed and put on the walls. Me and Ben in hospital, him brand new and still crumply, skin like paper, and me shattered and morphined up to the eyeballs. Eden shaking hands with Bill Clinton, standing behind Musharraf at a press conference, me picking up my award from Norman Tebbit (no, I swear). Inhaling deeply, I looked at the mail. There was a package in my hands from a bee-keeping firm in California, a price list for various types of hive and all kinds of information booklets. God knows what was happening to Eden. Breakdowns I can understand. But this was way beyond the kind of thing that most people experience. He had taken sanity and settledness so far that it had tipped off the other side of the scale into madness. What made him think that normal family-type people keep bees?

I flipped it over to see what other letters there might be and found a postcard addressed to me c/o Eden Jones with a picture of Palermo on the front. A big church against a fake-looking but obviously real sunset.

There was no denying it this time. Or, at least, no denying that somebody was trying very hard to frighten me. Because my dad had written me millions of postcards. I've got them all in a box somewhere. I say, somewhere. They are in storage off the North Circular along with everything that means anything to me. Or would mean anything to me if I let it. The floor seemed unsteady beneath my feet, seemed to shift and lurch as though it was turning to liquid.

Dearest Faithy,
Poor old Perry, eh? He never did get over his poofter boyfriend dying.
Drop the story now. It's just Fischer being vindictive.
Give it up and be happy, darling, while you still can.
Yours, as always.

No sign off. But it didn't need one. I put my hand up to my throat. Either it was from my dead father or it was from someone with enough examples of his handwriting to fake it well and terrify the crap out of me. It probably sounds strange that I can be so sure about the writing when he died so long ago. And it's not as if I scrutinise the cards and letters, most with silly labelled drawings on them of cars he'd hired or big dogs he'd seen. But I did scrutinise them then. They were everything to me. They were my escape, my way out, the real life I planned to have when it all came right, full of swimming pools, hotels and silver implements for holding snail shells. I toppled slightly and leaned back against the wall. The photo of me and Ben in hospital fell off its hook and the glass smashed on the floor. I looked down at it but didn't register it as real, didn't hear the noise.

I forced my feet to walk me into the kitchen and towards the potential sanity of another grappa. I poured it, sat down and drank it in one. I looked back at the card, half expecting to see a message from Don McCaughrean or something, the real card with real writing on it instead of the phantasmagoria my disturbed mind had come up with. But no. Not this time.

I tried to run my brain through the possibilities. Either, it was all true. Ghosts, messages from the tomb, signs from the other side. Like those awful films where you get all excited dying to know who did it and then it turns out to be Satan or something and it's so disappointing. Or, someone was so determined to put me off what had seemed like a completely silly and facile assignment a couple of days ago that they were willing to go to these *Gaslight* lengths to do it. Or, of course – and this was going to have to be faced as one of the possibilities – my father, whose funeral I had gone to, whose death I had mourned all these years, was, in fact alive and living in Sicily. Or, at least, having a nice holiday there. I tried all these theories out on my tongue. No, whatever the truth – and two of the options were too outrageous to be seriously entertained – this Cairnbridge thing was dangerous. If not for me then certainly for somebody. And another thing. It was dangerous, apparently, specifically because it was me who was on the story. Done absolutely to death by journalist after journalist, nobody had ever, as far as I knew, run into anything this sinister.

'You're not smoking down there, Zanetti?' Eden shouted from upstairs. Bloody hell.

'No!' I shouted back and went outside, holding the postcard in my hand. I wandered through the gates of the house

83

and walked up the path under the stars. Someone had lit a candle in the chapel that is built into Eden's garden wall. I peered through the bars to see a plaster of Paris statue of the Virgin Mary staring at me. For the first time in my life I realised why she touches people, why she is so important a symbol. Because, of course, she is a mother. Like me. Well, to some extent like me. Determined not to feel moved, I stomped on to the Piazza where an old man also out for a fag nodded at me and said, 'buona notte.'

'Buona notte,' I said, but it wasn't destined to be one.

Chapter Eight

It took me ten minutes to even find Pip's mobile number. I'm still using my state of the art contacts system – a twenty-year-old Filofax, worn black leather and overstuffed with the numbers and addresses of a lot of dead people as well as the living, all the pockets full of visiting cards in English, Cyrillic, Arabic, Hebrew and Chinese. Indecipherable and, in any case, almost certainly out of date.

'Hey!' I whispered loudly.

'Faith Zanetti? I think that's you, isn't it?'

'Yup. Sorry. You asleep?' I asked, pacing the kitchen floor, flicking my fingers against every hard surface I reached.

'Do I look like someone who goes to sleep?' he asked.

I laughed.

'I'm drinking whisky on the terrace. Back to bloody London tomorrow, for my sins. I do envy you having a house out here.'

'Eden's, not mine. I haven't got a house anywhere. You know that. Anyway, listen. Can you go and flick through Walter's computer for me?'

'Yuh. No.'

'Oh, go on.'

'Hmmm. Let me think . . . Er . . . NO! You're insane, Zanetti. He adored you. Call him and ask him for whatever you need. You don't need to steal it.'

'I'm not going to. You are. Seriously, Pip. Help me out. Old time's sake.'

'Not really?'

'Worth a try.'

'Hardly.'

'OK. Listen. Someone is fucking with my mind. I'm getting really scary calls and messages . . .'

'The police? First port of call for most of us.'

'Come on. Don't be silly. Anyway, it's to do with this Cairnbridge thing I'm trying to do. Walter set me up an interview with a guy who shot himself after lying to me . . .'

'Yes, he said.'

'But I do think the guy had something interesting. His boyfriend was on the plane . . .'

'The TAA plane?'

'Yes. And he thinks it was this huge drugs thing that got discovered and the plane was blown up as a way to get rid of the grasses. But, basically, I got the impression that he was trying to fob me off so that I'd stop looking for anything. So, I just want you to see what Walter's got under Peregrine's name – any extracts of the book he was hoping to write or anything like that. Will you? Boyd. Peregrine Boyd.'

'Why don't you ask Walter like a normal person?'

'Because Walter's not a normal person and, on the off-chance that it's him who's trying to fob me off, he won't tell me, will he?'

Pip sighed and I knew he was melting. I stopped pacing and waited.

'He's not dodgy, Faith. He's just a publisher.'

'Yeah, a publisher whose wife had an affair and an illegitimate kid with Karel Zanetti.'

'Whoah. Your dad? I thought he was a friend of Walter's.'

'He was. Phoebe was just here – at the house. Sobbing and wailing.'

'But I thought it was Walter who was always sleeping around. Which child?'

'She's called Jessica. Have you met her?'

'No. I've only met their eldest – Tatiana. There are portraits, some local artist, of them all when they were little. I think one of them's labelled as Jessica.'

'Does she look like me?'

'Jesus, Faith.'

'Please? One little glance? I'm going to Sicily tomorrow. Via London. It's cheaper, weirdly. I broke my mobile so I'll call you, OK? What time's your flight.'

'One fifteen, I think. BA.'

'OK. I'll try and get on it too.'

'God,' Pip said. 'I'm on a break, you know.'

I laughed and put the phone down. It was a mirthless laugh. Well, of course it was. I sat down at the table and put my head in my hands, ruffling my hair. It was about two in the morning. I stood up and kicked the dishwasher so hard it dented. And I hurt my toe. I swore and sat back down again. I found that I was breathless with rage. I had been strong for so long. I had stood alone in the dark and I had frozen solid. I heard a story about a little girl adopted from a Chinese orphanage. Her new mother played hide and seek with her but she hid too well. The girl didn't scream or cry or carry on looking for her mother. She just sat down and shut her eyes and waited. Locked down. I did this years ago – a kind of death, a kind of torpor but, also, a kind of safety. Nobody can get me in here, not even, perhaps, Ben.

87

But now, sitting in a Tuscan kitchen, surrounded by heavy-bottomed pans, a plait of garlic, a clock disguised as a big frying pan, bunches of herbs, a whole shelf full of Russian rustic stuff and a wide cook's cooker, its blue light flashing on and off, I was facing the possibility that it had all been in vain. That he was out there somewhere, looking after me in the way that people imagine dead relatives do – looking down from their star – or that God does – silent, supporting, invisible hands holding us up. Except not dead. Alive. I wanted to punch him in the face.

And then, realising the lunacy of the thought, I started laughing, loudly, madly, my face streaming with tears.

Wiping my eyes with the back of my hand, I stomped upstairs in the dark, hoping to creep into bed unmolested. But Eden wasn't asleep. He was sitting at his computer, back hunched, glasses on, tapping at the keys.

'Writing your column?' I asked, trying to sound normal, glad of the chance to say something normal, to try my other life's voice out.

'No. I'm looking up Rhett Summerman.'

'Who?' I asked, going up behind him. 'Oh, the boyfriend.'

'Wasn't he on his way to Washington to grass the drug shippers up? Anyway, he existed. He was on the plane, he worked for the Drug Enforcement Agency. Handsome. Look.'

He pulled the face of Rhett Summerman up on to the screen. It was a site for the victims' families, a memorial for the dead.

'Very eighties. T.J. Hooker,' I said.

Eden looked round and was about to smile but then saw my red eyes and swollen face and scowled. 'What's going on? Did Phoebe punch you or something?' he asked, spinning his chair to face me. A dog was barking on the other side of the village.

'Oh. God. Eden,' I said. 'No, it wasn't Phoebe. Not that she wasn't bad enough. Had an affair with my dad. A child, maybe.'

'I thought he was a friend of Walter's.'

'That's what Pip said.'

'Pip?'

'I called him. Asked him to raid Walter's study.'

'Mmm. Cunning.'

'But no. Oh, Jesus. No, it's this,' I said, and handed him the postcard.

'I love Palermo,' he said, to himself more than to me.

'Yuh. Not the point, Jones,' I hissed, tapping the postcard with my raggy-nailed finger.

'OK. OK . . .' He went quiet while he read. 'Um. Wow. What is this? How weird that I was just . . . What does it mean Fischer being vindictive? What? For putting you on this story? Who's it from.'

'OK, that's the problem. Eden. It's . . . Well, it looks like it's from my dad.'

'Who died some time ago.'

'Twenty-five years ago. Yup.'

'Right. So, we can rule him out then.'

'But the night I got here when I broke the wine glass he called. I heard his voice on the phone. I know I'm insane but it really . . . He said "Faithy". He used to call me Faithy. And I . . . Well, I just, I threw the phone across the room.' I couldn't tell him what I'd said.

Eden stood up. He put his arms round me and held me very tight. 'OK. OK,' he said, as though he was talking to a skittery horse. 'OK.'

I nearly rested my head against him but, in fact, pushed

89

him away and wiped my nose on my sleeve. 'Look, I know it's mad. I know I'm mad. But it really sounded like him and this is his writing and . . . well . . . I'm going to Palermo.'

'I'm coming with you,' he said, taking my hands in his.

'No. I want you to look after Ben until this is over. Please.'

'Well, you're not going on your own. What if I get Don over there?'

'Don't be silly. I've lived in a cave in Afghanistan by myself, OK? I think I'll be OK in Sicily.'

'It's not the point . . .'

'Eden. You wouldn't recognise the point if it poked you in the eye,' I said, and turned away from him, throwing myself into bed in the hope of hurting something on the way, ready for a night of blood-drenched nightmares sucking me into their dark twisting holes of horror. But, in fact, I slept like the dead.

Why do people say 'like a baby'? Babies don't sleep.

Eden and Ben took me to the station in the morning. We drove through Bagni di Lucca where the shopkeepers, standing on their doorsteps in their aprons like people in a plasticine village, waved at us and smiled. I think this is partly because of Eden's car. The cheese man, Mario, is rosy-cheeked and pot-bellied and very keen to get Eden to buy some of his lard. (This is a delicacy here. In the Ukraine people rub it on their chests when they have a cold.) For him we stopped the car and got out to shake hands, warm in the morning sun, even this early. There's no need to get all dewy eyed and naive about all this though. They wouldn't give us the time of day if we were Moroccan. The English bring money and that's basically that.

There is a fountain on the station platform, overgrown with weeds and populated with frogs, but left over from a time when Byron and Shelley came here for the spa waters.

In those days there was a casino and, almost certainly, a busy brothel and it was the very height of glamour. Now it is somewhere that a few discerning Italians travel to for the wild boar season, for the truffles (supplied by the florist's dad who has a special pig) and, oh yes, for the mushrooms. And some sunburnt English in shorts and sandals, of course.

I was quiet in the car and when I kissed Ben goodbye it was, as ever, my stomach, throat and heart that cried. My face smiled and cooed and promised I'd be back soon though I wasn't sure I believed it.

Eden pushed his sunglasses back on his head.

'Faithy . . .' he began.

'Please don't call me that.'

'Sorry. Look. Faith. It's not him, you know. Don't let yourself hope.'

'Hope?! Hope!? Are you insane?'

I pulled Ben out of his arms and pressed my cheek into his, breathing in the smell of him so that I could take it with me.

'Mama,' he said, grinning his toothy grin and touching my face with his fat hands.

'Baby,' I whispered in his ear, handing him back as my train came in, turning quickly away and not looking back, though I could hear him cry.

I found Pip at the bar, sitting outside in front of a lawn. None of your fluorescent sterile hell at this airport. He was trying to open a pot of pills.

'Arsing childproof,' he said, looking up at me.

I smiled and opened them for him. Pip snatched them, thin hands shaking, spilling a few on the floor and pushing three or four into his mouth, crunching them quickly and swigging his beer to help them down.

'Flying?' I asked.

'Mmmm,' he mumbled. 'Four diazepam and a couple of pints. Bob's my uncle.'

'Great, Pip. That's great. Any luck with Peregrine?'

I tried to sound a bit casual. An English family with a lot of big suitcases came and sat down, the parents rowing about whether or not to book a cab for Gatwick, both children playing with Gameboys. 'Fine. We'll walk then.' 'Fine.'

Pip looked baffled.

'Oh! Yes! Well, sort of. God, I felt like such an arsehole, creeping around in the dark. So undignified.'

'Uh huh. And dignity is your thing, is it?'

He stuck his tongue out. It was white and chalky-looking. 'Do you want this or not?'

I sat down. 'Sorry. Sorry. I do. I want it.'

'Well, there was nothing in the computer at all. I mean, not that I'm an IT genius, but nothing I could find. No files overtly named Peregrine Boyd or anything. Best I could do. BUT, I riffled through the stuff on his desk too, just to make myself feel more sleuth-like really, and I looked up Boyd on his Rolodex. Couldn't think of much else to try. And, listen. He's written 'Peregrine Boyd' and then a huge list of numbers in different countries, all scribbled out and re-entered and what have you. Obviously, he moves about a lot.'

'Moved about.'

'Moved about. But, next to the name at the top, he also wrote in brackets 'Ihsan El Sayed' and a question mark.'

'The Al-Jazeera guy? That's weird beyond weird.'

'I know, that's what I thought. Do you think it could mean him? I know him quite well. Or did, when I was more . . .'

'Isn't he based in London?'

'Yeah. Well, he was. But he travels. You know. Big star. Face of the station.' I heard a little twitch of bitterness.

'Always in Iraq uncovering more and more evidence that indeed the Twin Towers were attacked by terrorists.'

'Were they?'

'Ah-ha! That's the question . . .' he said, waving his fingers around mysteriously. We both laughed.

'Have you got his number?'

'Whose? Ihsan's? Yeah, should have,' Pip said, and got his tiny little Blackberry out. I don't know what's wrong with me. I mean, how much could one of these things cost? And so handy.

By the time our flight was called I'd arranged to see El Sayed at the Frontline Club that night before flying to Palermo the next day.

Chapter Nine

I took the stairs up to the members' area of the Club two by two, my suitcase (well, my brown leather doctor's bag) slung over my shoulder. It was raining in London and it had that surprising bright green of all the lawns and parks and trees accentuated by the light and dark greys of the sky, pavements, buildings and people. Everything looks sharply defined here in the grey light. It smelt like home. Taxi diesel and rain.

This club is one of the few places where you can still smoke inside in London and everybody does. El Sayed wasn't there yet so I collapsed into a leather sofa and a Dutch girl in a white apron brought me a vodka and an ashtray. I put my feet up on the table and relaxed. There were people I knew in here, some blokes from the *Chronicle* looking slightly out of place in shabby suits and ties, trying to buy a big scoop off an American TV correspondent, and that woman who got half her face blown off in Bosnia and adopted a Rwandan boy with her girlfriend. I waved vaguely to them but don't know them well enough to have to chat or anything. Oh, but, hello? There he was. My marine. The boy from the plane to

Pisa, the airport and then Villa Thingy. I was being tailed. Was I? Jesus.

I have always had trouble with this place. Partly it's nice to have somewhere to go where nobody will find me too weird, where you can smoke and the food is good and friends will come in. But, on the other hand, there is the issue of glamorising this job that the place cashes in on in a huge way. The bar is wallpapered with photos of dead photographers, cameramen and print journalists, most of whom I knew at least casually. When Dad was killed, so long ago now, not so many journalists died on the job. It was shocking then, especially in Ireland where you were more likely just to get kneecapped (can you imagine?). But now, with 24-hour television news, you don't just need the story, you need pictures. More and more daring ones. So it is mostly cameramen who die. Not that a lot of them aren't half trying to. There is one woman who married, and lost, two of these suicidal madmen. Two! And young children in both cases standing bewildered in little suits by the lily-laden coffin. Eden, and anyone else mildly sane, would say that she must only have fancied people who were, at least on some level, trying to kill themselves. But why?

Families left behind have donated stuff for the glass cases of the club. A camera lens, a favourite hat or jacket, a watch. There is one case full of stuff belonging to someone who nearly died but didn't (I ask you). He had a narrow escape, saved by his mobile phone. So there is his T-shirt with a bullet hole in it and here is the destroyed phone that stopped the bullet. For those of us who have had a bag of clothes returned to us by the morgue, this is beyond bad taste.

I saw him in here last time, actually – the bloke with the phone.

'Still alive then, Dave?' I said.

'In body, Eff Zed,' he said. 'In body.'

We could all say the same.

Personally, I got a new phone at the airport when we landed in London and made the mistake of calling the desk to give them the number.

'Jesus, Zanetti. Where the fuck have you been?' Tamsin shouted. 'The Editor is going crazy. He actually asked me if you were OK. Which is distinctly odd. Have you got anything?'

'Actually, it's more interesting than I thought it was going to be. Tell him to keep his hair on. I'll file on time. I always do.'

'No you don't.'

'I do.'

'Rubbish.'

'Bye, Tamsin.'

I hate mobile phones.

And there, on the left above the rack of newspapers and magazines that do not feature celebrities, is the photo of my father, now the godfather of dead journalists, of people who, basically, choose to leave the people who would rather they stayed and then to put themselves in the line of fire. Heroic or selfish? Well . . . Perhaps it is an addiction like any other. Neither heroic nor selfish – compulsive.

I lit another cigarette though the embers of my last one were still in the ashtray. Ben was safe in the Tuscan mountains so I could do what I liked, couldn't I? But wasn't this trying to kill myself? Fucking hell. I put it out and sighed. The nice lady brought me over another vodka and I winked at her in gratitude. Yet, there he was, staring right at me. A man of . . . what? Probably about thirty-two when that picture was taken, standing in front of a helicopter, shades

96

on, this jacket (I shrugged it off and let it fall behind me), jeans, notebook in his hand. He looks like a film star. And was it worth it, I wondered? I scraped my hair back into its ponytail and looked into his eyes.

The sliver of forbidden hope, a blade of rosemary, that's what it felt like, tasted like. Don't they use rosemary for funeral cakes in Italy? I could feel it in my gut, trying to get out, trying to get recognition. I wondered if this really was the taste of death, the taste of that last mad hope that it was all true, that there is a God and a Heaven and a long white tunnel to eternal life. A blade of rosemary. The tears inside, that I had started to acknowledge almost as real tears, the feeling of leaving Ben, the realisation of loss when someone I love dies, rose inside me and I was relieved when Ihsan El Sayed walked in.

His face was wildly familiar to me as it probably is to everyone. He's the only reporter in the world who has been filmed actually meeting Osama Bin Laden ('Ah, Osama'), he met a lot of the 9/11 terrorists before (well, obviously, before) they set off on their mission and, being unbelievably beautiful, he appears on British and American news networks and channels pretty much every day, speaking decreasingly broken English and fixing the presenters, especially the female ones, with his black eyes and his fervour for the truth. Or, at least, he looks as though he genuinely has a fervour for truth. Though, probably, it is just a fervour to be found attractive which presumably gets regularly satisfied. It was certainly going to be satisfied this evening.

There is a fantastic bit in the Bridget Jones film (I saw it on a plane) where she first sees the bloke she will eventually end up with and the voiceover goes, 'Ding DONG.' This is something like what I thought when El Sayed walked in. I smiled but couldn't quite manage to get up. I just raised my hand, though he had recognised me too. From my byline or, perhaps, just by my reputation of having mad hair. I can't help it. He reached out to shake hands and I realised I was going to have to get my feet down off the table in order to lean forward enough to reach back to him, so I rearranged myself and then decided to stand up. This seemed to make him think we were going to embrace, so we kissed awkwardly on both cheeks, and he was going for the Arab third when I sat down again, leaving him hovering. Unruffled (and, hey, this is someone who's been ruffled plenty and not by social etiquette) he lit a cigarette and offered me one, which I took. You only live once . . .

I say that, though I was soon to discover that it's not quite true.

I noticed that his hands were covered in scar tissue.

'Happened to your hands?' I asked.

'I was blown up in Cairo,' he said, looking down at them as if he'd never noticed before. 'My friend died.'

'God,' I said.

'It was a long time ago,' he shrugged.

'Still . . .'

'Yes.'

We both smiled and the waitress brought him a glass of Chablis which she slopped over the side of the glass, giggling nervously. Ihsan touched her sleeve in thanks and she blushed. The stripped sash window behind us was open and the rain suddenly got heavier.

'London!' Ihsan said.

'Yup.'

I paused to drink my vodka.

'Hey! Congratulations on your Afghanistan thing,' I remembered.

'Thank you. Yes. As you can imagine I have had a house full of camera crews ever since. The mighty CNN this morning.'

He had a heavy Egyptian accent and a quiet lullaby voice that didn't quite go with his self-consciously relaxed (and therefore not relaxed) clothes (all very expensive, Italian – a learned uniform, presumably adopted when he realised that suits weren't right for the image). I couldn't quite tell if he was being ironic about CNN or not. Surely he must be. They would snap him up in an instant, I would have thought. They must have offered. But I imagined he was probably an Al-Jazeera evangelist. The whole Arab world has been revolutionised by the station – bringing real news to people who have never had access to it before, many of them living under censoring dictatorships, many of them illiterate. Not that this is anything but hugely worthy, but those who take part have been known to disappear up their own arses about it.

'Are you an Al-Jazeera evangelist, then?' I asked, going in aggressive for no good reason.

'What do you mean?' he asked, eyes meeting mine with a sparkle.

'Sorry.' I sighed and threw my hands up. 'No. I am. I'm sorry.' I paused. 'I always turn into a bitch in here. That's my dad,' I explained, if explanation it was.

'I know,' Ihsan nodded, sipping his wine with what looked like enormous relief. 'I put the picture up.'

'?' my face asked.

'He was my hero. He came to my school . . .'

'In Cairo?'

'No! In the country. By the Nile Delta. He must have been doing something about the water shortages. There was drought then. I told him I wanted to be a journalist. I was very young. I cannot have known what it meant really. I think I wanted his sunglasses.'

'They were good sunglasses.'

'Yes. And he gave me this.' Ihsan stood up, very tall, and started rummaging around in his pockets. He pulled his keys out and showed me the keyring. It was a piece of lead with 'The London Chronicle' in tiny letters, written backwards along the thin bottom of it. A print block from when they used to have to lay the pages out letter by letter. It was like a fossilised bone, something from prehistory.

'And you were never tempted to get in touch with me? You know? Meet his daughter?' I asked, sobered, maybe annoyed. Jealous? Hmm.

'Faith. May I call you Faith?'

'What else?'

'Faith, I think if everyone who knew your father or who was influenced by him called you up, then you would do nothing but talk on the telephone.'

I laughed. He was right, of course.

'I didn't know he had died until I went to train in Cairo. Strange. I always wanted to tell him . . . show him that I'd done it!'

I looked Ihsan in the eye to check for absolute sincerity before I said, 'Me too.'

He couldn't have known, but this was a big realisation for me. Was that really what I'd being doing all these years, charging round the world being shot at, watching people do these awful things to each other, finding out secrets? Trying to impress my dad? Yes, it was. I supposed it was. And yet I was very aware of what he would actually have said if he'd known. 'Why do you want to do this bollocks? Why don't you want to be a doctor or do something proper? You don't want to end up like me, do you?' But I did want to end up like him. Because if I was him then I couldn't be me. Left at home in the rain while women with long red fingernails (I

100

had always imagined them to have long red fingernails) played with the olive in their martinis and laughed at his jokes under swaying palm trees and gold minarets.

'And you have a child now?' he said.

'Yes. Yes, I do. Ben,' I told him and got a picture out of my wallet of Ben in the bath with bubbles on his head.

'He is very beautiful. Children are a precious thing. The mother should be at home with the child.'

'Is this a morality lecture?' I asked. God, I am plagued by men who want the moral highground and have no entitlement to it whatsoever. 'Your wife's at home with the kids, is she, while you try and get yourself killed in the desert?'

'I am not blessed with a wife or children. I did not mean to offend you,' he smiled, quietly.

Ah, queer, I thought. But didn't say.

'No offence taken. Well, only a bit. We are the mothers we are able to be. I'm doing my best, you know. It's all I can do.' I shrugged my apology.

'Of course,' he nodded, all sage-like.

'Listen. How well do you know, did you know, Peregrine Boyd?'

I arranged to take another one of Ihsan's cigarettes with a brief exchange of eye and hand gestures.

'Peregrine Boyd?'

'Cairnbridge. His boyfriend died on the plane.'

He nodded. 'Ah, yes. Boyd. Always trying to sell an unproven theory. Some of it true, some maybe yes, maybe no. The two CIA guys were the targets, I'm sure. They'd come from Beirut, to Cyprus and on to London connecting to New York. I didn't know Boyd. Met him once. Twice. I never knew about the homosexual thing. I heard he was killed.'

'Killed himself. I was there. A meeting set up by Walt Irving.'

'Him I know. He will do my 9/11 book I think.'

'Another one?'

Ihsan laughed and shook hands with a very made-up American television presenter who was walking past our table with her microphone attached to her collar. 'Ready for you in ten, Ihsan,' she said. He nodded and looked back to me.

'Another one, yes.'

He appeared to be thinking for a while and I waved another drink out of the waitress, feeling, vaguely, that I ought to be eating.

'Boyd. Boyd. He must have been with the Russians, don't you think? I found some suggestion of evidence for this when I did my investigation. He spent time in Moscow. More than once.'

'It did occur to me. His boyfriend uncovered the drugs thing and was murdered. Or, more likely, Boyd TOLD him about the drugs thing – you know, pillow talk – and Summerman's professional conscience got the better of him.'

'Ah. Very very interesting. Very possible.' He thought about this with his hands clasped as though in prayer.

'Incidentally, Ihsan. Were you . . . did anyone try to deter you when you were working on this? Try to stop you?' I asked him. Wondering if I wasn't perhaps being too centre of the universe in thinking that only I was in danger on this story, or endangering someone else.

He waved his hand, batting the idea away like a gnat. 'I have more than fifteen death threats hanging over me. I cannot even remember from which story each threat came. Probably. Possibly not. But . . . to continue . . . you are aware, of course, that the Libyan men had nothing to do with this. I knew one of them, actually. Many years ago. Nice man. But the drugs theory is correct. I am sure of that. Operation Shorf. Israel Levy is a friend of mine . . .'

'The Munich guy who killed the hostage takers?! No way!'

'You are surprised?'

'Yuh huh.'

'A Jew and an Arab can't be friends?' he smiled.

'Well, perhaps not THAT Jew and THIS Arab!' I laughed.

'Hmmm. An education for Faith Zanetti then.'

Yeah, OK, OK. Don't push it.

'Levy is a friend and the findings of his investigation, though discredited by the governments involved, were largely accurate. Mostly accurate. His Interfor report to TAA alleged that Karim Mohammed, a Lebanese–American passenger with links to Hezbollah, had brought the bomb on board thinking he was carrying drugs for the Syrian dealers he worked for. In this respect he was not quite accurate. But it was clever. The West was clever. I mark this as the beginning of the world's anti-Islamic conspiracy. Well, for this century, at least.'

He laughed bitterly. As though bitterness were expected rather than felt.

OK. Interesting. Especially from a man who seemed to dedicate himself to proving that Al Qaeda does, indeed, exist and does, also, perpetrate atrocities. This is typical of people who get too involved in something. Clearly the general public has no doubts about this at all. But if you spend your life investigating this stuff you run into all these conspiracy theorists who say, 'No, no! The Americans did it themselves to give them an excuse to . . . blah blah blah.' And, being a martyr to the truth, you want to prove them wrong. Weirdly though, you just end up writing pieces for the kinds of people who never questioned the toed-line in the first place.

It's like my editor, Sam Fischer, and Cairnbridge. Most people assume that the imprisoned Libyan and his not-imprisoned colleague are guilty as charged. Anything else would just be too hassly. And I agreed with them too until a few days ago.

'You do?' I said, raising my eyebrows and leaning my elbows forward on to my knees.

'Yes. I do. You see, Cairnbridge happened so soon after the Iran Air flight was shot down by the Americans. And it is true that Monzer al-Husseini was trafficking drugs and had links with the US. It is true that Karim Mohammed did sometimes work for al-Kasser. But he worked for others, also. If we take the protected suitcase theory as fact, which I believe we must, then we are, of course, dealing with drug barons. So, it is assumed that the allowance to traffic drugs was granted in return for information from Palestine and Syria. But I believe, no, I am certain, that the people trafficking drugs through Europe to the United States were not Arabs.'

'Not Arabs?' I repeated in a mutter, just to encourage him to go on.

'Not Arabs, no.'

'Israelis?' I said, moronically. Imagining in my booze-addled brain that his theory would be one of these table-turning clichés with which the Middle East is so tediously saturated.

Ihsan looked stunned. He put down his now empty glass and picked up the full one that had been placed next to it on the low wooden table.

'Why would they be . . . ? Oh, I see. No. No. Not the Israelis.' He pronounced it Izrayeeeleez.

It was all I could do not to shake him by the shoulders and shout, 'Who?! Who?!'

'My story aired three years ago. Ignored by the west. No surprise there. The Italians.'

'The ITALIANS?' I squealed, bolt upright now. For some reason, having just got back from Italy, I was imagining architects, painters, cheese makers, olive farmers. Just for a moment, you understand.

'Mafia,' he said. 'You know Mafia is a word from the Arabic – mu'afah. Meaning protection.' People who feel that their culture is overrun by the west are always pointing out their culture's influence on that of the perceived oppressors. 'Many Arabs in Sicily once. Naturally.'

OK, so now I was really really interested. Mafia. Sicily. Palermo.

Unfortunately, I had said this out loud. 'Mafia. Sicily. Palermo.'

Ihsan was laughing at me, openly. I coughed and tried to get some dignity back.

'What evidence for this did you find?'

'What evidence did I not find? Even a name. Gianluca Caprese. He was living in Cyprus, running the family's heroin trade, selling a little on the side for himself.'

'Where is he now?'

Ihsan looked at the ceiling. I didn't get it. 'Up there. They executed him. And everyone disappeared. For five years the heroin stopped coming into America. From Europe, at least. Look. I'll give you a tape of my piece. And notes, if you need. Remember when the judges were being killed left, right, centre – in Sicily? It's public property, Faith. And I am relieved that at last a reputable publication is interested in my story.'

'I don't know about reputable . . .' I started saying, but stopped. 'Yes, thank you. That would be great. I'm actually going to Palermo tomorrow to . . . well, on another story. Sort of. On this story . . .' I was getting confused.

'You won't find anyone,' he shook his head. 'Not anyone who was involved in this. They just melt into the villages.'

'Maybe,' I told him. 'Maybe not.'

I had to leave so that I could go and let Pip into my flat where I'd said he could stay. Ihsan promised to bike the tape of his feature on this Mafia theory and anti-Islamic conspiracy round to my flat immediately.

'You know who can help you?' he said as I stood up to go, slightly dizzy now from the vodka. I looked at him expectantly. 'Walter Irving. I offered him a book on this, but he wouldn't take it. He told me I was right, as if he knew it. But we would have to wait. That's what he said. Perhaps, Faith Zanetti, the time has come.'

I smiled at him as I turned to go, the excitement burning in my stomach. 'Yes,' I said. 'Perhaps it has.'

I turned back and approached my marine. Now I was sure.

'Seriously. If you want to follow me without me noticing then you'll have to do better than that. And if you want to scare me then you'll need to DO something and not just lurk around. OK?'

He looked at me blankly. And I ran out down the stairs.

Chapter Ten

Pip was standing on the pavement outside my flat when I got out of the taxi. He had no umbrella and was not standing under the shop's canopy. It was dark and the orange glow of the streetlamps was reflected in the wet road. Men in clean jeans and new watches were taking girls with glossy straightened hair out to dinner. Pip and I would never belong to that world.

'Hey, Deakin. Let's get you inside,' I said, as though to a child. As though to Ben. He looked just as much in need of comfort. I think that's one of the strange things about being a mother. You do start to see people in a different light, knowing they were a child once, and probably as deserving of a hug now as ever they were. Hard to apply this to oneself, of course, though this is apparently a measure of mental health. The ability to have sympathy for oneself as a child. That's what my shrink told me. Puh.

Pip followed me meekly upstairs and I flicked lamps on and tidied up all the tiny socks, bright toys and dummies that might depress me if I let them. Kristy had left a note with hearts dotting the 'i's and I thought how much I was looking forward, really, to having her and Ben back here and me schlomping off to the office every day as normal. Normal. Hmm. Like the Joni Mitchell song about not knowing what you've got till it's gone. Or however it goes.

'Listen, Pip. Have a bath. Whatever. There's wine in the fridge. I'm going to get some of my stuff out of storage. Be back in an hour. If the bell goes it's a bike with some tapes, so can you buzz them in?'

'Thanks, Zanetti. I appreciate this.'

'You'd better do,' I smiled, and skipped back out again, getting soaked trying to find where I'd parked my bloody car before I went to Italy. Round the corner from Snappy Snaps as it turned out.

There is something incredibly bleak about the North Circular at night in the rain. Well, there is something bleak about it at all times. The huge yellow storage depot where most of my stuff lives is second only in grimness to those car pounds where you have to go when you get towed. The woman in the glowing uniform, who greeted me by lifting her eyelids slightly higher up her eyeball than usual, seemed dangerously depressed, a torpor somewhere a fraction above coma slowing all her movements to the barely perceptible. She gave me the forms to sign and, eventually, the key for and directions to my unit, a good mile or so's walk away up and down dimly lit tarmac avenues. It would be hardly surprising if all of these giant boxes contained corpses. I mean, it would be only sensible to put them here wrapped up in a carpet before leaving for Rio, or wherever you'd go. This place was designed for body disposal.

I unlocked my unit and put the light on. Strange to see all my stuff from Moscow again, lurking here, waiting for me to admit I had a child and to buy a proper place with a garden and big bedrooms, somewhere that could contain all these souvenirs from my life. The box I was after has 'DADDY' written on it in felt tip, written by a nine-year-old who was collecting everything she could, all the shreds of his life that she wouldn't ever share. Though I hardly ever looked in it, I never hid it either, always leaving it on top of a heap, in an accessible cupboard. I heard Ihsan's voice saying that maybe the time had finally come. It was, in many senses, true. I had some facing up to do.

When I got home, hauling my box, rain streaming down my face just from the run from the car, I found the downstairs front door on the latch. I didn't think I'd left it on the latch and I felt a here-we-go-ish feeling rise from my stomach, though I didn't let it past the censors who told me not to panic until it was necessary. Still, I crept up the stairs without putting the hall light on and, yes, the door to my flat (painted bright blue when Ben was born, so that he would know when we were home) was open too. The television was on inside; I could hear someone listing the grotesque 'procedures' someone had undergone before her 'final reveal'. But I could already tell. There is an atmosphere when you've been broken into. I remember it from when I was little before I was moved in with Dad and Evie. You can feel it in the air, perhaps the smell of people you don't know, perhaps things moved too slightly to notice consciously, but still a part of your brain registers.

I put the box down at the top of the stairs and tiptoed into the living room, already aware, I suppose, that whoever had been here had already left. Nearly all my books, hundreds and hundreds of them, had been knocked off the wall-to-wall shelves and Pip was lying under them, not moving at all, though I think I could tell before I even checked that he was still breathing. I wasn't about to be screaming or anything.

'Fuck. Fuck. Fuck,' I muttered to myself, kneeling down and moving the books off him, the corner of *Spycatcher* having hit him in the temple and drawn blood. He groaned in some kind of greeting and I let myself breathe. He was probably OK. Opening his eyes and smiling at me with pale cracked lips, he tried to haul himself up towards the sofa and I crouched down to help him.

'OK. I'm going to sit you down and I'm going to call an ambulance,' I told him, dragging him up to standing and carefully lowering him down again on to the cushions.

I reached for the phone and put the kettle on while I was, staggeringly, put on hold. 'Ambulance, please. Oh . . . and police, I suppose. Yes, my friend has been very badly beaten up. No, I don't know. OK,' I said, keeping my eyes on Pip in case he did anything untoward. Oh God. I hope this wasn't because I'd told my stalker he needed to be scarier. I didn't mean it or anything. Christ.

Whoever it was seemed to have left Pip's face and head (you know, like violent husbands and fathers do – so that nobody can see the damage in clothes) but his arm was perhaps broken, at least at a funny angle, and his clothes were torn and bloody in places. He couldn't straighten up and was clutching at his stomach. I shut the curtains, huge cream things with a kind of coloured pattern of Chinese scenes on them that covered the whole of the broad and high bay windows.

'God, Pip. What happened?' I said, sitting down next to him and trying to give him a cup of tea. He shook his head and I put it down on the table.

He was croaky and shaking with fear. 'Don't know. Three of them. Didn't speak. Didn't want anything. Ask anything. Just . . . did this and left. A lot of aftershave. One of them had fag breath.'

The thought of this, irrelevantly, worried me. Must give up. 'What did they look like?' I asked, not that this would necessarily have added anything to my understanding of the experience, since I would be unlikely to have known them personally or anything, whoever they were.

'Balaclavas. Cheap clothes. The usual,' Pip said, rocking backwards and forwards.

The usual? Did this happen to him a lot, I wondered. I looked round to see if anything was obviously missing, though this wasn't a robbery. It was about Cairnbridge – I was sure. But why on earth would an anniversary special investigation into a subject already done to death prompt this kind of thing? It's not as if I was uncovering some Russian oligarch's murderous past or exposing the Beslan operation as a shambles at the highest level (though it was). And also you usually get more warning before this type of crap kicks in.

I stroked Pip's head and waited for the room to light up flashing blue from the street.

After a brief examination, during which Pip screamed when they touched pretty much every part of him, the paramedics in their green jump suits went and got the stretcher and took him away. I told him I'd come and see him, bring him back in the morning.

'No thanks, Zanetti. Think I'll stay somewhere else,' he smiled, head turned painfully towards me. The police pounded in after that, a whole crew in jeans and T-shirts with truncheons raised in case the intruders were still on the premises. They were followed by some shorter people with thinner necks and wearing uniforms who started dusting for fingerprints.

'Detective Inspector Chowdry,' the main woman said to me after half an hour of my not being addressed at all. She flashed her card (which is rather impressive, actually). 'Very professional job this. No prints. No breakages, unless we count your husband's joints.'

I raised my eyebrows. Was this supposed to be a joke? 'He's a friend,' I said.

She nodded with a slightly upturned lip as though assuming I was sleeping with him. Or was that my own sicko imagination?

'Anything missing?'

'No.'

'Any idea who might have done this?'

'No.'

I paused.

'Well. No. But I am a . . . I'm a journalist and I'm doing an investigation at the moment that's getting a bit . . . I believe I'm under threat. But I don't know why Pip would be, but I think it might be some kind of warning. I wasn't here. I went to get a box out of storage . . .'

'Box at the top of the stairs?'

'Yes.'

I would never use the words 'under threat' unless I was talking to the police. The strange formality of their language always kind of rubs off and makes people say bizarre things. Like when people write. Suddenly they take on this incredibly pompous tone they wouldn't use in speech, along with a sort of laboured formal vocabulary that makes every email sound like a legal document. Why do people do this?

I sat down at the table feeling invaded, and glad Ben wasn't here, as they picked up Mallowy Bear and looked under the soft checked cot blanket. Chowdry asked me lots of questions without registering any interest in the answers and eventually left with a deep sigh that suggested her total lack of hope of finding the perpetrators of this efficient and damage-free break in. She clearly believed that Pip had let another few of my lovers into the flat willingly, left the doors on the latch in the hope that they would soon be leaving and then got into a terrible fight with them. This despite the fact that Pip had no injuries to his hands (the kind of thing that happens if you punch someone back) and the locks had no trace of any fingerprints on them (obviously they'd have had Pip's on them if her version – deduced by self from the pattern of her questioning – were correct).

I pushed the books to the sides of the room rather than picking them all up and went and dragged my box in from the stairs. Kneeling down in front of it, I pulled open the cardboard flaps as though I were doing something brave. I'd never been scared of this stuff before. At least, not in this way. Now I thought it was possible that there was 'something' in here. Something that would mean something not just to me, but to other people too. Even, perhaps, the thing that Pip's attackers had wanted. Though that, I thought, was, as I'd said to Chowdry, looking a lot like another 'warning'.

I picked up a pile of postcards. 'Dear Gleamer, Here is a pile of steaming dog's numbers,' Dad had written on the back of a desert scene. Malawi. And he had drawn a poo in blue biro. The next one said he'd hired the biggest car in the world and he had drawn a long thin car taking up the whole bottom of the card and then a few normal sized cars alongside. I knew this writing better than my own. I smiled and put them down.

All these piles of scrawled notebooks, all these little black books of contacts, the leather faded and curling at the edges, the doodles and plastic press passes on bobbly bathtub chains, the angry love letters from women scorned, the photos of me, laminated and signed in a pudgy childish scrawl. Fat passports, the big old leather kind, some of them bound together with red ribbon to contain all the coloured stamps, and a manual typewriter that had become an antique while confined to this box, through no fault of its own.

So here was my theory, unarticulated even in my own mind. It seemed that my father, Karel Zanetti, the famous and tragically murdered war correspondent who was known to have excellent contacts throughout the Middle East, had known some of the people who had been involved in the Cairnbridge bombing. Or had been in possession of information about one of them, or some of them. For whoever was impersonating him in an effort to terrify me knew that I'd been assigned to this surreal task, knew (at least knew of) Sam Fischer, my editor, and also knew the recently deceased Peregrine Boyd. This much was clear from the postcard, a document made all the more gripping (as if that were possible) by Ihsan El Sayed's belief that the drugs trade used to plant the bomb in question was actually Mafia-run. But they also knew me.

I lit a cigarette, shut my eyes and drew in deeply. Whoever had made that call to me and sent me that postcard knew exactly how to destabilise me. Knew what had made me who I am and what, perhaps, could much more easily unmake me. After all, the process of becoming a new person after bereavement, especially for a child, is slow and slowed even further by rebellion, by a refusal to accept a new personality and a desperate desire to be that other person again – the more innocent one who still had arrogant expectations of life. The unmaking could happen in a second. I knew how fragile my shell was and I could feel something tapping at it with a sharp claw.

Starting slowly, moving things with reverence from box to varnished floorboards, I got more breathless, more hysterical and was eventually throwing stuff around, glancing at notebook titles, dating things instinctively, showering the room with heaps of yellowing paper, mostly typed on that thin stuff especially produced for typewriters, lists of names and numbers, articles written but never delivered, stapled together documents from press departments and agencies. And then a page called 'Karim Mohammed', the name underlined.

I stopped, lit another cigarette, sat on the sofa and then looked down properly at the document. 'Potentially useful. Already being used by the Syrians. Boyd confirms his willingness to diversify.' There followed a list of flight numbers and dates. It looked like a list of Jafaar's successful missions so far. Dad had written a big question mark on the page in felt tip that had leaked to make the mark fuzzy round the edges.

The doorbell rang and I screamed, clamping my hand quickly over my mouth and scrambling up, almost running to the door, gasping. I stood collecting myself for a second, trying to bring myself into the present, to listen to the sirens across London, to hear the ordinary voices of people leaving the Indian restaurant a few doors away. Consolidate the bits of myself that were roaring around the planet, through time zones and countries, into terrorist cells and cockpits . . .

'Hello?' I whispered, surprised at the thin croak that seemed to be my voice.

'Bike for Faith Zanetti from Al Jazeera?' a bloke said, friendly, bright.

'Great. Come up,' I said, smiling with wild relief, and pressed the button.

It was after midnight now and I sat with my knees pulled into my chest, drinking frozen vodka from a delicate Moroccan tea glass, while I watched Ihsan's film, dubbed into English by, strangely, a Texan. Scoops like this are odd.

While you're investigating this stuff all the whispers and insinuations, all the smuggled documents and late night phone calls, death threats and disappearances make your pulse race and you imagine the world will be irreversibly changed by your revelations. Then, at last, you formulate what you've got into an article or, in this case, a short documentary, and, when laid down as fact, backed up with whatever evidence you've got, it becomes suddenly quite mundane. Once described and explained it's no longer a mystery. And, of course, you have discovered what you believe to be the truth, so you don't give space to other theories or to doubt, thereby making your piece utterly convincing, at least for the duration of reading or viewing.

Watching Ihsan's film, it suddenly seemed odd that any theory other than his had ever been entertained. Of course the Libyans were framed so that the US could justifiably attack Tripoli. Ihsan proved the innocence of the two patsies way beyond reasonable doubt, even including the baffled original investigators from Dumfries and Galloway who hadn't found a trace of evidence connecting Libya or Libyans to the mass murder. Everyone had, however, found links to Cyprus (you probably remember the traces of baby's clothes in which the bomb mechanism was wrapped that got traced to Cyprus, but Cyprus seemed a red herring and nobody serious was convinced by this). The thing about the Reykjavik warning – you know, the security screener at Frankfurt who was looking for explosives under the X-ray only heard of Semtex for the first time on an ABC News show a year after the bombing.

And they used those awful cockpit audio tapes. MacDonald did a 'Daventry departure' flying northwest out of Heathrow. Once clear of Heathrow, he steered due north towards Scotland. At 18.56 as the plane got near the border, it reached its cruising altitude of 31,000 ft, and MacDonald throttled the engine back to cruising speed (Ihsan had had a dramatic reconstruction of this done – hands, that thumb, in navy blue sleeves, blurry controls, voices, shots of clouds and sky). At 19.00 TAA67 was picked up by Shanwick Oceanic Control at Prestwick in Scotland where it needed clearance to start across the Atlantic. Archie Green, a tin pusher, made contact with the clipper as it entered Scottish airspace. And here's the tape Ihsan, and so many others used. MacDonald replied, 'Good evening Scottish, Clipper 67. We are at level 310.' Then First Officer Updike spoke. 'Clipper 67 requesting oceanic clearance.' Those were the last words heard from the aircraft. I mean, it can't not send a chill down your spine. Most of his quite boring talking heads (all men over fifty) seemed convinced of the protected drugs suitcase angle and then, when this was all firmly established, Ihsan went out on a limb to show his Mafia link. He showed a Mafia history in Cyprus reasonably convincingly. He showed that indeed there had been a heroin trade (with some quite funny inter-views from inside New York prisons) – no big shock – and with photographs of the guy, Gianluca Caprese, who was a known Mafia heroin trader living in Cyprus who had been, as he'd told me, executed immediately after Cairnbridge, his tortured body dumped in the Hudson (though no record of his having travelled from Cyprus to the US was ever found).

That was the last bit I watched. Though my very bones had been rattled by the emotional earthquake of the evening, the very threads of my personality seeming to fall away from me, I must have fallen asleep. I woke, trembling, to a crackling television screen, still wrapped in a dream about a huge black panther prowling round my flat. I knew in the dream that I had released him from the zoo and brought him home and that he was beautiful and benign. But then I suddenly knew he was dangerous too, that he might hurt Ben, that he might maul me, that he might run away into the street and be hurt himself. It was a stupid thing to do and I should take him back.

I had dropped my tea glass and it had broken into three neat pieces, a pool of vodka on the floor and the rose-coloured shards with flecks of gold in them lying on the leaf of paper entitled 'Karim Mohammed'.

I put my hand up to my throat and I knew that in my dream the panther was the truth.

I picked up the phone and dialled Walt Irving's mobile number.

'Yuh?' he answered, woozy with sleep.

'Walt. It's Faith. We need to talk.'

Chapter Eleven

I heard Irving climbing out of bed, the shrugging off of a duvet, the mumbling of a bewildered Phoebe, his padding across the floor, maybe putting on a dressing gown, maybe sliding his feet into leather slippers, picking up his glasses off a marble-topped dresser.

'Faith Zanetti. I know you. I remember you,' he said, and I could hear the smile in his voice, could imagine the dark outside his pale blue shutters, the noise of the insects, the low glimmer of the stars and the cold of the stone floors. God, I'm sounding like Eden. I really should get one of these dossing around columns for myself.

'Hi. Walt. Listen,' I said, still curled up on the sofa, almost afraid to move. 'So, I'm still on this Cairnbridge thing. Pip got beaten up at my flat by people who wiped their prints off everything and Ihsan El Sayed, the Al Jazeera guy, told me his theory about it being a Mafia job. Also, I've been through Dad's stuff and he seems to have known Karim Mohammed, who was almost certainly carrying the Cairnbridge suitcase, and Dad seems to have been aware of the kind of thing he did – that is, drugs trafficking. I also think that Dad knew

Perry Boyd. Or might have done. I want you to tell me what's going on and I think you know.'

I had babbled it all out in a hurry and I expected him to babble back, like he normally does. He didn't say anything though, and the sound of movement had stopped.

'Walt?' I said, straightening my limbs out now, reaching for my cigarettes.

'Yuh,' he said, sounding distant.

'Walt. I'm going to Sicily tomorrow. To Palermo. I'm going to try and find out who's threatening me and I want to see if any of Gianluca Caprese's family will talk to me. You know Gianluca Caprese?'

Walter paused a long time but I didn't rescue him.

'Yes.' He cleared his throat. 'Yes, I do know who he is. El Sayed thinks he was running a Mafia heroin trade, and we know he was executed Mafia-style after Cairnbridge, just before Christmas that year. Dumped in the river. I know all about Gianluca Caprese but I don't think you're going to find anyone in Palermo who will admit to being involved in drugs or anything else. You need to . . .'

He stopped again, not like him at all.

'I need to what? Tell me, Walter. Did my father know these people? Did he know about the heroin trade from Cyprus? Was he doing a story about it? Maybe he was killed because of that? Did they do it in Ireland to make it untraceable? Is that why I'm being threatened? Someone in the Mafia knows that Dad knew things about them? Things still dangerous now? And they're scared that if I, his daughter, perhaps with access to his documents, something they failed to get rid of, they're scared I might . . . what? Break the story he was on to all that time ago. Is that it, Walter? Tell me. Please.'

While I was talking I had stood up and crushed my

already broken glass into the floor with my boot. My mind was working as hard as I could force it to.

Walter Irving coughed on the other end of the line.

'Faith Zanetti. Faith Zanetti. Faith Zanetti,' he finally sighed.

This was not helpful.

'Faith Cleopatra Zanetti, actually,' I said, slightly annoyed.

He laughed. 'Yes. Faith Cleopatra Zanetti.'

Oh, for fuck's sake.

'Look, Faith, I'm going to level with you. I'm going to be as honest with you as I can. And you know my views on honesty, right? You want to be honest you don't need to say you're going to be honest. Start saying you're going to be honest and you're either gonna lie or inflict pain gratuitously. Now I'm not saying I'm going to tell you every-thing I've ever known. I'm not saying that. Hell, you wouldn't want to hear it anyway. You want to hear my Talmudic recitations? I don't think so. I don't think you do, Faith. Not a word of that. Don't understand Hebrew anyway, right? Do you, Faith? Of course you don't. So, I'm not going to give you the full Mighella. I would if I could but I can't. OK? Shoulda coulda woulda, right? Well, I can't do it. But what I will tell you is this. I will tell you that your thinking is pretty sound. Pretty, pretty, sound. You're not there. You're a long way off. You may never get there. But I always knew you could think. I've read your stuff. I love your stuff. We should do a book of your stuff. Did I already suggest that? Did we come up with a title? Yes! We did. *Battle Babe*. I love that. Gotta call Allegra. Gonna call Allegra. Where was I?'

'I'm a long way off,' I said, quietly.

'Right. Right. A long way off. But you can think. You're

a good thinker. Put Faith Zanetti on a story and you know she's going to come up with the goods. Right? And will you, Faith? Are you going to come up with the goods this time?'

I expected him to ramble on but he'd apparently stopped.

'Ummmm . . . Walter. You tell me.'

'Ah, answer a question with a question. Right. You're good. She's good. Very good. Very good. So, I'll level with you as far as I can. About as far as you can throw me, right? We all know about Sam Fischer. That we all know. The worst spook in the business. David Cornwell never used him as a model. You know? John Le Carré? He's called David Cornwell.'

'I know,' I said.

'Sure you do. And I'll be straight with you – he never took Sam Fischer out for lunch. Nor did the other guy. Freddie. Freddie Forsyth. Great way to a free lunch. Feed them some procedural bullshit – something to surprise the public and they're all over it like a rash. Brilliant. Brilliant. You know – tell them yes we do run protected suitcases for information, play the odds, weigh the risks.'

I was unsure whether it was fear, excitement or actual vomit that was rising now from my stomach. Or, let's face it, all three.

'We?' I whispered.

Walter laughed. And I realised without even forming the thought that the house in Frascati had been a safe house. A not very safe house.

'Look,' he said. 'This is not a conversation to be having over the phone. As the Russians would say: Eto nye telefon-niy razgovor. Right? I love that. As Perry would say. This is not a telephone conversation. And you're talking to them on the phone and you want to say, Yes it is! But, Faith, Faith,

Faith. We can't do this over the phone.' He sounded almost playful. 'You know what I'm going to do for you? I'm going to meet you in Palermo. We'll look together. What do you say to that? Safer, I think. Book into the Villa Egeia. I'll see you there. What time do you land? Well, you'll call me when you land. Call me when you land.'

'My flight gets in at half six,' I said, too stunned to comment further.

'P.M., right? I'll have someone meet you,' Walt said. 'Are we done? Back to bed? We're done, I think.' And he hung up.

I stood under the burning hot shower for as long as I could stand to. I knew what Walt was trying to tell me and I didn't doubt it. I was just stunned that I had never known, never suspected, never even thought about it. Which was ridiculous really, since they'd approached me a million times, for God's sake. Sometimes I would go to the meetings, a café in central London, a bloke in a suit with a name like Bob that you know isn't his name, if even he can remember any more. They offer you unbelievable contacts, interviews with anyone – the Pope, Osama Bin Laden, Fidel Castro – if you'll write the piece they want to see in the press. They'll pay your rent, kids' school fees. And they don't usually demand the kind of piece you wouldn't be writing in any case. But . . . But what? I don't know. Yes, I do know. I thought Dad would disapprove. I thought Dad would think I was compromising my ability to tell the truth. I was trying to be like him. When all this time . . .

And I remembered once. We were sitting in a hotel room somewhere in America – Stockbridge, Massachusetts – throwing tiny fish-shaped cheese-flavoured biscuits at each other. All day he had been making me dive to the bottom of the pool for a silver dollar. A silver dollar that I have in the pocket of my jeans right now. Then he had put me on his shoulders and run round and round the pool, making me scream by nearly toppling me in until Evie, spreading coconut smelling oil evenly over her perfect golden skin, told him to stop. He put me down and picked up her watch, presumably expensive, worked for in front of a camera. Pouted for. He threatened to throw it in and she chased him squealing while the white-jacketed waiters holding their silver trays of iced drinks smiled. When she caught him he threw in the watch and she called him a fucker and wouldn't come down for dinner with us. So we ate lobster with gleaming instruments and I had a strawberry daquiri without the daquiri – my favourite drink at the time. When we got up to the room Evie had packed and gone and I was secretly glad. Dad switched on the television and we threw the fish. Then something came on the news about a hijacking. The Air France one in Uganda. Palestinian hijackers, mostly Israeli passengers. Anyway, Dad went white and started packing our stuff up and rushing around the room, chain smoking and really hysterical. He called someone back in New York, a woman called Arla whose flat smelt of cats, and asked her if he could drop me at her apartment, he had to run to the airport. 'Keep calling Evie. When she gets home she'll come and pick you up from Arla's,' he told me, pretty much throwing me into the old Buick with all our stuff and hurtling the five, six hours back to the city down empty freeways, the lights and signs passing nauseatingly above my head as I lay in the back and he smoked and smoked and smoked.

Would I even have remembered this? I doubt it. And where did he go that night? Where did he fly to? He was often in Nicosia, getting the boat across to Lebanon because the airport was shut. Or it was safer. Safer or less detectable I wondered now.

'Honey?' Evie said.

'Hi. Sorry. I keep doing this, I know. But some very weird stuff is happening. Do you remember that time Dad threw your watch in the pool and I had to stay at Arla's?'

'Are we talking 1823, babe? Are you calling me at three a.m. to ask me a question about a time when I was so coked out of my tiny little mind I couldn't even tell my watch from my chacha?'

I laughed. Chacha is such a great word for it.

'Yes. 1976, I think. He had to rush somewhere when a plane got hijacked. Where did he go?'

'Honey. I guess he went to wherever the plane was and wrote a story about it.'

'Do you really not know?'

'I guess not.'

'Well, why would he have gone to Uganda? They must have had an Africa correspondent who was nearer. He wasn't covering this stuff. Eves, I think he was involved. I think he might have been a spy. I think he was working for the government. Might have been . . . or for someone . . .'

You see, here I was cowering on my sofa in the dark, having had ambulance and police round, having faced revelation after revelation, having not eaten, shaking with the earth-shattering significance of everything, so that it took me a second to realise that Evie was not choking to death or having a heart attack or sobbing uncontrollably. She was laughing her head off.

It was infectious. I was so tired and so frayed, so baffled by the turns this story had taken, that I started laughing too. I laughed until my cheeks hurt and I was doubled over clutching my stomach and begging Evie to stop. When we both caught our breath, sighing still with laughter, Evie spoke.

'Jesus, Pumpkin,' she said. 'I can't believe you didn't know that.'

Chapter Twelve

I fell asleep on the plane and when I pushed up my sunglasses to squint out of the window we'd already landed. I was sitting next to a nun. A lot of glinting, flashing bright blue sea, palm trees, higgledy piggledy golden houses and churches, a low white airport building like they have at the smaller airfields in remote Africa, and a beautiful dusky woman in a khaki uniform and reflector shades waving the plane in with big red lollipops. It looked more like Greece or the Middle East than Italy and I suddenly felt more ready to like the place than I had done – I could see, even from 43F, that it had the heat and chaos I need.

I'd been on the phone to Evie practically until dawn, mostly just shouting at her for not having told me. But again, a bit like watching Ihsan's film, once something is a fact it is absorbed as a fact, almost as though it has always been known. Her explanations sounded reasonable – we talked about him more as a person, about how much we missed him, especially when I was little. Not about his job, about the man he was when we weren't around. And then she'd moved on and got remarried and she'd felt that he was my property now. I'd never asked about his work and she'd never thought to tell me, hadn't thought it was important. After all, lots of journalists end up doing a bit of espionage on the side. You know when journalists are captured in foreign countries and accused of spying? It's because they're spying. Nobody but an idiot is remotely surprised by this. I remember looking up at the TV in some hotel room a while ago and seeing this bloke from the *Telegraph* protesting his innocence in handcuffs somewhere – Malaysia, maybe. And what I thought was, 'Oh, I didn't know he was a spy.'

And Pip, of course. He left me a message saying he'd discharged himself and gone to stay with his ex – 'for my sins'.

Anyway, I was getting my bag out of the overhead locker ('Ladies and Gentlemen welcome to Falcone-Borsellino airport'), the heat and the smell of the sea and, perhaps, lemons had already come into the plane through the open doors, and I heard someone up front causing a commotion.

'Oi! Woofter! Don't touch that. Did you touch that? I said don't touch that. Are you deaf?'

I stood on tiptoes to see above everyone's heads, though I knew perfectly well who it was.

'Hey! Don! McCaughrean!' I shouted. How the hell could he afford to be in business class? Annoying. I once went on a TV talk show, you know, where you sit round opining about the news (no knowledge required), and we had to get a train to Manchester. They bought the CNN bloke a first class ticket and I was in slime. I couldn't decide if it was a TV/print thing or a British/American thing. Either way, I had a cheese sandwich in cellophane while he had a full English breakfast served at his poncy little table. Bastard.

Don spun round, bashing the man behind him with his camera bag. The injured party was one of those blokes with complicated thin strips of facial hair and sunglasses resting oddly in the middle of his forehead. How do they do that? And is that why it's supposed to be cool? Because it's so incredibly difficult to do? The man said something about Don's 'culo' which I was glad he didn't understand, given his pre-existing state, presumably related to his camera bag and his old bloody Nikon. But, God, I was glad to see him.

'Eff Zed! Fuck me! It's as bloody tight as a virgin's minge in here!' he yelled, hustled off the plane and into the blurry-edged heat by a harassed steward. A hippyish-looking woman with a baby in a sling and three other small and smeary-faced kids tutted loudly. English, obviously.

I shoved past people to reach him, taking the stairs down to the runway sideways and tripping over a folded push-chair that was waiting for someone at the bottom. Funny how things come into your line of vision only if they relate to you. I had never knowingly seen a pushchair on or near a plane before I had Ben. Now there seemed to be hundreds of them waiting by the steps of everything I ever got off. The sky was lapis lazuli blue like Mary's headdress in those medieval paintings. Almost sharp.

I finally got to Don as he toddled into the arrivals shed thing, waving his passport around drunkenly. 'All right. All right. Keep your knickers on, Zanetti. I've come to work with you. I'm not trying to sodding well run away,' he said, kissing me on both cheeks, his sweat running on to my face.

'Yuk,' I said. 'What do you mean work with me? What the fuck are you doing here?'

'Jonesy gave me a bell. Told me to come and keep an eye on you. Shoot whatever you come up with, you know,' McCaughrean said, putting his bag on the table for the caramel-skinned customs babe to examine. 'I cleared it with your foreign desk.' 'Careful, love,' he told her. 'It's a fucking classic, that.'

Quite rightly, having fixed him with a sultry glare, she ignored him. 'What? He told you to come and babysit me? What is WRONG with that bloke? I am practically a hundred years old. I bloody well dragged you out from under that car in Grozny and I'm not even going to go into the number of times I've saved Eden Jones's scabby little life (four). I don't need a bloody bodyguard,' I said, breaking into a sweat myself now, swept forward by the shouting, gesticulating crowds to the heap of suitcases in the centre of the hall, tugged at by taxi drivers and limousine peddlers. No, not peddle in that sense. Don got carried off a few people in front of me.

'Fine. I'll go back to Moscow then, Zanetti. Nice to see you and everything. It was fun. Arrivederci,' he said, looking backwards, red-faced.

'No!' I shouted. 'Don't go! Stay! It's just that . . .'

And suddenly we'd been spat through a pair of glass doors and into the noisy swelter of a bus stop and taxi pick-up where a driver was standing with a card that said 'Zanetti' on it in that European handwriting they all have.

Don shook the bloke's hand and stuffed himself into the back with his bags. 'Where are we staying?' he asked, wheezing as he lit his fag.

'WE are not staying anywhere. I am staying at the Grand Hotel Villa Egeia. You are staying in whatever hovel you can afford.'

'Hey. I might just book myself a little suite at the Egeia. I'm corporate now, you know. Cunts in suits. Make a fucking fortune.'

I sighed. Poor Ira. How did she stand it? Don had married a Russian woman he met in Baghdad and they lived in the suburbs of Moscow with their little son and were occasionally visited by Don's older kids. He was always on the wagon and going to meetings at the British Embassy and then toppling off and going into Russian-style week-long drinking binges with old blokes he found in the pancake bars.

The car choked into gear and set off throwing up a cloud of orange dust. The driver had a crucifix glued to his dashboard and a photo of his daughter at her first communion in a gold plastic frame. We were obviously driving down the coast but I only got occasional glimpses of the sea through the trees, as bright as sapphires. There were a couple of families sitting in the shade finishing lunch on a blanket and a pair of tously girls cycled out in swimming costumes, pigtails flying. There were olive groves and lemon groves, oranges and green walnuts. Young men on rusting Vespas overtook us constantly. One of them, a fag hanging out of his mouth, had his girlfriend on the back in a flowered dress that billowed up as she clung to his brown and half-naked body. I wanted to be her.

Everyone was going home from the beach now and there were women and children standing around the vans that had parked up to sell fruit, bread, garlands of red chillis, salamis and cheeses from their open doors. The light was going that deep dusty pink and the old men crouching at the side of the road over their vats of olives and capers were smiling gold teeth at each other.

'This is beautiful!' I said, leaning out to breathe the sea in. I should have known better than to say an openly enthusiastic thing in front of Don McCaughrean.

'What do you mean?' he wheezed, flicking his fag butt out of the window. The driver spun round and told him that was illegal because of forest fires, but Don didn't understand.

'What's up his arse?' he mumbled, complaining.

'You know. Beautiful. Nice place. Sun. Sea. Natural abundance. That kind of thing.'

'Looks like Lebanon to me,' he said. 'Which, as everyone knows, is a shit-pit full of nutters.'

It was true, it did look a bit like Lebanon, actually, which, as everybody knows, is extremely beautiful. Sea and mountains. No volcanoes in Lebanon though. And poor Sicilians aren't as poor as poor Lebanese. There was something about the ease and languor of these people that betrayed the fact that their country hasn't been ravaged by war in the past half century. That they're used to the harvests coming in, the sun shining and the fish practically hopping out of the sea on to their plates. Here was a guy in a black felt trilby he'd bought in about 1952 standing proprietorially in front of an enormous heap of watermelons, hundreds of them, piled opulently on top of each other, gleaming green and stripy.

'Anyway, fuck are we doing here?' Don moaned.

'God, I was pleased to see you for a second on the plane back there,' I said. 'I'm planning my Sicilian life column. What are you doing here?'

'Oh. Really? Am I shooting terracotta jars of marinaded lemons with wooden spoons then? I thought we were on a Mafia story.'

I laughed.

'We're on a Cairnbridge story,' I said, lighting a cigarette.

'Cairnbridge???? That was YEARS ago,' Don said, his flesh shaking with indignation.

'I know. I know. That's what I said. But you know our editor's totally obsessed with it and it's the anniversary coming up.'

'Fifteenth? Is it?'

'In your dreams McCaughrean. In your tiny little dreams. Twenty-fifth.'

'Oh shit.'

'I know. Anyway, someone issued a warning to the embassy in Reykjavik . . .'

'Spooky,' he said, and wriggled his sausagey fingers in a ghostly manner.

'Well, not really. They did usually used to warn. But it was basically ignored and normally with a warning you then have the warners claiming responsibility. But that never happened so it was a bit weird in the end. ANYway, here I am looking for the Reykjavik caller,'

'But, like, Eff Zed though. He'll be dead or insignificantly junior anyway and who cares and what kind of story is that and I want to go home.'

'Look. I agree. I do. But then it got interesting. I interviewed this old poof of a spy who then blew his head off after claiming he did the warning to save his boyfriend. Which was just absurd and a lie. And then Pip got beaten up at my flat while I was out . . .'

'Pip Deakin? Oh. Yeh. Sorry about that.'

'Don't be silly. And, well, other shit that I don't want to go into. But it's more interesting than it looked. You know Ihsan El Sayed?'

'Al Jazeera?'

'Yes.'

'Tosser.'

'Oh, I liked him. Cute.'

'Exactly. Tosser.'

'Anyway, he did a thing ages ago about how it wasn't Libya or Syria or Iran or Palestine or any of the . . .'

'Terrorists.'

'Arabs.'

'Whatever.'

'He thinks it's a Western conspiracy, you know how they

133

do? Well, I think in this case it is. It was an Italian Mafia job. This is his theory, anyway. The CIA were about to grass the protected suitcase up and stop them doing it so they basically murdered the boys who were on their way to report it. Then America used the Arabs as an excuse to do what they'd already planned to do anyway – bomb Libya.'

'Help me here,' Don said, craning round to look at me as we bounced across deep potholes and swerved violently to avoid a goat. 'I thought it WAS the CIA who was protecting that suitcase.'

'Well, it was. But a rogue thing, you know. To get information about the people here . . .'

'Right here, you mean?'

'Yes. Sicily. Who were murdering judges, remember? The airport's named after two of them. This is what Ihsan reckons.'

'So they had a Mafia grass, did they?'

'Must've,' I shrugged.

'Whoah.'

'Yeah.'

We were quiet then as the city started growing up around us. We were in narrow dirty streets now, lined with those hole-in-the-wall shops lit by one bare bulb that swings under a canopy and whose goods spill on to the pavement. Shops that close as suddenly as they open with the clang of an iron shutter. They mostly seemed to be flogging sacks of coloured spices or boxes of pink Turkish delight and nougat with pistachios, green sugary jellies and caramelised nuts. The ones with the biggest crowds (six fat old ladies in black dresses with black headscarves, 60-dernier flesh-coloured tights and black slip-on shoes four sizes too small so their feet spill over the sides) were the hardware stalls with plastic washing up bowls, dustpans and brushes and detergents with unknown labels. Occasionally, we'd take a corner with a handbrake turn and skip up a no-entry alley where one-eyed stray cats and three-legged dogs would lurk, hunched and cowering, while women would empty slop (or perhaps just washing water) and plastic bags of rubbish out of the back window and down into the street.

'Holy fuck,' Don said, and actually retched. He is very sensitive for all his bravado.

'Do not vomit in the vehicle,' I told him.

'Right,' he nodded.

Then it all got a bit elegant. Tourist centre, I imagine. Clipped gardens with healthier looking palms and iron fences around slides and swings, a candyfloss stall, enormous baroque villas painted yellow and pink, with cascading stair-cases and bright flowered bushes outside in pots. Here were all the flashy shops and cafés with good looking people sit-ting outside over a granita or a red wine, these dogs on slim leather leads, waiting nicely with their fur puffed up from their mistress's comb. I didn't see a woman here of any age who wasn't wearing high heels. Couples strolled, the elderly sat on benches in front of a grand church that looked, weirdly, almost Islamic in terms of architecture, but had a give-away cross on top.

Sinking into the warmth of it, I was almost dozing off with my face against the rattling window, when a handsome boy in a top hat and tails opened the car door for me, dragging a shining brass luggage trolley behind him.

'Signora?' he said, bending to assist me.

'Oh. Wow. No. No. Grazie,' I said, clambering out all by myself and showing him that I only had hand-luggage anyway. He looked disappointed and went to help Don. Yuh.

Good luck, I thought, skipping up the ornate steps to the hotel entrance, which was flanked by palms, gleaming with marble inside and all shivery in the icy icy cold air conditioning.

Chapter Thirteen

Champagne steaming in a silver bucket on a stand, vase after vase of pink, yellow and white roses and butter muslin curtains billowing inwards in the sea breeze. Now, that's what I call a hotel. Not too shabby for Faith Zanetti. I threw myself down on the duvet, boots on the floor, lying on my back, and lit a cigarette. The bed linen was as white and squeaky as new snow and I knew my jeans, jacket and even, let's face it, hair, would dirty them. A mosquito – it was that time in the evening – screamed round my head and I put my hand up and caught it in my fist.

Don called to say he was going out to do a few Palermo a notte shots to see if he could flog them to some travel pages. 'Don't you worry about old Don,' he said, coughing.

'Well, that's a load off, thanks,' I said.

'No, honestly, I'll be fine.'

'I! KNOW!' I shouted, and hung up.

I think before I'd had Ben I would have found Walter's flowers, the champagne, the grand romantic gesture of it all a bit much, a bit sleazy, not in good taste. You want to get laid? Ask me if I'm interested. I wouldn't have needed or wanted all this. If I didn't want to, it wouldn't change my mind and if I did, you wouldn't need to do it. But now it was, frankly, nice to know I could still get the attention. Amazing what babies can do to your self confidence. I think it must be that knowledge that you've fulfilled your biological purpose so there's no longer any need for sex appeal.

I stood up and poured myself a glass of champagne. An antique glass with tiny patterns engraved into it. I took my drink out on to the balcony and couldn't help smiling all over my face. Despite everything. I mean, you have to know when you're lucky, right? Boats were twinkling out on the sea and starched tablecloths were being flicked out on the terrace below me, silverware wheeled to the tableside and black-haired uniformed waiters making complicated things out of the napkins, chatting and laughing. And the sea.

There was a note on my coffee table embossed with the hotel logo and written on thick cream card. 'Dinner on the terrace at 9? W.' Wandering towards one of the vases of roses I noticed that they came with a card too. God, he was really going for it. Or, actually, was he? 'The people of Sicily welcome Faith Zanetti,' it said. Okey dokey. Well, Faith Zanetti is jolly glad to be welcomed. If a trifle taken aback.

I lay in a huge iron tub on lion's feet in a cloud of rose-smelling bubbles and I combed conditioner out of a blue glass bottle with a real silver lid through my frizz, just like my mum used to tell me I should. Fresh white T-shirt, clean jeans. Hmm. Not exactly knocking them dead. I found a weird sort of sponge in a plastic box that said it was for cleaning shoes and I wiped the front of my boots with it. There. I mean, what more could a gentleman ask? I knew the answer to this, OK. I just didn't have any of that shit. Lipstick. Jewellery. Nyetu. As they say in Russian.

Walter stood up as I walked across the stone flagging to

our table, dropping his napkin and kissing me on both cheeks. 'And here IS Faith Zanetti,' he said, sitting down and scrutinising the wine list. 'So, I ordered for you, Faith. Take a liberty. Took the liberty. Gavi, Gavi, Gavi. That's what we want I think. How was your trip? Good? Good. Fine. Great. And here we are. What do you think? Not too shabby huh?'

Exactly what I'd thought, myself.

The oil-eyed waiter came and Walter ordered wine.

'The best for Miss Zanetti here.' He smiled, glancing over the top of his glasses with irony and affection all at the same time.

'Miss Zanetti?' the waiter said, as though mulling my name over, impressed, awed. And he performed a sweeping bow.

'They're going to love you here,' Walter nodded. 'Or they're gonna pretend to, right? And who are we to scrutinise the difference? Who are we anyway? Listen, Faith. I shocked you didn't I? On the phone? I know I did. Fact is, I was interviewed years ago, back in the States. Went out to Arlington on a crack course, wore us down, tried to break us, build us up again and interview us some more. Well, what can I tell you? I was a younger man. A younger fitter man back there. I don't know. It's not so bad though. Not too bad?'

He held out his arm and flexed his muscles, inviting me to feel them. I laughed.

'Looking good,' I said. I can't remember now if it was true or not. I think it was starting to feel true what with the champagne and the sea and the stars. The tables around us were mostly taken, old couples, women with set hair and ostentatious décolletage, men in shirts, open at the neck, though they looked as though they'd feel more comfortable in a tie.

'Look at that guy. That one. See him? In the blue shirt? You think he's her father. Look. They're close. See how he looks at her. Oooh. In't she purdy.' He was smirking. 'That ain't no daddy, Faith.' I agreed with him. He was not the girl's father. She was wearing shoes with diamante straps.

Walter seemed entirely unaware that he was old enough, just about, to be my father, though perhaps these age gaps narrow the older you are. Maybe people can't see much of a gap between forty and seventy. Perhaps at my age one is supposed to be grateful for whatever attention you can get. And, hell, I am.

The waiter brought us huge grilled prawns on a white plate. Walter grabbed one before the boy had completely let go and started gnawing at the shell to get it off.

'God, I love these. Grazie mille. Love them. So, they put me through the mill and then I didn't get the job and, Faith Zanetti, you know what? Nobody ever gets the job. So there I am, jobless, kicking about in Beirut, Cyprus, drinking ouzo, seeing what I could see, researching book projects. And, hey, there's Perry Boyd sitting at the same cafés as me, reading Pravda. Well, I'm exaggerating but you know what I mean. And you know who else? Sam Fischer. Sam Fischer, that idiot. No clue. No clue at all what was going on. Brits must have been the worst informed government in the world. God, I loved Beirut though. Most beautiful women I've ever seen. Green eyes . . . perfect skin. Well, you know how that feels, Faith. How does it feel?'

'Right now, not bad,' I said quietly, easing into the evening and the lull of Walter's voice telling me stuff I would probably wish I'd never known. I peeled a prawn.

'Cyprus I never warmed to. Too much going on. Worse than Beirut. Dangerous work for those with a job. If I'da had one I'da known, right? Nobody ever gets the job, Faith.

Nobody ever gets the job. And I'll tell you another thing – nobody ever wants the damn job.'

'And Karel Zanetti? Was he there too?'

Walter dipped his hands into a bowl of iced water with slices of lemon floating in it. He dried them on his napkin and wiped his mouth. He took a swig of wine and sighed, taking his glasses off and folding them, putting them down on the table.

'Ah. So, you got there. We were waiting for you to get there,' he said, glancing at the boy to come and take our plates away. And his gaze got taken to another table now too. A young man, sitting alone, short back and sides, neat shirt, pressed trousers. He was so similar to my guy that I almost thought it was him. But I realised, even before Walter spoke, that he must be my guy's replacement. Aah. I'd got him sacked. I felt sorry really. I'm not sure if they were being sent to scare me or make me feel safe but, perhaps perversely, I had found him reassuring. Just to be watched and to know that my instincts were right. This was a big deal to someone other than me.

'Have I got shit in my teeth?' I asked him, baring my teeth like a gorilla. I have a phobia about this.

'What, you mean, like, actual faeces, is this what you're asking me?'

'No, you idiot. Broccoli. Or spinach?' I bared my teeth again.

'We haven't eaten either of those items, Faith Zanetti,' he laughed.

'Parsley then?'

'Nothing. Honestly.' He laughed again. 'You're sweet,' he said. 'You know that?'

I didn't.

'Look at that! They're here. Who're they following? Me

or you? Spot these people from a hundred miles away. It's ridiculous. You'd think after all these years, wouldn't you? I mean, at least try and mingle, right? Did we look like that back then? That obvious? I don't think so. But then I wouldn't would I? Would I, Faith?'

'I suppose not. He's for me, I think. I've had someone on me since I started this. Thought I was going mad for a while. I approached him yesterday and the poor thing must have been fired. Now we've got this one. The other one was better looking.'

Walter laughed.

'Turbot with morels,' the waiter said, in English, producing a huge white fish with mushrooms arranged around it. He put it down on a trolley and filetted it with spoons. The hotel lights had been turned down and out here it was just the candles in glass globes, showing the faces of all the couples leaning in towards each other on a dark night by the sea.

'Ah, yes. Morals. Well, we know you love those, Faith Zanetti. We all love those. Get those morals down you. Right? Yes. Karel Zanetti. He was around, Faith. He was. He was around, but he was different. Always with the prettiest girls, always slouched at the bar with a martini in his hand. Up with a twist,' he said, and mimicked the way Dad had ordered his drink, turning his hand to demonstrate the twist to the waitress. 'Up with a twist. Remember? You probably don't. Up with a twist.' Walter sighed and popped a mushroom into his mouth.

I pushed my food away. I took my napkin off my lap and put it on my plate. Finished. I lit a cigarette.

'Look, Walter. This is all gripping stuff, but I am baffledissimo. I'm being tailed by the CIA, my friends are being beaten to a pulp, I am receiving extremely odd calls and cards and I don't know what kind of role you're trying to play? I feel as though I'm working my arse off to find out things you already know, that you could have told me in the first place. I don't really understand what you're up to.' As I spoke I suspected he'd scrawled Ihsan's name on his Rolodex just before Pip got in there – knowing I'd send him to look. Ugh.

A champagne cork was popped at the next table and we both glanced round nervously, smiling then in acknowledgment of our shared twitch.

'Ah, yes. What I'm up to.' He rolled up the sleeves of his linen jacket and his shirt at the same time and ran both hands through his salt and pepper hair. Women aren't allowed salt and pepper hair, are they? It's just grey. Or, worse, 'streaked with grey'. 'What I'm up to. It has long been a mystery to me too, Faith. What can I tell you? But can I tell you? Perhaps I should tell you? Should I? Should. Ought. Hmm. Never liked them. I didn't know about the bomb. I knew about the drugs and we were watching it. I wasn't involved but I planned to report it. There but for the grace of God. I knew Summerman and Leith. Perry was in love with Summerman. I think there was a brief fling before he found out Perry was a double agent . . . Was he double? You know what, I can't even remember. Maybe it turned out he'd completely sold his soul. He did in the end. Sell it. Not to the Russians though. I didn't know about the bomb, Faith. But a lot of people did. I believe they knew, I do. And I want to . . . I will be happy if they could be found. I am not authorised . . . It's not something I can do. But it's time.'

I waved for an espresso and beckoned the waiter to bend down to my ear. 'E una piccola vodka per favore. Senza ghiaccio. Grazie.' I winked at him and he twinkled back. Walter looked disapproving, an expression that slapped twenty years right on him. He lifted a finger. High up behind him a woman came out on to one of the hotel balconies in a long silk nightie. The whole scene was like an idealised past. Apparently Caruso stayed here. I could imagine it.

'Let me give you a tip. That's not going to help. That's not going to help with anything. Not ever. Not short term. Not long term. But it's your business. Your business. Of course it is. The exclusive business of Faith Cleopatra Zanetti. Her domain.'

I leaned my elbows on the table. Someone started playing the white grand piano that stood under a twisting tree in an alcove by the edge of the terrace that dropped to the sea. Frank Sinatra. That kind of thing. These trees looked like they should be in Louisiana. You know, with that hanging stuff. Makes it look hot even when it isn't. Though, this evening, it was.

'Yeah, but Walter though. What is this? You and that guy sitting over there are waiting for me to somehow break an enormous Mafia story that might get me killed so that you can follow along behind and get some kind of vicarious revenge for an age old grudge? Something that you are "not allowed" to follow up. I mean, that's ridiculous.'

'Ridiculous? Well of course it's ridiculous, Faith. The whole business is ridiculous. I learned that many years ago. Long before I got out. Though of course I can't have got out if I never got in, right? Long before I got out. Yes, it's ridiculous. But it's people doing their best. Trying to do their best. That's all it is. Can't live with us, can't live without us. That's how the world is. We were trying to keep the peace, Faith. Most of us. Nothing else. And you must know that nobody is about to let the protected drugs thing out – let it be proved. It will always be denied. It's a matter of public record – you remember the guy who said, "Both our governments know what happened and they will never tell." That's about right.'

Sanctimonious crap! I thought. Keep the peace? Pah. What peace? Where is this peace being kept?

'Sanctimonious crap!' I said. 'Don't give me this world-saving shit. I don't believe it. What is your interest here? What, Walter? Come on!'

Our guy had got bored and ordered a bottle of wine. I was tempted to go and tell him off for drinking on the job. But then my vodka came and a violinist joined the pianist, throwing me off my thought train.

'The children. My interest is the children,' he said, and I noticed that his lip was trembling slightly. All romance over, he stood up, put his glasses back on and looked at me. 'The children,' he said and walked away, back towards the hotel.

Everyone had turned to look at me and I smiled and waved. Yup. Here I am. Had a row with my boyfriend and he's walked off. That's what it looked like. My guy stayed, pretending to read his book, so that cleared up whose he was if it needed clearing up. Which it didn't. This was about me. My centre of the universe complex was getting way out of control. I lit a cigarette and finished my vodka, then my wine. They were playing 'Love Me Tender' and I remembered that first phone call and how mad my reaction had been. God. I shook my head and felt cold all over, my skin tightening. The physical phenomenon before the conscious thought. I realised. Suddenly realised.

I nearly knocked the chair over standing up and I pretty much ran over to the waiter to ask him to charge it to my room and then into the hotel and up the marble stairs, into my lavish room where one of the vases had blown over, spilling roses and giving the room a ransacked, sad look. And on to my computer. Switch on the computer. Passenger list. Passenger list. Passenger list. I scrolled down, willing it not to be true. Please don't be true. Please don't be true. How could I not have realised this? How could I not have noticed? Not have known? How could you not have known? This seemed to apply to me a lot at the moment.

Illaryan, Ipswich, Irving. Jessica Irving. Unaccompanied child. Seven years old.

I leaned forward and put my head in my hands. Jessica Irving. Jessie. Oh, but I hoped she hadn't had time to be scared. Did somebody hold her? Tears were seeping through my fingers and I picked up the phone.

'Hey,' I said, barely able to get a word out.

'Hi, darling. You OK? You sound funny,' Eden whispered.

'No. I'm fine. I just . . . Is Bennie all right? How is he? Can I talk to him?'

'He's right here. He couldn't be better. He's asleep though, love. Do you want me to wake him up?'

I sighed and smiled. These things, these things that wrench your heart out, really they just remind you how selfish you are. Because there is only one thing I care about. Perhaps it is good to be reminded.

'No. No, don't wake him up. I'll call you tomorrow . . .'

'Don't go! I'm awake now. How's it going? Anything new?'

I sighed hard. 'God, Eden. So much. But I don't want to talk about it to be honest.' I smiled to myself. To be honest! 'I'll call you tomorrow. Night.'

'Night babe. I love you,' Eden said. I put the phone down. Well, there you are.

I hated seeing her name there on that fucking list. My sister's name. Maybe. Well, it explained why Phoebe had got so hysterical and left. Not about Dad or about me. Her daughter died. Her little girl had been on the bloody plane. How old would she be now? Only a couple of years younger than me. A couple of years. We could have been friends. I could have had a little sister just like I'd always wanted. And I realised that when I didn't ask questions, when I banished her from my mind and refused to acknowledge her, I realised that it wasn't because I didn't care. I had invented a life for her, imagined her crossing a road in jeans, holding a handbag with her sunglasses on her head. I had given her a school life and three years at university, boyfriends and piano lessons. All in an instant. Not this. Not her lungs exploding as the air rushed through the fucking cabin. Did she have little fat hands? Did she like butterflies? And I hated myself for muttering my prayer in the night for having conceded anything to a God who either doesn't exist or is evil. I threw the fallen vase across the room, making a slash of water on the sage carpet and scattering the stupid roses. I don't even like fucking roses. The people of Sicily for Christ's sake.

For a moment I thought he'd gone. When I knocked on the door. 'Walter?' I said, knocking again. 'Walter? Are you there? Please let me in.'

And then I could hear movement and a click as he pulled the door back, wearing an oversized grey T-shirt and long shorts, blinking, confused.

I threw my arms round his neck and hugged him as tightly as I could. 'Oh, Walter. I'm so sorry. I'm so so sorry.'

And, when he realised, he hugged me back and began to cry.

Without switching the lights on we walked over to his bed and lay down. I kissed his cheeks and his forehead and his eyes and I kissed his mouth, gently, trying to kiss the pain away. And I remembered a woman whose son had died saying to me once, 'Well, I have to believe in God. I have to. I have to believe I'll see him again. Otherwise I'd go mad.'

And I wanted to think it was true. That someone might look after Jessie and hold her hand until I get there. Because I so want to give her a hug. And it won't be long really. In the scheme of things I won't be far behind. And Walter just held on to me, one hand in the small of my back and the other in my hair. 'Faith,' he said. 'Faith.'

And I understood that he really didn't know. Should never know.

I dreamt about Heaven that night. I knew it was heaven because everything was white and there was mist every-where. You know how they do get through the dry ice in the afterlife. For some reason. Anyway, in the dream it was seri-ous and desperately sad, but wonderful at the same time and I didn't feel cynical about the dry ice. I had arrived and was walking towards a line of people who were there to meet me, all smiling completely openly, almost sadly, as if apologising for the ridiculous ways in which we hadn't been able to love each other, really appreciate each other, when we'd had the chance. My dad stepped forward to hug me first, wearing my leather jacket, looking as though he'd been expecting me, had wished he could tell me that it wouldn't be long now, and behind him Dimitri, my Russian ex-husband who shrugged as if to say, 'Yeah, well. Here we are. What are you going to do?' Then Shiv, who hanged herself in Jerusalem years ago, laughing and kissing my cheeks and, at the back, Jessie, who jumped up into my arms, wrapping herself around my middle and burying her face in my hair. 'I waited and waited!' she said and I squeezed her as tight as I could.

In the morning I walked out on to the balcony in a white robe and I even put on the slippers to feel the towelling on my clean toes. The toes of a new person who'd had a sister and lost her. Walter came out from behind the curtain, his

148

face grim, older somehow, without his bravado on. Was that why he kept up his reassuring rambling all the time, never pausing, never deserting you for a moment? Was it for her? Was he trying to comfort her? He was holding a small photograph. It was a school photo in one of those brown cardboard frames and she was grinning, told to say 'sausages', into the camera, her eyes scrunched up, dimples in her pudgy pink cheeks. She had brown hair that Phoebe had put into plaits on either side of her head, making her look even more cheeky, and curls were springing out of them round her face.

'What was she wearing?' I whispered. 'That day. What was she wearing?'

'I was meeting . . . I was supposed to meet her in New York. I promised to take her skating at the Rockefeller Center. I can't look at that place now. And they use it so much. In every film, you know? Phoebe told me, when she called to say she'd sent her through with the stewardess and another kid flying alone, she called to say she was wearing a striped sweater. And jeans. Jeans with flowers embroidered on them. Little flowers.' He took the photograph out of my hand and turned away, back inside.

The sky was a searing blue and the sea sparkled under it, completely clear to the sand on the bottom. Straggly deformed and windswept trees were scattered around the top of the beach and up towards the terrace where Don McCaughrean was eating his breakfast. I rustled my personality up.

'Hey!' I shouted down.

'Zanetti, you fucking slag? I was banging on your door all night expecting a shag. Did you take a mogodon or what?' he yelled. He was joking. At least, I bloody hope he was joking.

'Ah. Don. You're sweet,' I said, blowing him a kiss. 'Down in a sec.'

Chapter Fourteen

Don had tucked his napkin into his collar and there were already dribbles of hot chocolate on it. He'd put a fag out in the cup and was now buttering the underside of a croissant with a tiny little glinting knife that looked miniature in his ham hand. 'You are never going to believe this, Eff Zed, but our luck is way in. Guess how many Mafia-related killings there have been this very morning within a ten – one, two, three, four, five, six, seven, eight, nine, ten – mile radius of here?' I sat down and was brought a heavy silver pot of black coffee.

'Dunno, Don. Two.'

White birds were swooping in the sky. It was so blue I put my shades on.

'Seventeen. SevenTEEN?! Can you imagine? I was watching it on the news. Can't understand the Italian channels but BBC World's got it. Haven't got a correspondent over from Rome yet but they're using RAI thingy's pictures. They think it's a war. This huge inter-clan war. Icing each other like nobody's business. Fucking morons.'

As he was speaking, my phone, which was in the front pocket of my leather jacket, rang.

'Hi, Zanetti. It's Tamsin. Listen, are you in Palermo? Did you find Don?'

'Yes and, oh yes. And, yes again, I've heard the news. Do you want something on it?'

'Do we? Are you crazy? It's the front page. No question. It's all happening up in the hills near . . .' she left the receiver to check. I heard her shouting at someone. 'Hey! You lot. Where're the mafia murders happening?' She came back. 'Near Bis-ac-quino.'

Funny when you hear the names of these places and things for the first time. Like Cairnbridge and Zeebrugge, Aberfan, Hungerford. Just little places but their names get associated forever with death. And Bisacquino would be the same.

'Mafia heartland blah blah blah, you know. Up where they finally found that bloke who murdered all the judges and hundreds of other people. Prizzi or something. Remember? He just lived there perfectly happy until his driver, honestly, his DRIVER, turned him in. But that's where you go . . . it shouldn't be far from you. Give me eight hundred words for four o'clock our time. We'll do a box. You know – top ten Mafia massacres and top ten Mafia films. Godfathers One, Two and Three . . .'

'Tamsin? I get it,' I said. 'You should get Sam to do a cover mount of the DVDs.'

'Not at all a bad idea. No time though. Maybe for Saturday. Any luck with the other thing? Tell me later,' she said, the receiver halfway down before she'd finished speaking.

I looked at Don who was wiping his mouth and lighting another fag.

'We're on it, McCaughrean. I'll get reception to hire us a car. Up to somewhere called Bisacquino, in the hills. You know, near all those places like Corleone and Prizzi. Not far, apparently,' I said.

'Can't you borrow a motor off your boyfriend?' Don asked, burping loudly. A fat wasp was buzzing round his head .

'God. How do you KNOW this stuff?'

Don put his hands over his ears and rolled his big head around in what he must have thought was some psychic sort of way.

'Anyway, not my boyfriend but a friend of my late father's and, if you must know, he's gone to visit some writers' commune over on the other coast for the day. I'll get the car.'

Don burped again.

'Jesus,' I said.

'You do realise,' Don started, hauling his flobulating body from his seat, already sweating into his shirt though the sun wasn't even hot yet, 'that we'll be in a traffic jam all the way up there. Every fucking news organisation in the world is going to be driving to this shit pit, flying in from bloody Doha, you know. People love this shit. Especially if we've got bodies in black suits lying in the streets. Al Pacino, you know.'

'You think HE'S here?' I laughed.

'Hey! I walked past that church this morning, you know when he's shot on the steps at the end of *Godfather Three* and—'

'Yup. Yes, Don. *The Godfather*. I know. It's a famous film about the Mafia. Tamsin's putting a box together on it. Christ. People actually died, you know . . .' I found myself saying.

'Ooooooooh!' Don mocked, waddling behind me with his camera bag, mimicking a prissy school mistress, whatever that even means. Something misogynistic.

'Anyway,' I turned round and walked backwards. 'We

152

might be first up there. It will only be the locals so far. It's at least an hour's flight from Rome. Nobody will be here yet. Especially if they only kicked off this morning.'

It was a relief to be leaving my Cairnbridge nightmare, especially after last night, and, somehow, going off on an ordinary news job with Don made me feel sane again. I suppose that, though obviously it was a touch on the shocking side, the spying thing had made me relax a bit about my eerie calls and the card. I imagined spies being the kind of people who were good at doing voices and forging handwriting that must, I now realised, have been well-known to them. Not that something reeeeally weird wasn't going on, but it had lost its scare and, leaning across the brass and mahogany reception desk to ask for my messages didn't come with the shivering horror of hallucinations and ghostly apparitions. Somebody didn't want me to turn up Karel Zanetti's information on Cairnbridge and they knew how to try to stop me. That was all.

We had to hang around in the lobby waiting for the car and Don spent the whole time slumped in a yellow silk-upholstered chair under a Moorish glass lamp polishing his lenses and occasionally muttering, 'Hasselblad.' It sounds like a swear word. Or Rumpelstiltskin or something. The magical password whose very utterance turns grain to gold. Apparently it is a type of camera. A woman walked in with a little girl in red ribbons and my stomach twisted. I wasn't going to be confiding in Don though. Not about this stuff. He would only cry.

When the bell boy told us our car was ready he gave a little bow and very very nearly clicked his heels together. 'Miss Zanetti,' he said, with this immense reverence that, frankly, a person could really get used to. Perhaps it was him that left the flowers.

Don bustled down the steps to our little Fiat, out through the grand iron gates and past the bright oleander bushes. 'Ah,' he said, reaching out for the door handle. 'Back behind the wheel, at last.'

'Yuh. Don't think so, Dondon,' I said, shoving him out of the way and leaping into the driver's seat. I mean, honestly.

It was fun driving here. We got stuck and had to go round a big stone fountain three times when the other drivers wouldn't let us through to take our exit and, by the time we were out on the hill roads, the sun was really beating down on the car, cooking us on the inside. The landscape reminded me of Crete, with cliffs down to the sea, scraggly olive groves and tumbling white rocks, wandering goats and abandoned-looking churches baking in the sun, huge grave-yards with ornate white tombs behind railings and long alleyways. The roads were pleasingly terrible and I was beginning to feel all intrepid again, just knowing that I was driving out into craggy Mafia country to look at some fester-ing bodies.

We passed more than a few people riding horses with none of your hard hats, whips and silly boots, obviously using this as a means of transport rather than some status-ridden recreation (is the status thing left over from when the number of horses you owned was important?).

Bisacquino, it turned out, was a hilltop village with those narrow, vertically sloping cobbled alleys that I often dream about – walking up these lanes as my legs turn to jelly and I can't make it. Balconies hung out over the streets, stream-ing with red flowering plants and lines of washing. The age of the population seemed to average at a wizened-faced, toothless and headscarfed ninety-three. The place also had that very Araby feel to it like a lot of places here, and there were buildings with pointed archways and views through

154

to potted lemon trees in internal courtyards strewn with rugs.

It wasn't hard to find what we were looking for. We just followed the Carabinieri. And the Pronto Soccorso. And the fat white television vans with dishes and aerials on top of them and 'Sicilia 1' written on the side in slanting graphics. I pulled over when they did, dumping the car off the tarmac in an olive grove right on top of a mountain with views out across the sea to the horizon on every side.

'Fuck me!' Don said, catching sight of the deal and almost falling out of the car with his camera stuck to his face. His shirt was drenched and he ran as fast as he could over to the police lines that didn't look as if they'd been up long. And it was, after all, like a scene from a film. It's the scenery. You expect this kind of country road on a Mediterranean island to have, at the absolute most, an old man selling olives out of a bucket in the dust. Or perhaps, if you were feeling more like a pastoral idyll, a young girl decorating a crumbling roadside chapel with garlands of red flowers, her hair blowing in the breeze that swept all the way in from the glittering sea in the distance.

What you don't expect against this sort of backdrop is a heap of corpses, young men in expensive city clothes, their blood slick on the tarmac of the road, soaking into dry earth at the side and in the olive groves and, in the case of one of them, spattering the bonnet of a bullet-speckled car. A red vintage Alfa Spider. One correspondent, his company's van chugging next to him, was already going live in front of the scene, shouting into his microphone and gesticulating wildly. Don was lying on the floor under the police tape taking a close-up of one of the dead men's faces. It did look like a war. Like a meeting gone wrong. There were tyre skid marks all over the place showing that another car, or maybe cars, had left in a hurry, so there had been survivors. The driver of the Spider was sitting in his seat, his head flung back, his eyes open, blood everywhere. I've never seen anything like this. Not an execution of pathetic prisoners of war, marched to their death in a freezing forest, but a real battle and actual bullets still rolling about on the floor. No shortage of ammunition, obviously. There were small grey birds looking at us all from the trees and, not far away, a goatherd, his goats rambling about in the white stones, their bells ringing. I imagined he'd be questioned in a fairly big way tonight, however far over there he tried to amble.

I stood as close as I could get, listening to the Sicilian journalists shouting their questions at the police. Everyone wanted names but they weren't telling and, because we weren't in a village, there wasn't anyone about who we could grill, who might know. A policewoman in very tight trousers, her gun in its white leather holster at her hip, was drawing chalk lines round the Mafiosi. Nobody was in any doubt that that's what they were. The first reports that Don had been watching at the hotel went straight in with that as though it were a provable fact. I guess they've just seen it all before. But not on this scale. Not recently. This was real Chicago Valentine's Day stuff. I tried to work out who went with who, who was on what side. They were all wearing the Italian uniform of over-designed jeans, slim white trainers with slanting stripes on them or Campers, and tight T-shirts, some with a little pocket on the front, some with a wavy line sewn through in coloured cotton, a lot of broken sunglasses on the road and a few of them still wearing them. There was a set of keys in a sticky pool of blood, the key fob a solid gold 'G' and, yup, a whole load of guns. One guy was holding a submachine gun, maybe a Colt, a bit like the kind the police now carry cocked at English airports. Most of them had hand-guns either still in or lying near their hands. I could see a silver Beretta 36.2oz thing, a black Smith and Wesson double action and a Russian police issue, Makarov 9mm, surprisingly. Strange diversity. I pulled my notebook out of the back pocket of my jeans, my Biro from behind my ear (I know, I know, but my hair is frizzy enough to keep it there so it is, in fact, the handiest way to carry it. If naff. If a tiny bit naff) and wrote it all down. Don had managed to wriggle his way past the police and was now crouching by the car, still shooting. But then the woman drawing with the chalk started shouting at him. 'Via! Via!' and he shambled away, swearing.

'Stronza!' he said, under his breath. I didn't know he spoke Italian.

The weirdest thing I noticed, and I always try to ask myself what the most striking thing about a scene is (apart, of course, from the bleeding corpses, you know), was that a few of them were blonde. Well, not white blonde like Siberians or anything, but two of them, as far as I could see, had very curly dark blonde hair, a bit like mine actually. Always so odd to see people here without that black glossy stuff that I want to run my fingers through. But that meant, I decided, that these were brothers or, at least, cousins, close in age. And, as the Sicilia 1 correspondent wrapped her piece up, lowering her microphone and making a cutting motion with her fingers that made me want to shout 'Stone!', I shut my eyes slightly and thought about the women who would be weeping tonight. Tonight, and every night from now until the end of time.

I sat down on a rock and lit a cigarette, bringing my sunglasses down and dragging my hair back into a ponytail with an elastic band. I watched a lizard darting its glassy eyes about, not aware of me or of any of this. 'Love Me Tender, Love Me True . . .' I picked the phone up.

'Pronto?'

'Faith?'

'Yes.'

'It's Ihsan. Am I interrupting?'

'No. No. Not at all. No. I'm up a mountain in Sicily with seventeen dead Mafiosi. You?'

He laughed. 'Wow. They must have known you were coming. Did you get the tape?'

'Oh, God. I'm so crap. I should have called you. Yes, yes, I did. It's pretty convincing, Ihsan. I think I worked out why me investigating is more dangerous than anybody else investigating. It turns out my father was a British spy who was somehow involved in Cairnbridge. I guess he found something out that they think I might have access to.'

'Allah! That's huge. How did you find out?'

'Oh. You were right about Walter. He told me. He was out in Cyprus dicking around with them all too. And you're right that he knew it was the Italians and not the Arabs. God knows what else he knows. Whatever it is, I think it's the thing I'm looking for.'

'Any ideas?'

'Well. I got everything out of storage but there's nothing much. Just proof that Dad knew Karim Mohammed and was interested in him. In perhaps using him. I suppose paying him for information. And that Boyd knew them both.'

'Interesting. Interesting. But not . . . well, not the front page. So far.'

'No,' I agreed. 'Also, his daughter was on it.'

'Whose daughter? Your father's?'

Goodness. What an odd and difficult question. Eden would say I had engineered it because it was on my mind. Or that I wanted to confess to someone. My shrink would have agreed. Sod them both.

'Yes. No. Walter's,' I chose.

'You mean Irving had a daughter on the plane? Allah. Allah. Allah. You sure? How old was she?'

'Seven,' I whispered. 'Seven,' I said a bit more loudly. His gentle voice made me want to tell him what Phoebe had told me. To tell him that she was my sister. But I couldn't. Knew I shouldn't.

'So, Faith. I'm in Rome right now. At the airport. They're sending me to Bisacquino which I'm assuming is where you are. So, I took a guess that if you were in Palermo the *Chronicle* would get you up there pretty fast. And I have news . . .'

I sat up straighter. You've got to love news.

'I love news. Gimme news,' I said.

'You owe me, Faith Zanetti,' he laughed.

'Not yet, I don't. Not yet,' I said, rapping my fingers on the hot rock and startling my lizard. More and more television vans and cars full of reporters were now blocking the road and the police were having trouble dealing with them all. The chalk woman was shouting so that her tonsils showed.

'So, as soon as I see this story on CNN I call my Italians in New York, the people who helped me with my Cairnbridge story back then. One of them got out of jail last year – I won't tell you his name. But when I said "Bisacquino" he says, "Hey! Caprese was from Bisacquino. The guy you were bothering me about when I was inside." Quote, unquote.'

'Oooh. Wow. What does this mean? Something. It means something.' A siren was screaming up the hill.

'OK. They're calling my flight. I'll see you this evening.

Where are you staying? They checked me into the Grand Hotel Elegy or something.'

'Yep. That's where we are. Where I am,' I said, standing up and turning my back on the commotion for privacy. 'What does it mean, Ihsan?'

'I don't know. I just thought you'd like to know. I think it means that the place is Mafia country, though that particular village was never known for it before. I imagine somebody moved house. And, obviously, you can go and find someone who knew him. I never got a lead on where to start. I did try up there, but – nothing. That's why I'm telling you. It's not a big place.'

I laughed.

'Not big, no.'

Don was in a very good mood when I stuffed him back into the car. I lurched it into life and, throwing up a cloud of dust, spun round and hurtled back to the village, swerving to avoid the endless snaking convoy of cars that was coming up. I parked outside a tiny bar called 'Ristorante Borghese'. Ristorante, my arse. It had three big buzzing fruit machines, a pinball thing and two plate-sized round tables where two old men were playing cards and consuming nothing. The floor looked greasy and the proprietress was smearing more grease on to some glasses with a greying cloth. In a glass cabinet were the ubiquitous three stale croissants, cheese and ham sandwiches with flies on them and some solid wedges of pizza.

We ordered espresso with brandy in it and the woman looked pleased, heaving her enormous bosom up to reach the bottles and wiping the dust off with her hands. The coffin-sized espresso machine was gleaming chrome and flaking enamel and the radio, on very very loud (perhaps for the deaf old men) was doing a live broadcast from up the road. Interestingly, I thought the announcer mentioned 'local' boys. Ragazzi was the word she used for boys. These people never ever tell anything though.

So I asked the woman about Gianluca Caprese. She threw her head back and laughed. She had dark grey curly hair that she had last dyed orange about six months earlier. The men turned to look at us with toothless contempt.

'Non siete la prima e non sarete l'ultima,' she said. You aren't the first and you won't be the last. Meaning, I supposed, that she wasn't about to be talking about Mafia executions to strangers, least of all today.

I muttered something that I hoped meant, 'Terrible what's going on, isn't it?'

And she, schlomping our coffees down in front of us and schlooping the brandy in, said something that I thought meant, 'They've all got it coming to them.'

I drank up quickly and passed the woman a five hundred euro note, meeting her eye and raising an eyebrow (being able to raise one eyebrow is probably my most useful journalistic skill).

She scrunched it up and stuffed it in her apron. 'Oi. Giovanotto. Take these people to Ornella's,' she shouted.

One of the old men snarled at her. 'I'm winning,' he said. He had been handsome once. Had that kind of swagger and still a twinkle in his eyes. Now he looked as though he was covered with a thick layer of dust. Though he probably wasn't.

She glowered. He stood up, got his walking stick off the back of his chair and shuffled towards us. Without beckoning us to follow or addressing us in any way (though he talked quietly to himself incessantly) he took to the street, four foot high, ancient black suit, felt hat, stick, bow legs. My boots

161

were loud on the cobbles and I could see the lace curtains and the shutters move as we walked by, everyone feeling nervous today, their village becoming famous as we walked. And not in a good way.

Chapter Fifteen

Ornella lived on the square. It was a cobbled square and, in a tourist village, would have had shops selling soap made with olive oil, bunches of lavender and religious figurines, jars of olive paste, preserved oranges and all that stuff that people think of as quintessentially Italian but is in fact produced exclusively for tourists. Of course, now that tourists and film crews would start flocking here, things were probably about to change. But, for now, the square was a car park and striped plastic curtains obscured all the wooden front doors. Geraniums stood in neat pots on the balconies and it was so quiet that the televisions of the bedridden could be heard outside.

The old man pressed Ornella's bell and she came to the door in her apron, wiping the dough from her hands. She smiled at the man but then saw us and stopped smiling.

'All right?' Don said, and I kicked him. It was getting very very hot. The man shuffled away back to the bar and Ornella called after him but he didn't respond. She patted her hair and looked at us expectantly. She was thin and about fifty with her jet black hair scraped back into a bun, tiny gold earrings swinging in her ears and flip flops on her feet. She invited us in, not because she wanted to, and she pursed her lips to show it, but because she didn't want to be rude, knew what her mother had taught her about hospitality.

Inside it was very dark and cool, a narrow corridor of a room with a wood-burning stove against the wall and plastic flowers in vases on all the surfaces. Christ hung in bleeding agony on his cross above the dresser where what looked like the good china was displayed. The floor was green lino and the table was covered with net curtain material. The huge television was also draped in net curtain and she took a heavy crystal bowl of sweets off the top of it and offered them to us. Don took one, unwrapped it noisily and then sucked it as if he was slurping down a milkshake.

Hospitality done with, Ornella, who had put us on the sofa (a stiff and uncomfortable velour thing that probably opened out into a bed), sat on a kitchen chair, clasped her hands in her lap and cocked her head on one side.

'Umm ... cerchiamo gente che conoscono Gianluca Caprese,' I said, wishing I could smoke in here.

She crossed herself and brought the crucifix round her neck to her lips to be kissed. Right. So. She knew him, then.

'He was my big brother,' she said, looking calmly at me, speaking, oh thank God, English.

'Ah! You speak English,' I smiled. She did not smile back.

'My mother lived in England during the war,' she said. 'She taught us.'

'Right,' I nodded. 'Um. Well. I am a journalist from England. From the *Chronicle*.' Yup. It worked. It often does in places like this. On people who remember the old reputation of the paper and don't know that it was bought by a right-wing tycoon, who sacked all the printers and basically tabloidised the paper (well, we're all tabloids now, but, you know what I mean) and moved it to Docklands. She lit up with admiration, reverence and awe. This was good. People who (bafflingly) respect the press think they have to tell you stuff, as if it's the law or something.

'I know your brother was . . . was murdered . . . and . . . well, everybody thinks that his murder had something to do with what he knew about Cairnbridge – TAA 67, the plane that was blown up over Scotland twenty-five years ago?'

'Yes.'

'And, well, I wondered if you thought there was any connection. If there is a story about your brother that you would like to tell. It is generally believed that he was trafficking heroin from the Middle East and Afghanistan to America for the Mafia. This has been widely publicised . . .'

I'm not proud of it. I was using a technique. I mean, not exactly consciously even. But with stuff like this if you explain how maligned the deceased relative has been, you will get people telling you what they believe to be the truth. And, hell, very occasionally, it is.

'Yes,' she said.

'You were aware that he was a drugs trafficker for the Mafia?' I checked.

She crossed herself again, but didn't say anything.

'Ornella . . . Signora Caprese . . .' I paused. 'My sister was on that plane.'

Don lurched himself into an upright sitting position and stared at me. 'Oh, Shalom?' he asked.

I glowered at him.

Ornella's eyes were filling with tears and, despite myself, I recognised this as a good thing.

'He had to do it. He was . . . Carlo's father helped him. This is how they do it. All the good boys. This is what they do. He needed work. Look at this place. What is a young

165

man going to do? And it was worse then. He needed work and his friend, Massimo, God rest his soul, took him to meet Carlo's father. I never knew his name. They called him Grandfather. Nonno. He found him work in America. Good work. In a warehouse, he said. But then he asked him favours, always to go to Cyprus, and Gianluca, when he finds out what the favour is, he says no. And they came here, to my mother's house, God rest her soul, and I was young. I was very young and . . .' She had been getting more and more hysterical as she told her story and now she put her face in her hand and sobbed.

'I don't get it,' Don whispered to me in the gloom. 'What's she on about?'

'They raped her. And presumably her brother carried on working for them. Get it now?'

'Got it,' Don nodded. He got up with enormous effort and helped himself to another sweet.

I went and put my arm round her shoulders, aware of how hopeless a gesture this was. How ludicrous. But she reached up and put her hand over mine, so perhaps it meant more to her than I had thought it could.

'Who is Carlo?' I asked.

Now she laughed a bitter laugh. She wiped her nose on the hem of her apron and rallied herself to speak. As if there was nothing much to lose now.

'Carlo?! You a journalist and you don't know who is Carlo?' she said. 'Not an Italian journalist obviously.'

Don coughed. 'Went down the wrong way,' he explained, spluttering. 'I know who Carlo is. Elusive bloke. Nobody knows if he really exists or not. He took over the whole thing when his dad was killed by the police in this huge raid years ago. Ten, fifteen years ago.'

'More than twenty,' Ornella corrected him. 'Nonno was

killed more than twenty years ago, and he is burning in the fires of hell. He will burn for all eternity.'

Hmm. Harsh, I thought, though, let's face it, he probably deserves it.

'How do you know this shit?' I asked Don, throwing my hands out. 'And why do you not mention it, when you know we're on a Mafia story?'

'Yuh. Faith. If you'd said to me, "Ooh, Don, do tell me who the head of the Sicilian Mafia is reputed to be since we're on a Mafia story," I would have told you. I imagined, in my stupidity, that you bloody knew.'

'Well, I didn't,' I muttered. Another thing everyone thought I knew. To be honest, I hadn't even realised it was still like that. I suppose I thought of organised crime to be a whole network of people, most of them in politics, with an allegiance to some greater thing, like the Freemasons or something. OK, OK. I was realising that I am, basically, none too bright.

'We don't use the word Mafia here,' Ornella corrected us. Now that I had known. 'They have . . . euphemisms,' she said, looking as if she might spit on the floor.

'Great sweets,' Don said.

'Please. Finish them,' Ornella told him, holding the bowl out again. He took three.

'But, really, nobody knows, do they?' Don went on. 'They've got so many people taking the rap, pretending to be them when they need it. It's like that film. You know. When Kevin Spacey is like the underworld king but you don't find out until the end and even his mates don't know.'

'*The Usual Suspects*,' I said, sighing.

'He phoned me before . . . it happened,' Ornella interrupted, not understanding what we were talking about, entranced by her own story, and it was hardly surprising.

'Cairnbridge?'

'No. Well. Yes. But before they . . . before they killed him.'

I stayed quiet. Waiting for her to tell me what he'd said. Feeling the significance of it tingling on my tongue, clenching my fists in my jacket pockets, curling my toes in my boots, tensing my stomach muscles.

'Wad he say?' Don asked, breaking all my rules. I let my breath out.

'He said the Americans had found out about them. That he had been disloyal to Nonno and they would all be punished. The men my brother met in New York, they were, many of them were arrested at that time. The drugs business was in trouble, so I understand. This is what I think. I think he was giving names to the Americans and they protected him.'

'Protected the suitcase,' I said, as things slipped into place.

'I don't know about a suitcase,' Ornella shook her head and looked up at a photograph on the dresser. A smart boy with smiling gap teeth holding up a woolly dog. 'But somebody found out. He said he loved me and I should never say anything about it to anyone.'

I nodded, wondering vaguely what had made her elect to disobey him so long afterwards. But she told me before the thought really became conscious. 'I decided then and there that I would tell whatever I knew. I had already been punished and now they would take my brother. It killed my mother. Killed her dead. But you know? Nobody ever asked me before. If they ask me I will tell them, I said to myself. And they never asked. They believe this lie. This myth. That the cosa nostra "melt into the hills". That's what they say.'

'Yes, they do,' I smiled. 'That is exactly what they say.'

'One man. An Arab came once. To the village. Asking. Asking. But I don't like Arabs,' she said. 'Very sly.'

'Ihsan El Sayed?' I asked, suddenly hating her, for all her pain and tragedy.

'All their names are the same. How should I know?' she said.

And Don and I got up to leave. As we pushed our way past the plastic exit curtain and into the light, Ornella grabbed my arm.

'I'm sorry for your sister,' she said. 'God will protect her.'

He didn't though, did He, I thought, though I knew that's not what she meant. I turned back.

'Thank you. I hope you're right,' I said, and my heart started trying to get out through my mouth as I realised how much I hoped she was right.

A Jesuit priest in Israel once said to me that hoping there is a God is some people's way of reaching out to Him. It is the chink in the armour of the unloved into which He will pour his love, he said. I had pretty much ignored it as the babbling of a psychopath at the time, but now it made me want to cry.

'If you pass Borghese, could you ask my husband to come home for lunch now?' she called after us.

Hello? I thought. Obviously it showed in my face. My absolute stunned horror.

'He was a friend of my father's,' she shrugged. 'Nobody else would have me after.'

Oh but, Jesus Christ, the world just makes you want to weep.

And she shut her front door on us and on the world.

So, was that it? Was this the end of my Cairnbridge story? Gianluca Caprese just like Ihsan had suggested? Just what he had basically aired on Al Jazeera three years earlier? Gianluca Caprese, who had known his number was up, had known that Nonno, whoever the fuck he was, would blow the plane up to get the CIA guys going back to the states. Summerman and the other guy. He would probably have handed the suitcase to Mohammed himself. And, so, he was probably the source of the Reykjavik warning. And it would look like a scoop. Why not? Nobody had seen the Al Jazeera piece. But what had my postcard meant? That Fischer was being vindictive? I'd got the story. Not so difficult. So not, therefore, very vindictive. There was only one answer. I hadn't got the story. Not yet. I puffed my cheeks out and let them go. There was a banner over this saying 'the end' but it didn't feel like it.

'So, Eff Zed, though, yeah?' Don began, screwing his face up into the sun and hauling his bag on to his shoulder. 'How come you never said you had a sister on the plane? That was way out of the blue. Did you make it up so she'd like you?'

I laughed and strode off towards where we'd put the car. I hoped it was still in the shade. 'I didn't know. Only found out last night.'

'Last NIGHT?!' Don spat, kicking a mangy cat out of the way.

'Yup. Walter Irving's wife showed up at Eden's a couple of days ago in the middle of the night sobbing about having got knocked up – MAYBE – by my dad a hundred years ago. Then at dinner yesterday, Walter, who's basically CIA and knew Dad in Cyprus, tells me his daughter, that daughter, was on the plane. Flying unaccompanied to visit him.'

'He doesn't know that she wasn't his daughter?'

I wished I hadn't brought it up now.

'No. He doesn't. And. Don. He never will know. And, anyway, Phoebe isn't even sure, so it's not . . . you know.'

'Not really, Zanetti. Not really. So, basically, this spook tells you your sister died and this inspires you to fuck his brains out all night? Genius.'

I stopped walking and turned back to face Don who wobbled towards me across the narrow cobbled path, red and gasping. Seeing my face, he realised he had gone too far.

'We didn't have sex,' I said, leaning into his face. 'We just held each other. Because we were sad. Oh, and Don,' I continued, and punched him as hard as I could in the stomach. I can punch hard. He doubled up and retched as though he might vomit. 'See you at the car,' I said, and went into the bar to deliver my message.

I have always wondered why I got doled out such a short tether. It has always been insufficiently long and now, well, there just wasn't any left.

While we'd been at Ornella's the world's press had discovered Borghese. The place had never seen business like this. All the journalists from Palermo and a couple of hacks who'd already made it from Rome (better dressed and with more expensive shades) were ordering coffee, and my barmaid friend was rushed off her feet. She'd make another five hundred before the day was out. She'd even brought a ham down from upstairs. And, standing in the corner, playing a video game where the player is a fighter pilot, was a young American man with his head shaved like a marine, glancing up at me. I smiled and waved but he looked away. It is strange, I always find, how one's outer self ploughs on even when the inner one is finished. I daresay my shrink would have a brilliantly insightful comment to make.

The game of cards was still in full swing at one of the ristorante's two tables. I leaned down to the old man and told him to go home.

'Just finish my game,' I think he said, and he patted the chair next to him to invite me to watch. Then he put his gnarled, liver-spotted hand on my knee. Or, actually, just above my knee. I froze but decided not to move.

'What do you know about Carlo?' I asked him, in crappy Italian. He sort of yelped, a bit like a small dog, the kind whose eye fluids run into the white fur and congeal there. It took me a breath to realise he was laughing. He drew his finger across his throat.

'He's dying,' he said. 'That's what the boys are all fighting about! The successor has come home. Didn't you know? Didn't you know?'

God, but I was fucking sick of being asked that. The other old man stood up and tipped the table over, knocking my suitor off his chair and on to the floor. He shouted something at him and stormed off, struggling to the door with his cane, still shouting insults at his drunken, talkative ex-best friend. I helped my man up and, in the end, escorted him all the way home. If it looked like altruism to anyone peering round their net curtains, it wasn't. I just wanted to be sure that he couldn't tell this news to anyone else in the café. Maybe they already knew, but maybe they didn't.

Don was standing by the car when I got there, his face streaming with tears. When he saw me he opened his arms and beckoned with his fingers.

'I'm so sorry, Zanetti,' he said. 'Give me a hug.'

What could I do? I held my breath and put my arms round him while he buried his face in my hair and sniffed.

'I'm so sorry about the little girl, Eff Zed. It's so sad about the little girl,' he said, his whole body shaking.

'I know, Don. I know,' I told him, soothing him. You see. This was why I hadn't wanted to tell him. I knew he'd cry.

Chapter Sixteen

I left Don in his room (he did book himself a bloody suite, as well) trying to send his pictures to London, digitally. He doesn't know I know this, because it is his secret. He made such a fuss about using digital cameras (even though Pentax offered him billions of dollars to be in their advert) and said he'd rather have a red hot poker shoved up his arse than use one, clinging in obsessive compulsive manner to his trusty old Nikon. People interviewed him about it and he came up with all sorts of pseudy bollocks about how the clunk of the shutter on the old ones made him feel that all was right with the world and God knows what. Anyway, basically he was just frightened that he wouldn't know how to work the new ones but, when he realised it was really easy, he took whatever one it was they were trying to force on him but he STILL carries his old Nikon around and gets it out, all ready, only swapping them over at the last moment when he thinks nobody's looking. It's sweet really, but it does mean he has to pretend to have a headache quite often while he goes off to download them.

The roses in my room had been replaced. Frankly, I had

gone off them. I was cutting it pretty fine for Tamsin's four o'clock deadline, but I'd checked on the Internet and there was nothing concrete on Carlo. All rumour. There were a few references, if you translated the Italian articles, to someone having taken over from Nonno (of whom there even existed one grainy, if fairly familiar-looking, picture) but clearly nobody had a shred of anything.

I left my jacket behind and set off to walk round the city, hoping I would have a brainwave before I had to file. I mean, I could get away with what everyone else would be doing. The pictures would be spectacular, everyone has the cultural references from the films and most of the *Chronicle*'s readers have been on holiday in Italy, so it's all there. I could just say how many were dead, talk about the possible reasons for in-fighting (rows over territory, succession, honour and all that jazz) and then do a brief history of all the Mafia stuff that's gone on over the past seventy or so years, with the emigra-tions to America and the retained links, the growth of the businesses and all the rest. It wouldn't take long. Oh, but I did want to mention Carlo. And I'd need more proof than I had. Not that the paper wouldn't run pure speculation. Hell, they would, they would. But I didn't want them to have to.

On my return I checked my messages at reception and a girl with a black silk ribbon tied round her neck and waist-length black hair plaited down her back handed me an envelope. 'You are very welcome here,' she said, bowing her head, and I raised my eyebrows, taking my stuff and walking away. Yeah, yeah. Very welcome, very welcome. I'd had enough of being welcome. I wished they'd all just been buried under a pile of dust when Mount bloody Etna last erupted. And I shivered, sitting down in Don's lobby arm-chair and putting a cigarette in my mouth and my boots on the brass tray table, Moroccan-style thing. And I remembered holding a little glass bottle stopped with a tiny cork. 'Volcanic dust from Mount Etna,' Dad had said, and he quoted something. I tried to fish it out from the clouds in the back of my mind, but I couldn't get to it.

I shook my head to try and get rid of the thought and opened my message, hotel stationery thing that I assumed would be from Walter, back already from his writers' thing, though, at this point, who could say if that's really where he'd gone. So nobody ever gets the job, fine, but does anybody ever leave the job? I mean, after all, he definitely was a well-known publisher. So he must concentrate more on one thing than on the other these days. It was one of the postcards of the rooms and very beautiful they are too. But it wasn't from Walter. It was that handwriting again. The handwriting that makes my head spin and my heart hurt, that makes me feel everything I've ever thought was real is just made out of jelly or cobwebs and I will never be able to get hold of it.

It said, 'If you don't leave, Faithy, this will not stop.'

What will not stop? What will not stop?

I stood up, ripping the postcard into pieces and I shouted, 'WHAT WILL NOT STOP?'

All the people milling about the lobby stopped what they were doing and froze. A prostitute in a business suit lighting her cigarette, four men drinking granita with mint leaves in it over a brass table like mine, in pink cotton shirts and linen slacks, the bell boy pushing an old woman's luggage along, the receptionist who'd given me the message in the first place. I ran over to her.

'Who left this?' I shouted at her. 'Who left this message? Was it a tall man?' I asked her, raising my hands above my head to show how tall my father was. 'Was it?'

She looked very frightened.

'No, Signora. A boy ran in. People often . . . He probably got a Euro for running in with it. You know, from the playground across the street. They stand outside and ask people for errands. Especially on a Saturday, Signora . . .' she said, shaking now.

I leaned forward and rested my elbows on the reception desk, putting my head down and trying to make myself breathe normally. And as I lay there, making such a spectacle of myself, but only for a second, not for long, not so long that anyone would do anything about it, I remembered.

I remembered sitting in a hotel courtyard in the English countryside in that teapot dress he loved so much, holding my stuffed dog, Bernard, on my lap. And he walked towards me in a dark blue shirt, clean but rumpled jeans, an oyster Rolex on his wrist, the shirt sleeves rolled up, white tennis shoes, a fag in his mouth, wet hair and smiling slightly, leaning forwards, not quite hunched, but rushing. He was described as hunched because he was so tall, but it was more a kind of eager leaning forwards, legs bent as if to run, always smiling, or looking as though he might smile and hair always wet, smelling of Head and Shoulders shampoo. He hated his hair to smell of smoke so he washed it in the shower all the time. It was always wet. Like mine. And he was so real in my mind that I realised, in remembering him, that I had, until now, completely forgotten him without noticing. Not forgotten ABOUT him, of course not. But forgotten him. The real him and what it had felt like to have him walking towards me. As though if I fell over someone would pick me up. And it was that feeling of someone standing in front of me, and behind me and underneath me, carrying me on his shoulders, that had been gone all this time. It is this sudden exposure, as though someone had stripped me naked and thrown me out of a plane, that constitutes loss. My loss, at any rate. And I was still falling, though I had understood it as quickly as I could, and I had spent twenty-five years pretending to be standing upright in my clothes when really I was falling naked.

'Oft liquid lakes of burning sulphur flow, Fed from the fiery springs that boil below.' That was it.

'Faith?' said a gentle voice behind me. 'Faith? Is that you?'

I raised my head and turned round, frightening poor Ihsan with my swollen, red eyes and terrified expression. But I should have known better. He wasn't frightened. He held me by the shoulders looking at me and then he pulled me into an embrace that I would normally have refused. I rested my head on his shoulder and let him hold me like that until I could breathe again. Probably only seconds, but long enough for me to breathe in the smells of mint and lemons, Black and White hair lacquer and cigarette smoke.

'Hey,' he said, quietly. 'You OK?'

This made me laugh and come back to myself a bit. I stood back and let him hand his credit card to the still nervous receptionist.

'NO!' I said, pulling my hair out of its ponytail and giving it a shake. Eden says I look like a lion shaking its mane when I do this. 'No. Not really. I'm being followed by this marine,' and I glanced around but, unusually, he wasn't in sight. 'And I'm getting these cards . . .' I looked down at my hands and realised I'd chucked it on the floor. A boy in an olive green uniform with gold tassels was dutifully sweeping it up as I stood there. 'And I think . . . I think someone might want to . . . kill me. I know it sounds ridiculous and nothing's happened but . . .'

Ihsan took his key and laughed. 'Not to me it isn't

ridiculous. Everyone wants to kill me. I have threats from Al Qaeda . . .' he did that lovely gutteral 'q' '. . . And I have had threats from the Americans – from when I ran the story about them bombing our office in Baghdad on purpose. I have . . . well, they are countless, Faith. This is part of our profession,' he said.

Oh, well, I see. He was one of those. Because, you see, I don't want to be part of a profession of which getting death threats is a part. Thanks. I'm not an intrepid warrior for the truth. Or, at least, if I am I don't mean to be.

'Well. It's a crappy profession then,' I said.

Ihsan shook his head in disbelief. 'You don't think that,' he said, picking his suitcase up off the floor (covered in the stickers and labels that advertise our trade) and made for his room.

'I have to go up to Bisacquino,' he told me, and beckoned me to follow him.

As he said that I realised I was going to have to write and file in the next fourteen seconds.

'Hey! Thanks for that! I found Caprese's sister immediately. She basically confirmed what you already thought. I guess he's my man. The Reykjavik caller. I guess . . .' I said, knowing he wasn't, somehow, but not knowing why it mattered.

'Well done, you,' Ihsan said. You see, I like foreign men and I'll tell you for why. They don't know the cultural tags well enough to be scared of me, to prickle at me and compete with me and feel that I am belittling them by my very existence. They treat me . . . well. No, I can't say it. They treat me like a woman. Argh. God, and I hate that I care.

But his being here reminded me of the thing he's famous for. He went off intrepidly to find the 9/11 masterminds somewhere and spent days locked in a room with them, interviewing them. The day he left for somewhere with running water they were taken, very very dramatically, into US custody. They follow us around and pounce when we've done their work for them. It happens all the time.

Ihsan was on a higher floor to me and we'd got into one of those old cage lifts with ivory buttons and someone who turned the big brass handle for us when we said what floor we wanted.

'But in return for your help I'll give you some back,' I said, looking up at him. 'Apparently, this war has broken out because "Carlo", who took over from his dad, only ever known as Nonno, is about to die. It's supposed to be some kind of succession battle, but I have no way of confirming this. It's not the sort of place where you just meander up to someone and say, "Oh, by the way, have you seen Carlo about lately?" You know?'

Ihsan laughed. 'Let's see what our friend Walter Irving says about it, shall we?'

'God. Of course. He's probably his best friend or something,' I laughed, and found myself standing outside Ihsan's room as he put his key in the door. I was leaning against the wall. A maid walked towards us in a humiliating uniform, presumably designed by a man, her trolley of towels parked by an open door.

'Oh. Sorry. Um. I'll leave you. I have to file, anyway. I'll just . . .' I babbled, practically running away down the corridor back to the lift while Ihsan went into his room laughing at me and my English embarrassment on the issue of standing near a man's bedroom door. Well, it's only embarrassing if . . .

I wrote my piece at the computer, forgetting to switch the lights on, and, by the time I'd finished, the grey glow of the screen was the only light in the room. You know how people go the colour of a computer screen – a screen tan – from over exposure? I used lots of clichés and even the word Godfather more than once, to my shame. I had to spend an hour or so on the phone getting quotes from all the local officials and then the departments in Rome who all promised to crack down on this stuff and allow law-abiding Italians to live in peace, free from the shackles of organised crime and blah blah blah about the European Union. Still, to be fair on Don, my piece was only really a caption to his pictures which couldn't be anything but spectacular. The guy from oped (that's 'opinion and editorial' to you, darling) who everyone knew was gay until he married this huge-breasted feature writer from the *Telegraph* called me up to run his oped piece by me. It was about how relatively benign the Mafia had come to seem what with global fundamentalist Islamic terrorism. Didn't look very benign up that hill today, but I knew what he meant. No immediate threat to Middle England at the moment. Though nor was Al-Qaeda in my view. Still, let them rant on if it makes them happy.

It was late now and I called Walter's room to see if he fancied dinner again. Fancied. I noticed my own mental choice of word and worried about it. All mixed up. It rang and rang but then, just as I was about to give up, I could have sworn someone picked it up and whispered something.

'Walter? Walter? Is that you?' I shouted into the receiver, feeling faintly ridiculous. The sky was black outside and the breeze from the sea was cooler than it had been yesterday. I could already hear the pianist and the buzz of conversation from the sparkling terrace below where silver globes were being whisked off plates of lobster and crêpes were being flambéed at the tables.

I hung up and went downstairs to his room, a bit nervous. I knocked on the door but nobody came. I put my ear to the door and definitely heard movement. So, I could either go and ask reception to open the door which they might well not do since they had no proof that I wasn't a jealous wife or a just a random lunatic. Though they did seem to love me here . . . OR, I could go and have dinner by myself like a normal person. Or . . .

Oh fuck it, I thought. I stepped back and kicked the lock as hard as I could with my boot. The door swung open and the curtains billowed into the room. I flicked the lights on and saw Walter lying on the floor by the bed, fully dressed in his linen trousers, sandals and baggy shirt, his glasses on the floor beside him. He was moving his arm and rolling slightly. No blood. Not beaten up. Heart attack. Went my thinking.

I launched myself at the phone and asked reception to call an ambulance and then I knelt next to Walter and held his hand.

'My chest,' he said, talking as though he was winded, his face bloated with pain.

'I know,' I said, wanting to scream but also wanting to calm him down so he might not die.

'I'm dying,' he said, looking into my eyes.

'You're not. It happens all the time. They'll give you an aspirin and clot busters and you'll be fine by morning. Gianni's your uncle. They'll be here any second. I promise.'

Promising is a bit like being honest, isn't it? If you have to promise then there's an element of doubt creeping around. And if there's an element of doubt creeping about it must have some good reason for creeping there. He knew this. And he knew I knew he knew.

He smiled weakly.

'Not this time,' he said, shaking his head a little. 'I'm going to see my Jessie. This time.'

His eyes glazed, rolling backwards, and I thought he'd gone, but he was talking to her. Oh God, but he was talking to her. 'Daddy's here,' he whispered. 'Daddy's here.' I scrunched my face up in an effort to absent myself in some way, in any way, but he squeezed my hand and brought me back.

'Faith,' he said, apparently alert now. 'When they get Carlo, when you get to Carlo with them, tell him I'm sorry. But I've waited my whole life to do it. He knows.'

OK. So this was huge. Ihsan, as ever, was right. He fucking knows fucking Carlo. I leaned into his face, all sentiment banished.

'Walter. Walter. You have to tell me where to find Carlo. Is it him? Is that what Dad knew? Who he was? Where he is? Walter!' Suddenly I knew I was right. This was the information I'd been looking for all along, though I hadn't known it. This was what my father had known. Why he had been killed, I was sure now. And why they were using him, resurrecting him to scare me.

But Walter had glazed again. I felt like someone in a film. You know. When they say, 'I've hidden the treasure just behind the . . .' and then they die. This was absurd. But awful and tragic at the same time. Perhaps death is always like this. Faintly absurd. A strange last gasp in the face of eternity.

I shook him by the shoulders which is probably a medical textbook error. Though it worked, briefly. He unglazed again, his eyes trying to focus, but instead of making contact with me he put his hand up to his chest and seized up in agony.

'Tell Phoebe . . .' he said, and that, I was sure, was that.

*

182

I was sitting on the balcony having a cigarette when the para-medics rushed in. I had shut down like a bank's security system – huge steel doors coming down from the ceiling like guillotines, blocking every exit, sealing in the cause of the alarm. No exit. A couple was actually waltzing down by the piano. And not an old couple either. I had a rush of life envy before I turned back into the room to face . . . what? The music? Hardly. They practically threw him on to the bed, the body I had held less than twenty-four hours ago, that I had taken such comfort from and, I hope, given such comfort to. Perhaps.

They tore at his clothes, pumped his chest and breathed into his mouth. I probably should have done this myself. But I knew. He knew. When their machine was plugged in and bleeping, whirring, flashing ('Andiamo!') they seemed about to give his limp corpse electric shocks, jolting him into flail-ing life. But one of the doctors stopped them after the shouted command. He shook the cardio monitor and looked incredulously at the sats machine.

'Respira bene,' he said, baffled, holding his stethoscope against Walter's chest. He slapped Walter slightly too hard in the face. And Walter sat up.

'Hey!' he said, stunned. 'Faith Zanetti, what in the name of God is going on!'

I walked towards him, not sure what to think. Was this some kind of epileptic fit? Or panic attack?

Well, he wasn't going to be finding out at this rate. Alert as a meerkat, he refused to go to hospital for tests and insisted, leaping up and putting a shirt on, that he was absolutely fine what on earth is the matter with everyone. The stunned paramedics left and, when he had shut the door behind them, Walter Irving looked at me quizzically.

'Must have been heartburn,' he said.

Open mouthed, I left the room. I went upstairs and didn't switch my lights on. I just curled up in a ball against the wall and screamed silently until I was gasping for breath and there was nothing left inside me. I couldn't take much more of this.

Chapter Seventeen

I took three Valiums before I called Phoebe and I drank a vodka out of the mini bar. I don't have any other way of processing this stuff and, frankly, I don't think anyone else does either. Short of a swift slide into insanity.

'Phoebe. It's Faith. Faith Zanetti.'

'Oh, hello, cara. I meant to apologise to you. I know it's the last thing . . .'

But I interrupted her. 'Phoebe. I'm in Palermo with Walter. He just had some extremely strange kind of seizure. Said his chest hurt, seemed to be dying. I called the ambulance and they started their cardiac procedures but then he turned out to be fine. Is this a regular occurance?'

She was silent.

'I'm so sorry, Phoebe. I didn't mean to . . . I just. I was so shocked. He wasn't suffering or anything. I don't think.'

This reminded me of my father. They said he hadn't suffered. Which is absurd. It's exactly what they said to me and Evie. He didn't suffer. Didn't suffer? Fuck me, he was shot in the chest. If that isn't suffering I don't know what is.

'Faith, cara,' Phoebe finally said. 'My husband is not a

sane man. The anti-psychotics don't always do all they should. I don't know what else I can tell you.'

'No, well, um . . .' I began. But she hung up.

I lay in a hot bath for as long as I could, cleaned my teeth with the hotel toothbrush and miniature tube of paste and lay down on the bed and shut my eyes, hoping that oblivion would wash over me now. I think I passed out. I was dreaming or thinking about Ben and how he felt against me when he was asleep, so when someone knocked on the door I wasn't sure if I was sleeping or waking. I stood up, feeling as though I was floating across the carpet in the towelling robe, my hair still wet.

'Who is it?' I said, though I couldn't tell if the words had come out or not.

'It's me. Ihsan,' he whispered and I remember smiling and opening the door. He picked me up like a bride across the threshold and carried me back to the bed, taking the robe off me slowly, like undressing a doll, kissing every bit of flesh he exposed as he exposed it. He laughed at my tattoo – Elvis Presley's signature on my pelvic bone – and licked it. I was completely naked in the warm night by the time he kissed my mouth, taking my face in his hands, pushing my hair back off my forehead and looking at me, his black eyes half shut. He had very long eyelashes and was the colour of honey.

'You're beautiful,' he said and I smiled.

'Take your clothes off,' I whispered, wanting to feel my skin against his and to lose myself.

He stood up and I watched him in the light from the terrace, the pianist doing his greatest romantic hits. Ihsan unbuttoned his white shirt, head bowed, serious, like a little boy. He had scars on his back that looked like evidence of torture and I wanted to cry. When he came quietly back to bed I ran my fingers across them, but I didn't ask. Didn't want to know. I thought we probably both understood what the world is like without having to discuss it, were both trying to escape. I felt as though we might devour each other entirely, leaving shreds of flesh and splinters of bone on the bed where we had been. I bit his shoulder when he pushed into me and he kissed my eyes. I hardly knew this man and I probably never would, but he'd seen me in here and he'd come in to get me and I was grateful. It felt like being in love.

'I love you,' I said, lying there on his chest afterwards. He didn't laugh. He just stroked my hair.

'I love you too, Faith Zanetti,' he said, and I knew he understood.

I have never been able to grasp the protocol by which you have to be one hundred per cent certain that you not only love this person with all your heart, but that, in order to say the words, you also have to swear to love them forever with all that that entails. It is incomprehensible. People change, they change their minds, the type of love that they initially meant changes. One could qualify the statement until the end of time. It is ridiculous. Why can't you just say it when you feel it, the fact that you might have rethought your position within five minutes understood? Because it doesn't make the sentiment insincere. Can't it count just like that? Just for the instant it is felt and meant and whispered and never mind the future and the rest?

For that's how I said it and that's how Ihsan took it. He kissed me on the cheek.

'There's nobody like you,' he said.

'Fuck me again, then,' I said, smiling.

'Oh, sure,' he laughed. And he did.

Later, when he was asleep and the dark terrace was empty, the sea still twinkling out to the horizon in the moonlight, I stood on the balcony with a cigarette and the last vodka out of the mini bar. Sex and death. That's what it's all about, I thought. Nobody likes admitting it, but it is. And I would happily have carried on this existential-angst thought train, wondering about Walter and Jessie, tasting Ihsan and smelling him on my skin, gazing out at the stars and thinking about all the things I hadn't known about my father. But the phone rang. Ihsan rolled over and put a pillow on his head.

'Signora Zanetti? There is someone to see you at reception,' the receptionist said.

'It's the middle of the night,' I whispered.

'Signora?'

'Who is it? Who is there to see me?'

'A man, Signora. He does not say his name. Please come,' the boy said. He sounded a bit desperate so I pulled my jeans, T-shirt, boots and jacket and crept out of the door. Walter? The thought made me feel guilty. I clomped down the marble stairs feeling woozy and exhausted from the pills and the vodka and I couldn't remember when I'd last eaten anything. I didn't actually look up at reception until I got there, emerging from behind some potted palms. I suppose if I had I might have run back upstairs and thought out some different course of action. But when I did look up I saw why the caller had sounded so keen that I come down.

He was trembling in his green and gold uniform, one of his ears pierced with a big fake diamond, his goatee beard silly on such a young boy. And someone who shouldn't have been there was standing much too close to him behind the desk, a bloke who looked at me expectantly and was clearly pushing the barrel of a gun into the night receptionist's side, not caring that he must have been on about ten cameras. Black cropped puffa jacket, green T-shirt, clean jeans, purple and beige campers, gel in his hair so it stuck up in hedgehog spikes.

As soon as he saw me he pushed the boy aside and moved away, lifting the flap in the desk that brought him out towards me, letting it slam down hard behind him, the sound echoing in the empty lobby. There was nobody else around, but I could see a car waiting in the street outside.

'You must come with me,' the gunman said in English but with a strong Italian accent, as though he was following a script, gesturing me out with the gun that stayed in his inside pocket.

'Um. No?' I said.

He almost smiled. He pointed his gun out towards the car again and this time I took the cue. In any case, I wanted to go really. Anything that brought me closer to knowing what was going on had to be a good thing. If they wanted to kill me they'd kill me, wouldn't they? If they were taking me somewhere then I must be getting closer. Though the idea of a remote beachfront, hilltop or woodland execution certainly crossed my mind, I banished the thought quickly and I tried very hard not to think about Ben because it made my heart ache with sorrow and longing.

And as I walked through the doors, behind one of the lobby trees, peeking out, I saw my marine and smiled. Stockholm Syndrome thing, I suppose. You rely on the people around you, pretty much whoever they are. And he'd been a constant for nearly a week now. I had started to depend on him. Or, rather, them.

Perhaps I should have been frightened, but I didn't have the energy. I came down the grandiose steps and could hear Palermo's traffic still screeching round the streets, the wail of the night insects and the crashing, even here, of the sea. Though I suppose I was being kidnapped, it didn't feel like it, exactly. I hadn't tried very hard not to get in the car and I doubted he'd have killed me or seriously hurt me if I had. It had not escaped my notice that, although sinister and unpleasant things had been happening, they hadn't been happening to me. Well, not directly at any rate.

It was a big new BMW and I got in the back while puffa jacket got in the front. It smelt of leather . . . and . . .

'Don?!' I said, stunned.

'That's me,' he said, raising his eyebrows.

'What the fuck are you doing here?'

'I was hoping you might be going to tell me, Eff Zed. Know what I mean?'

I didn't.

OK. Weird, weird, weird.

As soon as Puffa had shut his door the driver, another bloke in a similar uniform and a lot of aftershave, pulled off aggressively. Puffa put the radio on and the pair of them commented occasionally about the drive.

The driver would swear when whoever he'd gone up very close behind and flashed at didn't move quickly enough and Puffa occasionally pointed out obstacles. 'Attenzione al cane!' or whatever. They didn't seem tense, like people who kidnap me usually do (and let me tell you . . .). They seemed like Sicilian boys out on the town or, rather, driving into the countryside for a party.

'Seriously, Zanetti,' Don growled. 'If I get killed I am going to be really really pissed off.'

'Right,' I nodded. 'I'll bear that in mind.'

I thought about this.

'Are you somehow holding me responsible for this?' I asked him, glancing down at a flash of white on the floor of the car which turned out to be Don's feet.

'I was in bed when they came, OK? Couldn't find my shoes. And, yes, I am holding you responsible.'

'Fair enough. Fair enough.'

As the buildings slid into the distance Puffa remembered something and got his friend to pull over near a porchetta stall. The roast meat smelt delicious and the pig's head was balanced on the counter. Smiling reasonably politely Puffa leaned round and passed us two aeroplane eye masks.

'Per favore,' he said, and I took them off him and gave one to Don.

'Fuck me, Zanetti. Last time I had to do this I got taken to a fucking cave to be shown six chopped off heads.'

'Chechnya?'

'Noop.'

'Rwanda?'

'Noop.'

'Afghanistan?'

'Yup.'

'Well,' I told him. 'It can't be worse than that then, can it?'

'Could be if we're the heads,' he mumbled, putting the thing on.

'Hmmm. Sort of relaxing,' I said, shutting my eyes and abdicating responsibility.

I wanted to tell Don about Walter but I was afraid he'd say something terrible so I kept quiet. And there was no way I was telling him who I'd been with tonight. But, of course, I didn't need to.

'Been doing a fair bit of bed hopping, Zanetti,' he said blind, as we trundled over some pot holes. He grabbed my knee to steady himself as we took a tight bend.

'Not really, Don. Nope. Stayed in my own bed last night,' I said, pushing his hand off.

'Yeah, but you can't have had much room. What with all the enormous Egyptian . . .'

I kicked him very hard and he screamed loud enough for one of our friends to ask, 'Tutto bene?'

This made both of us laugh. I mean, hey, we were being driven fuck knows where in blindfolds by armed people.

'Oh. Si. Si. Benissimo,' I said, and we carried on giggling. It was hysteria really, because God knows, there wasn't much to laugh about.

Now I'm not saying it isn't very strange because it is, but when the car stopped, however long it might have been later, both Don and I were asleep. I could taste the memory of waking up in cars when I was little, with sleep still in your mouth and no sense at all of where you are or might be, just that the motion has stopped. I took my eye mask off and Don's had slipped off while we were driving.

'God, they're great these things,' I said.

'Oi! Geddoffme!' Don shouted, waking up.

'Oh, McCaughrean!' I sang. 'We're here!'

He shook his head like a bloodhound and came to. Puffa was opening the car door for me as though I was Princess Diana and I stepped out (not like Princess Diana) and stood up. Don crawled out after me.

We were standing in front of a grand villa on a cliff top just above a white beach that shone in the moonlight. We'd parked on a curved gravel drive and there was a lawn with bright rhododendron bushes and a path that led up between them to the front door. All the windows glowed with that deep golden light that means money and comfort (in fact it's just no central light but lots of lamps in cream shades in the corners of the room, in case this is a lighting effect you are wanting to achieve) and, as we walked towards the house followed by our escorts, a woman in jeans and a stiff white shirt opened the door. The boys understood that they weren't invited and, nodding to the woman, they walked off back towards the car, chatting.

'Avanti,' she said, smiling, and she then kissed me warmly on both cheeks. OK then. She had long dark hair in a ponytail, very white teeth and well kept nails and she smelt of shampoo and expensive perfume. She wore a glittering diamond ring and gold hoops in her ears.

The hall was tiled in blue and green Middle Eastern mosaics and there was a bike leaning against the wall. Over a marble wash stand hung what looked an awful lot like a Cezanne. It had a brass picture light over it, suggesting that it hadn't been knocked off in a market in Palermo.

'Someone's rolling in it,' Don commented, hugging his camera bag to his chest in case this woman ripped it from him and hurled it into a pit of fire. He suspected everyone of being on the point of doing this.

'Sono Annarita,' she said, sort of affectionately (well, I know) and showed us into a living room with enormous windows looking over the sea. She was wearing Tods. The bobbles on the bottom of these shoes make me shudder, I don't know why. She was tanned (and already dark) and healthy, looking as though she'd been playing tennis all day.

'Um. Well, I'm sure you know. I'm Faith and this is Don.' She reached out to shake Don's hand. 'Piacere,' she said.

OK, so this was beyond weird. It was like arriving at a dinner party or something, when, in fact, we'd been kidnapped and brought here blindfolded and it must have been three o'clock in the morning.

There was, in fact, a fire burning wildly in the grate here (though not awaiting Don's camera) and more real-looking art work. A Repin sketch from *Ivan the Terrible Killing his Son* (my favourite painting), a Surikov sketch, a very big Dufy and some little portraits that looked Dutch and very familiar but I'm too ignorant to place them. There were big leather sofas in here and standing lamps in the corners with those little brass bits that you twist to turn them on and off. The French windows to the sea were closed, but we could see the moon and the dark distance towards the horizon.

'Qualcosa da bere?' she offered, moving to a drinks trolley with crystal decanters on it and ice with tongs, a little tray of lemon.

I shook my head.

'Ooh lovely. Brandy if you don't mind,' Don nodded, warming, obviously, to this kind of captivity and this kind of captor. It was hilarious seeing him trying to be dignified and, oh God please no, even flirtatious, with no shoes on in this magnificent house.

She poured him his drink in an enormous sparkling globe and then asked me if I was tired. Of course I'm fucking tired, you lunatic, I wanted to say, but didn't. I just said, 'Si. Molto,' and smiled like a guest who doesn't want to inconvenience anyone but does, embarrassingly, have needs that can't be denied.

She took me by the arm and led me back into the hall and through a deep velvet curtain to the stone stairs behind.

'Bagno,' she gestured with her hand, and I saw a big iron bath and fat white towels warming on a rail. 'E, Lei siete qui,' she said, pushing open the door to what was, clearly, going to be my bedroom.

There was a floor-length, long-sleeved Victorian nightdress with smocking on the front laid out on an antique four-poster bed, the headboard painted with cherubs and harps, the paint cracked and beginning to peel. The bed was hung with white lace curtains and there was a dressing table with a silver-backed hairbrush and mirror on it and two pink leather boxes, one almost the size of a chess board, the other smaller. 'A domani, allora,' Annarita said, smiling and closing the door behind her. I opened the big box. It was an enormous set of make-up with every colour of lipstick, eyeshadow, blusher, nail varnish you could possibly imagine. It made me laugh. When I was little I always wanted one of these. I fiddled with the tiny gold clasp of the other box and found a pearl necklace and earrings. It was beginning to slightly freak me out and I went to the wardrobe, a vast imposing thing, also painted hundreds of years ago with angels and their instruments. Turning the key I pulled it open to find it full of evening dresses, one in grey silk, another sage green chiffon, another cream satin. For every dress there was a matching pair of shoes standing on the wardrobe floor. Whose room was this? I sat on the bed and buried my face in the nightdress. It smelt of roses. Something was making me want to cry. Feeling unreal, like a part of someone else's dream, as though I would melt away when they woke up, I took my clothes off and put the nightdress on, standing in front of the roll-over full-length mirror like Jane Eyre in her wedding dress, disbelieving. I wanted to scream but no sound came out. The person who looked back at me was a little girl.

I crept over to the bed, wondering if perhaps I had died in the car. I could hardly breathe but I leaned down to my clothes and got my cigarettes out of my jacket pocket, lighting one with my comfortingly heavy Zippo and sitting, in this Victorian nightie with my wild blonde hair bouncing down my back in ringlets, my feet bare, having a fag. I looked at my hand. It definitely belonged to an adult. But, even so, I didn't dare look back in the mirror. There was a white ceramic ashtray with flowers on it on a bedside table, so I needn't have worried. My every whim provided for. Unless my whim happened to be a can of macadamia nuts from the mini bar.

I tried not to have one single thought until I had finished my cigarette and then, taking a swig out of the bottle of San

Pellegrino, also on the bedside table, I crawled under the down duvet and put my head on the pillow. Where it met something hard and cold. I sat up, thinking it was a frog or a snake or I don't know what and looked down at where my head had been. There was a gold heart-shaped locket on a heavy-linked gold chain, both of these things very old. Worrying that I might faint with fear, I stuck a bitten nail under the catch and opened it, imagining maggots or spider's eggs or a miniature photo of some unspeakable horror. But it was more frightening, in a way, than any of those things. The locket contained a photo of Ben, taken, I think, less than a month ago. Holding it tight in my fist and hoping that my heart wouldn't give out, I fell asleep with the lamp still on, the waves pounding against the rocks outside my window.

Chapter Eighteen

I dreamt about a plane and a big table. Ben was grown up and an air steward, showing me my place in a huge plane all done out in the dark purple of my old school uniform and draped in gold curtains like a pasha's palace. I wasn't supposed to be on the plane so he hid me in a luggage cupboard where I crouched willingly, laughing. After take-off the plane started to bank violently to the left and then it tipped over on to its back but carried on climbing. I shouted to everyone to take off their seatbelts so that, instead of hanging from the ceiling, they could sit on the floor with me. We flew low over endless fields of ice under which we could see whales gliding. And then Ben said he wasn't sure who the pilot was but that we should go and look, so we walked together, him holding my hand as though I were the child, into a big ante-room on the plane where a huge table stood. A giant's table towering above our heads. We reached up but couldn't even touch the edge where the blade of a huge knife glinted. And it was then that Ben told me there was a bomb on board, that he'd been told by a DEA contact from Cyprus that there was a bomb on the plane and there would be no survivors, that our lungs would burst in our chests and the FBI wouldn't be able to find a thing.

When I woke up I felt as though I'd been asleep for a hundred years. The room looked completely different in the light, all the clothes and the paintings of angels, the strange gifts (if that's what they were) on the dressing table all now bright and benign, almost funny. I stretched my arms up and looked at the light streaming in past the white linen curtains, realising that it probably was at least midday.

When I padded across to open them I saw a few sailing boats far out at sea and, nearer the shore, a speedboat buzzing up and down . . . well, yes . . . along the back of the house. Guarding or attacking? I couldn't tell. I shut the curtains again, not wanting to think about it. I couldn't hear any voices or footsteps so I put my old clothes on, not for a moment considering the absurd dresses, but I did take the locket because I couldn't bear to leave it behind if I wasn't coming back to the room – I didn't imagine I was likely to have much control over what I'd be doing. I thought about stuffing the pearls into my pocket but decided against it as being in slightly bad taste . . .

Clomping across the varnished floorboards of the upstairs hall (which also had a window to the sea at the end and was painted dark red), I went into the bathroom and splashed my face with cold water. There was a Crabtree and Evelyn heart-shaped tea rose and glycerine soap in a dish but I didn't use it. Yes, you might have thought I would have tried to guess what was going on by now, but I didn't. I didn't know how to start guessing anything. I imagined that it would soon become clear. I was confused, but at the same time strangely comforted by the house and Annarita and the effort that had been made to accommodate me. I knew it was sinister but all I can say is that it didn't seem sinister. I felt . . . well, I felt as if it wasn't me in charge and so, at last, I could knock off. Surreal? Maybe. But there we are.

I came downstairs and went back into the living room where we'd been the night before. Don was sitting with his legs crossed reading the *Guardian International*. There was a cafetiere of coffee on the table, some tomato and basil bruschetta and a plate of salami, ham and melon. Freestanding was a silver wine bucket with an open bottle of Pinot Grigio in it. Don was drinking some from a delicate glass. Prosciutto's delish,' he said, seeing me and peering over the top of the paper. He was wearing some white towelling slippers. 'Any idea what the fuck's happening yet? I went out the front door and got sent back in by that bloke from last night waving his little fucking erect gun at me. Dicksplash.'

He didn't sound any too fussed though, actually.

'No idea at all. Annarita around?' I asked, sitting down and pouring some coffee into a blue mug.

'Not a sausage. Not a soul. Not a fart,' he said. 'Slept like a baby though. After a good wank.'

'That's great, Don. Really superb. What is with you this morning?'

I picked up a bruschetta (I could hear Eden in my ear saying, 'I don't understand why people in England insist on saying "brusssshhhetta" when everyone knows that the Italian is pronounced "brusketta". I mean, it's like saying "expresso" for goodness sake.' I switched him off) realising that I was starving.

Don prodded the front page. 'Ah ha! Look at this! They've had to use fucking Reuters pictures! Twats!'

'Mmmm,' I nodded, with my mouth full. 'Totherth.'

When I'd stuffed my face I went over to look at the sea again. 'There's a boat patrolling this place,' I said. 'And we're not allowed out the front, you claim.'

'Yeah, I saw the boat. On the other hand, I'm pretty happy here so far, Eff Zed. They'll get to us in the end.'

'They're doing a fairly good job of getting to me already,' I said. 'Lots of very weird shit in my bedroom.'

'Like bondage gear, or what?' Don asked, putting the paper down and burping.

'No. Little girl stuff. Weird stuff. Hey! Have you got your phone with you?' I asked him.

Don slapped his shirt pocket and then his trouser pocket, eventually pulling out a teeny weeny state-of-the-art phone. 'No reception,' he said. I looked around but there wasn't a phone in here. I hadn't really expected there to be. Was this some kind of safe house? Something to do with Walter? Or maybe it was my CIA boy, handing me over to his bosses now that I'd traced my Reykjavik caller, found Gianluca Caprese's sister? Or were Walter and my minder working for the same people in the end? 'Oh no. Hold up a second,' he said. 'If you stand over here . . .'

I took the phone off Don and went over to the window, leaning my cheek against the glass. Eden picked up straight away and a shard of pain went through me. Or guilt perhaps, about last night. It was none of his business, of course, and there was no need for him to know. Quite apart from the fact that he could barely keep his trousers on for half an hour. But I suppose that was the point. I know he's always going to be fucking around but that his heart belongs to me (should I choose to know that or think about it, which I don't) and the rest of him probably would too if I'd only take it (this according to him, obviously). But he knows that I don't do this kind of thing all that often, only when I am in desperate need to reach out to someone and get lost in someone and, of course, it is only a certain type of person in whom it is possible for me to get lost. So, a more dangerous scenario from his point of view. I wasn't even going to tell him about embracing Walter. And it hardly mattered now.

'Hey, baby! Where are you? I saw your Bisacquino piece online this morning! Congratulations. Huge splash. We've been waiting for you to call. We've been waiting for Mummy to phone us, haven't we, Scrumbs?' he said.

Mummy. God, I hadn't felt like Mummy for what seemed like years but was actually, one-two-three, only three days.

'Do you know what? I've no bloody idea where I am. These blokes came to the hotel last night and kidnapped me and Don and brought us to this house . . .'

'Jesus, Faith. What house?'

'No. No. Don't worry. It's OK. Well, I mean, I think it's OK. They weren't very forceful or anything. Well, you know, I mean, they had guns, but they didn't touch us and were all very polite about the blindfolds and then, when we got here . . .'

'They kidnapped you at gunpoint and made you wear blindfolds but not in a forceful way?'

'Exactly. And then when we—'

'Faith?'

'Yeh?'

'What's going on?'

'That's what I'm telling you. I've no idea. We're at this very grand villa on a cliff in these lemon groves and I've got a beautiful room with a four-poster bed that's got these angels painted on to it, you know, like an antique thing, with—'

'Faith? You're sounding very weird. Is it a hotel? Who are these people? What do they want?'

'I don't know yet, but everyone's being very nice and hospitable and I slept like a log. We had this brushetta . . . sorry . . . brusketta . . . for breakfast and there's wine, and Annarita left a Victorian nightie out on the bed . . .'

'OK. Listen. I'm going to leave Ben with Carolina and I'll be there by this evening if I can. A cliff and a lemon grove? Is that it? Anything else you can tell me? I'll call the police in Palermo—'

I interrupted him. 'No! No! Don't call the police! Don't leave Ben with anyone for God's sake. We're fine. It's just . . . I don't know. It might be a safe house we think. We're not being threatened, it's . . .'

I stopped when I heard Ben say, 'Mama.' And my heart dropped out.

Eden put the receiver to Ben's ear and I could feel my whole body soften to become a mummy thing, comforting and gentle.

'Hello, baba!' I said, and other things like that. Things that told a lie. The lie that I was reassuring, had the strength to protect and heal. And the lie that I was safe and well and on my way home any second. Home. Ha! There I go again.

'Listen, Eden,' I said when he came back on. 'This is Don's and we haven't got a charger or anything, so, do me a favour. Call me on this number tonight. So far, we're fine. Looks more as though we're going to be questioned or given an interview or something. But just so you know the situation. OK?'

'Whatever you say, Faith. But just so that you know the situation, OK? I don't think you should be off on these mad things at this point. What does Walter say? Any movement on the postcard or anything?

I wanted to tell him that Walter has turned out to be seriously mentally unstable, but somehow it froze on my tongue. I didn't like being lectured. Even to this degree. So I went for, 'Talk to you later, Jones. Kiss my baby for me.'

Strange to be torn apart like this. Bits of myself in another life entirely. I sighed and noticed a television in an alcove

202

over by the window that looked on to the bright flowers of the front lawn. I hadn't seen last night, but around the rhododendrons, stretching for miles, there were lemon trees, the fruit gleaming in the sun. I flicked the TV on and went back for my coffee. I watched a series of adverts all of which involved naked or semi-naked women writhing about. I remembered this about Italian TV. The entire population boycotted it once for a whole weekend in protest at its being so crap. This had little or no effect, apparently. Or maybe when they boycotted it it was all big budget drama, searing documentaries, live opera and nature programmes with ground-breaking photography.

They were in the middle of a garish news bulletin in which another woman with not much on was telling us about the Bisacquino massacre and showing live coverage from the scene which had, in fact, been cleared, just the grotesque stains remaining.

'Hey, look,' I said, and Don lumbered over.

'Why are they showing shots of fuck all?' he wondered, slumping on to a chaise longue that creaked at his weight.

'Fuck all to show, I suppose,' I said, and then they went back to yesterday's footage of the dead boys strewn about the place.

'Shit, there were a lot of them,' Don commented, wiping his nose on the back of his hand.

'Eden says it was a big splash, by the way.'

'Fucking well hope so, Zanetti. I am a genius.' He held his fingers up in the shape of a gun and blew on the barrel.

'Yes, Don.'

He looked back at the screen.

'I hope my Donchik doesn't grow up like that.'

'What? Dead? Or in the Mafia? It's not looking that likely, is it?' I said.

'Not that likely, no,' he agreed.

Then they went to an official standing outside a grand building in Palermo with a bank of microphones in front of him. People were shouting questions and he was ignoring them. It looked live. And then he started reciting a list of names. He was naming the dead boys, reading from his list, looking nervous. As he started the crowd went into a kind of frenzy – some of note taking, some of mourning, some of rage.

'Gianfranco Pici,' he said, and coughed. 'Massimilliano Pici, Marcello Pici, Alessandro Pici, Jacopo Pici.'

He was interrupted by a woman, a mother perhaps, who wailed at the sound of her son's name, knowing, presumably, the truth, the worst, but hoping anyway, as we all do. Though I tried so hard not to. He began again, 'Marco Zanetti . . .'

I shouted. 'Hey! Hey! Did you hear that? Did you hear that! Hey! Don! Don! He said Zanetti! Marco Zanetti!'

Don was about to speak.

'Shhhhhhh!' I hissed, waving my arms about.

The list went on.

'Fabiano Zanetti, Matteo Zanetti, Andrea Zanetti, Giovanni Zanetti, Paolo Francini, Mario Lagnoni . . .'

I was running up and down the room now, but I bashed my leg against a coffee table and ended up hopping wildly on one leg.

'OOOOOOOoooooooooooh Don! Why do I share a surname with all these dead dudes?!' I yelled at him.

'Search me, love,' he shrugged. 'But I mean, right now, that's probably the least of our fucking worries.'

'How do you mean?' I asked, and he gestured out of the window. Three cars had pulled up on the blistering gravel and a lot of blokes had got out of the front one and the back one and were rushing around, scanning the area, one of them with his hand up to his ear piece and another sweeping a semi-automatic machine gun around in a just-in-case way. The light was rich and golden and the vast expanse of the sky made the scene look incredibly odd. They needed a slummy city backdrop of stripclubs and abandoned cars. Not a tiny church on a distant hill and . . . well . . . paradise.

'Yuh oh,' I said, stepping back slightly.

The one with the ear piece opened the rear passenger door of the middle car, a Mercedes limousine, and a guy got out, with slight difficulty, forgetting something on the back seat and leaning back in for it, a newspaper, pushing himself up to standing with one hand and looking around. He patted the pockets of his leather jacket as though looking for cigarettes and then scrounged one off a bodyguard, making a joke as he did so, the younger man laughing and offering his boss a light as well.

He was wearing slightly worn Levis and shabby trainers, a green shirt open at the collar. He glanced up at the sky and ruffled his thick grey hair with his left hand, checking his jacket was on with a slight forwards hunch of his shoulders, before he started loping towards the house, chatting to the two men who flanked him, leaning down to hear what one of them said and laughing, saying something funny back.

'You OK there, Eff Zed?' Don asked me, as though from another room. The blood had drained out of my face and I was swaying by the window, the whole view blurred in front of me, my head pounding with the noise of rushing blood. As I slid backwards Don leapt to catch me, his camera, which had been swinging round his neck, now slamming into my spine.

'You weigh a fucking ton, Zanetti. Stand up!' he wheezed, pushing me forwards to standing. 'And you stink.'

Even now a part of my brain bothered with, 'You've some need to talk.' How does it do that?

The front door opened and there were footsteps and voices in the hall. We both turned to face the living room door and I dug my nails into the palms of my hands.

'Is she here? Is she here? Is she? Is she?' he was saying to someone.

And I heard Annarita, who must have come down from upstairs when she heard the cars, say, 'Si, si,' in a soothing way.

'Do my teeth look yellow?' he asked her, nervously. 'Do I look old? I look old!'

'Shut up and go in there,' she said, in English.

I had my hand over my mouth and I was standing but doubled over, my face drenched with tears, the breath refusing to come as the living room door swung open and my dad walked in.

Chapter Nineteen

I couldn't look at him, couldn't look up at all. Don walked forward to shake his hand, having no clue what my problem was. I heard them talking, but I was doing everything I could to absent myself. You know when people say they wish a hole would open in the ground and swallow them up? I think it's quite easy to make that happen. One second you're there, one second you're not. The fact that your body remains intact and even, sometimes, motor functions in general do too, does not testify to your actual presence.

'Hi,' Don said, boisterous and bright, excited. All the bodyguard types had been left outside, apparently.

'Ah! Don McCaughrean! Yes. It's so nice to meet you,' said . . . my dead father.

My not dead father. The man whose absence had left a hole right through the middle of me, who had taken my hope and my confidence and all the sparkle that life might have had to the grave with him. The grave on to which I had thrown a clod of earth, a little bunch of wilted freesias. The man who had left me curled in a tight ball of fear and loss night after night for years and years muttering prayers to a

207

God I'd been told didn't exist. The man to whom nobody else could ever compare – how could they? He was the Big Table, the father who was still so huge to my younger self's mind when he died that everyone else had always seemed tiny by comparison, reaching up to grab a crumb from his table, and be grateful.

But I didn't curl up and die. I gritted my teeth, pulled my socks up, got hold of my boot straps, got a grip, pulled myself together, soldiered on, bore my cross, woke up and smelt the coffee, looked on the bright side. And I became like a cast of a person, a fragile shell that I poured concrete into, so that I stood solidified, unassailable. But empty of anything but grey fuzz.

And now here he was, standing in front of me, showing me that it had all been for nothing, that the foundations of my belief system, my personality, were flawed. Like the end of Communism when all the people who had worked and struggled and fought and obeyed and believed were walked into the factory to hand their red Party cards in – the cards some of them had died for, reduced to a piece of cardboard in an already antique-looking wallet. It wasn't true. We lied. We lost. Go home now.

And yet, and yet. If you had asked me my whole life what I would wish for if I had a magic wand, a handful of beans, a lamp to rub, a pair of red sequinned slippers, I would have wished to hug my father again, to laugh with him and to walk at Kenwood, throwing shekels into the pond. There is that song that I hate to listen to about someone who, if granted one last dance with his father, would play a song that would never ever end. And that's what I would have said. That, before Ben was born, was all I had ever wanted. To feel whole again.

And here he was. But I was emptier than ever. With every

last bit of strength I had I stood up and looked into his face, pushing my hair back, jutting my chin and squaring my shoulders.

'Hi,' I said.

It was a challenge. And an attack. What I meant, of course, was fuck you. I knew I looked older, that I was unrecognisable as the little girl he'd left. Would you know my name, if I saw you in heaven? I often wondered this. Would he? Would he see me in here, in this gritty, exhausted, ageing face? Would you hold my hand? Because I had understood when he died that nobody would want to hold this ragged-nailed hand again. So, as soon as I could, I put a cigarette in it instead. At least, that's what Eden would probably say.

'Yeah. I'm a grown up,' I wanted to say. 'I'm not her any more. You're horrified? I'm hardly much younger than your girlfriend. Well. There you are.'

But I didn't say it. Didn't say anything else. I kept my eyes fixed on the tiny white sails of the boats in the Dufy painting.

'No hug for old Daddikins? Hey?' he said, throwing his arms out and walking towards me, putting his arms round me. He smelt of cigarettes. I pushed him away.

'What the fuck do you think you're doing? What? WHAT are you doing here? Don't give me this Daddikins shit. You're dead! You pretended to be dead? Did you think I wouldn't mind?' I was screaming now. And Don had cottoned on.

'Whoah. Resurrection city,' he said and sat down on the arm of the sofa taking shot after shot of us until I said, 'Don, can you fuck off?'

And so he stopped.

My father looked hurt now, crestfallen, the big reunion not going quite according to plan.

'Well. I didn't think you'd be like this about it. I thought. I thought you'd be pleased to see me. I'm pleased to see you,' he said, still standing in front of me, almost meekly. I could smell pasta boiling in the kitchen. Even a few feet away, life was going on.

'Wouldn't you have been pleased to see me before? At some other point over the past twenty-five years. I'd have been pleased to see you when you got back from fucking Ireland. Why? Why did you do this to us? Why?'

'Didn't you like the stuff?' He seemed genuinely baffled by my rage, whispering. 'The bed? You used to say you wanted a four-poster bed with angels on it! And a gold locket, a nightie like Wendy in *Peter Pan*. Faithy, I got you everything you ever wanted. I thought . . .'

And I put my hands up over my face as it began to dawn on me. I think I'd known and not known, like Phoebe was saying about affairs. When you just can't face it and some part of you chooses not to know. I couldn't stand to drag this stuff from my memory. And my dream flashed back at me – Ben, grown up, in my old school uniform colours. Perhaps my acknowledgment, in my sleep, that I didn't need this stuff any more – the dresses, the bed. That it was his turn now – to be a child and take on that uniform and then to become an adult. I'd had my turn.

And I felt sorry for him, for Dad. He was hurt that I wasn't pleased. And I should make that better because, oh God, he was giving me emotional responsibility. Me whose world he had destroyed, as it turns out on purpose. He was asking for forgiveness. Not a saviour. Another person asking for something.

'Um. No, it's . . . it's beautiful stuff . . . Look. I'm wearing the locket. How did you get a photo of Ben? No. Don't tell me. It's beautiful stuff. It is. But . . . D . . .' It was impossible to choke out. Like when you know you're supposed to say I Love You and can't. 'Karel. I'm a grown woman now. I don't wear make-up. Or dresses. I might sell the pearls though.'

He laughed and lit a cigarette.

'You won't need to. Call me Dad. Please,' he said, drawing the smoke in and hollowing his cheeks, coughing as the smoke hit his lungs. 'Christ.'

'Give me one,' I said, sighing, reaching forwards.

'No! You don't smoke, do you? God! No!' he said, genuinely appalled.

'D . . . ad . . . I am someone's mum. I started smoking when I was fifteen. Give me a cigarette,' I told him, sitting now on the arm of the sofa myself.

'Oh, go on then,' he said, tossing a packet of Silk Cut at me and then throwing the matches high so that they would have gone over my head if I hadn't reached quick to catch them. 'But I want you to give up.'

I blew the match out, looking at him.

'Late for the fathering. Late,' I said, raising my eyebrows.

'Anyway, why don't you wear make-up for God's sake?' he asked, laughing now, the atmosphere lightening, if that's remotely possible. 'You look like shit.'

Now I laughed too.

'You think I should be prancing about in high heels and short skirt with a face full of make-up so that fat old men will approve of me? Do you?'

He walked over to the coffee and leaned down, the shape of him pouring, leaning, so familiar it made my heart ache, like all those times at airports when I'd seen a flash of him and chased without admitting it to myself, only to see the hideous face of a stranger. Not for me. He put his fingers through his hair, grey now, but still thick, but his face fallen, the lines deep.

'Christ,' he said. 'Don't say that. No! No. But you might want to put something pretty on. You'd look stunning in one of those . . .' He flicked his hand up towards where my room was. My room. Ha.

He came back towards me with his coffee in a mug. I was beginning to focus, to take it in, to feel.

'Dad. Really. I don't care how I look. OK?'

He snorted. 'That's ridiculous. Nobody wants to look like a pile of rat's numbers.'

'I do not look like a pile of rat's numbers,' I said.

Don was laughing.

'Shame about Walt's brain, though,' Dad said, taking a big slurp of his coffee and then spitting it back into the mug. 'Cold as penguin's wee-wee.'

I smiled, wondering. How the hell could he know this? 'Yes. Incredibly weird. I wonder how Phoebe copes. Did you . . . did you know Phoebe?' Though I knew the answer I wanted to see what he'd say. Now that I knew he was a liar and a fraud.

'Yup,' Dad nodded. 'Yup. Knew her.'

'Uh huh,' I smiled and he smiled back.

'Should have got his years ago. Tedium-related drive-by.'

'He's not boring! I don't think he's boring.'

'Well you must have the tedia threshold of a stoat then,' Dad said.

'I've no idea about a stoat's threshold, but I think he's lovely and I don't think you should have been fucking his wife.' Hmm. Not so easy-going with an alive person, was I? So easy to be all-forgiving and ultra-mature about the dead.

'About thirty years ago!' he whined, looking sheepish.

'Yes, but, Dad. That's the last time any of us saw you, of course.'

He took a deep breath and puffed his cheeks out, a familiar

thing that I often do when I can't take any more of something. Then he sat down at the table with the food on it and picked the tomatoes off a bruschetta. 'Got any HP Sauce?' he shouted, presumably to Annarita, but there was no answer. There were swallows swooping out by the cliff edge and I wished I was one of them.

'Twenty-five, actually. Twenty-five years. If I'd had any choice, Faithy . . .'

I was about to punch him or something but Don suddenly piped up. He'd got out of the sofa and had his camera bag on his shoulder.

'Listen. It's ever so moving and all that shit, but I think I might just hit the road now if nobody minds . . . Spare prick at a wedding, what have you?' he said.

'Ah!' Dad said. Even the word Dad in my mind made me into one of those women. One of those forty-ish women whose parents are both still alive and who still partly see themselves (nauseatingly) as a little girl. 'Oooh, Dad, can you buy me a pretty dress!' And some old man does buy a dress for a woman who no longer looks good in it, but still thinks she does because Daddy's eyes are full of love (and, by now, perhaps, pity too). And I was one of them. I think you can tell people whose parents are dead – they relax into the age that they really are, have had to acknowledge that they're next in line to go over the top. Whereas the old women in the frilly skirts are fighting for it still to be their turn.

'Yes, I've got a car for you,' Dad said. 'But if you want to take a few photos of me, that's fine . . . God. How do I look? No! Don't tell me,' he muttered, taking his glasses off and putting them in his shirt pocket, licking his teeth, ruffling his hair again and putting on a strange mirror face, pulling his cheeks in and pouting. I laughed, but it was painful. Like someone doing such a good imitation of my dad that I felt sick.

'Uh. Sure,' Don said, fiddling about for a lens and getting on the job. He looked at me questioningly. I shrugged.

'Why do you want your picture taken?' I asked. Dad looked baffled, moving from foot to foot awkwardly.

'I don't! Do I? Oh! I see. No. No. You do. You want a picture of me. For your piece. I'm the Reykjavik caller. I gave the warning. I thought you knew.'

I looked at Dad and smiled and then I walked over to the bottle of Pinot Grigio and poured some into a white mug. I drank it as quickly as I could and then took a long drag of my cigarette before putting it out in the ashtray. Then I went back to where Don was doing slightly frantic portraits of my father.

'Raise your left hand a bit, mate . . .' he said, just another story. Just another day for Don McCaughrean. For me it was The Day. Definite article. Capital Letters. The Day.

'Ah. No. Well. No. I didn't know. Not as something I could write down. I suppose when I got that card and it seemed so . . . I think the call I didn't believe in. Didn't think it could have been . . .'

'Me?' he smiled. 'If not me, who?'

It was a joke. The Talmudic line, 'If not now, when? If not me, who?' Though apparently the last bit is a mistranslation and should be, If I am not for me then who is for me? But Dad said it to me once when I was little, a Rabbi had said it to him in Jerusalem where he was interviewing him for a story (or, God knows, getting information from him to pass to MI6) and, apparently, I said, 'If not now then in about six minutes. If not me, you.'

I didn't laugh. I couldn't. Not at this.

'Dad. I thought I was going mad. In fact, I still do.'

'Well, you always were a little unstable. A couple of republics short of a Union. But listen. We'll get Don back to Palermo and then the family's all coming for dinner. To meet you, Faithy. So if you want to file your story, you can do it in my study. I knew about the protected suitcase, I found out about the bomb. They'd have killed me if I'd really gone public. And you too. They said they'd kill you. I believed them,' he said, taking a strand of tobacco off his tongue with his fingers. 'The splinter CIA people who were being paid off would have, straight away. And others too. I risked my life to make that call. I went to Reykjavik specially. What a slimy snake pit that place is. The murderers were Cosa Nostra from New York and the targets were Summerman and Leith. They were CIA and they now had enough information to screw a whole network of Italians whose lives depended on the business – more people would have died or gone to prison than died at Cairnbridge. So, you two have the scoop, such as it is. I mean, there hasn't been a scoop since Watergate, really, has there? Ihsan El Sayed, the little twerp – why DO they have to wear so much aftershave? – pretty much had it a couple of years ago. The English-speaking world didn't take any notice, of course. But nobody was ever looking for the caller before. Nobody's ever looked for me before. Until Fischer, may his last strand of hair fall out . . .'

'It already has,' I said, and as he spoke I realised that I had carried the way he spoke into the world with me and it had spread so that Don and Eden and I all used turns of phrase, a way of talking, that had started with him. And I would say that it was strange the ways in which the dead live on in these tiny little flickers of themselves in others. Except now it turns out he's not, in fact, dead at all.

'Good! Until Sam Fischer decided the time was right. Bastard.'

215

Don was standing on a pile of books that he had created for his oeuvre, leaning down as the shutter clicked. He was wheezing and beads of sweat were erupting on his forehead while he worked.

I went back to the wine and swigged it straight from the bottle. Lit another cigarette and sat down on the sofa, facing Dad who was standing in the nicest bit of natural light for his photo. I mulled all this over, though I'd file it, of course.

'But . . . But if they'd have killed you then . . . and me . . . for leaking this, then won't they kill us now?'

'Who?' he asked, as if I was just overcomplicating things for no obvious reason.

'Well. The Mafia. And the CIA.'

'Fuck!' Dad said, and glanced wildly over his shoulder as if people had started firing at him from every direction. 'No. Um. Yes. Yes. They probably will. I had hoped . . . I heard . . . Well, I hear everything about you. Of course I do. But I heard that Sam had put you on this Cairnbridge thing and I hoped I could . . . I hoped I could stop you. You don't need all this. Faithy. You don't need me. You don't need this. You were doing so fucking well! And Ben. And that what's his name. Eden. Sneeden.'

I bounced up and down on the edge of the sofa. I mean, my shrink, and, hell, I was booking right back on in with him the second I got back to London, was going to just keel over and die. Like that film with Robert de Niro, you know? Psychoanalyse THAT!

'But! But! But! Couldn't you have stopped me without letting me know . . . without letting me think . . . letting me hope that you . . .'

Don was packing away now. 'Think I've got it,' he said to me, keen to get back to Moscow, to Ira and Donchik now the

216

story had been got, like a horse on its way back to the stables, a day's trekking achieved.

'Right,' Dad said to Don and then looked at me and shrugged.

'Well, I suppose some part of me . . . I suppose. You know. Once I knew Sam had set you off and I imagined you arriving here, thought about you getting out of a car and ringing on the bell . . . Well . . . I knew I shouldn't let you. We're in trouble now, Faithy, you and me. But . . . Fuck it. Here we are!'

'So Sam Fischer knew? My editor, who I see practically every day, knew my dead father was not dead and that you were the Cairnbridge Reykjavik warning?'

'Not knew. Suspected. He suspected. But he's still being paid, so there's diddly squat he can do about it. Can say about it. Without getting himself poked up the bum with a poisoned umbrella that is. He's spent twenty-five years hiring people he hopes will nail the story without him having to tell them anything. But now you . . .'

Don coughed loudly.

'Yup. Yup. Come on then,' Dad said, showing Don the door and the car that was waiting to take him back to the hotel. He shook his hand. 'I loved that picture you took of the bloke with the grenade in Kashmir in the snow – flying through the air!' he said, waving his arms in imitation of the soldier flying through the air in Don's iconic photo. You must have seen it.

'Yeah. Thanks,' Don nodded. 'Um. See you, Eff Zed,' Don said. 'I'll get Ira to call you with some dates to come over. And . . . er . . . I've got the shots of the first bit of this family reunion if you ever do the big feature . . . you know . . . "My Dad Came Back To Life" by Faith Zanetti.'

'Yeah. Drop dead,' I nodded, realising that nothing I could

do or say would convey the enormity of all this, the absolute earth-shattering hugeness of this deal. 'See you McCaughrean.'

I watched out of the window as Don waddled in the yellow heat towards the BMW that was taking him back to the real world. There were a few brown floppy-eared goats out on the road, chewing at some scrub under the olive trees. A man wearing a flat cap was clopping up and down by the gate on a white horse. Inexplicably.

I faced the man whose absence had defined my life and whose presence was starting to feel normal. That is, I had absorbed the fact that he was alive, with the same long fingers and brown forearms that I remembered. The fantasy of a dead man had become the reality of an ordinary, non-supernatural, living one.

'But. But why? Why didn't you tell us you were dumping us instead of lying? Instead of putting us through a funeral and a . . . and this LIFE? How did you do it for fuck's sake. It was on TELEVISION?!'

He laughed, sitting down now and having another sip out of the cup into which he'd spat the cold coffee. 'Christ,' he said, tasting it. 'It was easy to DO. Physically. Someone pretended to shoot me in that crowd – a big demonstration – I can't remember what it was . . .' He couldn't remember! He couldn't even remember!

'The Orange men. The parade.'

'Was it?'

'Yes.' I shut my eyes.

'And I pretended to fall – like this!' I opened them again. And he stood up, clutched his chest and staggered. It was not funny. It was . . . it was appalling. 'And I had a blood capsule thing, you know. And they took me away and that was that.'

I shook my head in disbelief. 'And they brought you here to some safe house with some new identity forever? To protect you? And me.'

And ludicrously, even now, part of me was pleased. He screwed me over in the kind of way they make long documentaries about. (In fact there is a house near Eden's, Sneeden's, where some English people knocked a wall down in a cellar and found the skeleton of a guy in a suit, with a suitcase and a gun in his hand. He'd said he was leaving to make his fortune in America but he bricked himself into the cellar and shot himself instead and his family only found out fifty years later, those that were left, when some English people knocked a wall down – a worse way round? Perhaps.) But it was for my sake. My dad was still a good guy.

'Well. That type of thing,' he said, pushing his shirt sleeves up just like he always had.

'But why NOW? Why are you suddenly all Mr Public now?'

He took a huge deep breath to explain and it made him cough. But then I remembered something.

'But Evie . . . Evie SAW you!? SAW your dead body. I even asked her the other day when you started the *Gaslight* shit.'

'No. She saw some bloke from the morgue with my clothes on and his face fucked up and she was off her head anyway. We'd already agreed to split up, you know?'

He said this as though that was OK then. I turned away from him and then turned back and punched him in the jaw as hard as I could. I kept doing this lately.

'You hadn't agreed to split up with me!' I screamed.

He put his hand to his face. 'My tooth!' he mumbled.

And then he said, 'No. No. I hadn't.'

'Sorry about your tooth,' I said, and walked out and upstairs to my room. My little girl's room that I grew out of that evening twenty-five years ago. When I stopped wearing dresses.

Chapter Twenty

So, guess what I did? Did I cry and scream and run away? Noop. I found the office (full of all those old books about the Middle East that he must have had to buy second copies of, and, among a lot of others, a photo of me in a silver frame, shaking hands with Goofy at Disneyland) and I filed the piece. This was the man, a British spy, who had heard about the planned bomb on the TAA flight and had flown to Reykjavik to warn the world (without success), while the people of Cairnbridge pottered about their business. It would go in the anniversary edition, but I knew it was incomplete. I knew this wasn't the story I had really been sent on.

Then I had a bath and put on one of the weird dresses (he'd guessed right) and a pair of the weird shoes and I came downstairs for dinner. I did this for a million reasons. Partly, I suppose, because I didn't want to lose him, wanted to give him a chance. Partly because I didn't want to make him unhappy or, no, worse! Didn't want to disappoint him. God, had I really come to that? Because in the fantasy of this happening – which I only ever allowed myself to have in dreams, even when I was little – he had somehow been in suspended animation all this time, and now he marvelled at Highgate's new one-way system, the internet, teeny weeny mobile phones (he'd had one of the ones in a suitcase), being able to fly trans-Atlantic at any time of day, the Berlin wall being down, the Twin Towers having disappeared, the Soviet Union having disintegrated. I would tell him and show him, walk him round the new world as he stood stunned. In no fantasy had he lived through it all, had a whole life with women and friends and a beautiful house while I, ignorant, had put my T-shirt on every day and faced my hangover.

And, of course, these reunion fantasies that take place in some version of heaven, a place full of nice kind people and all the time in the world, they involve fictional people: the kind of father who will say, 'I love you and I'm so proud of you. You are a marvellous, wonderful person and as beautiful as the day you were born.' What is this? *Oprah*? I never had a relationship with anyone in which this kind of stuff gets said. Understood, maybe. At best. But my father never told me he loved me in life. Or that he was proud of me or pleased. Perhaps a 'Shame your old father with nine out of ten in your spelling test, would you? Drag the Zanetti name through the mud?' All with a smile and maybe a hug. All understood. But this is not *Richard and Judy*. This, it turns out, is two very damaged, perhaps mad adults meeting in cir- cumstances so strained they involved blindfolds.

So, I could be true to myself, a myself that was very sub- stantially hinged on a murdered father and a fundamental disbelief that A has any relation to B. Or I could pretend to be someone else, an old chestnut of a policy which, so far, had never failed me.

This recalibration of personality took perhaps a couple of

hours, a pack and a half of fags and all the champagne that had appeared in an ice bucket next to my bed – at last an acknowledgment of my actual age. A teacher at school once told me (as he so loved to do) that we would all soon be old. That hair would grow out of our noses and our trust funds would be wiped out in a stock market crash (this did not apply to me but some people looked worried) and that we would turn, as surely as rivers run to the sea, to alcohol. At the first few school reunions, he said, people drank white wine and then some water before they drove home. Nowadays there were only spirits on the table and people arrived wankered in any case. Well, I'd arrived. Thanks Mr Griffiths.

So, by the time I came back downstairs, the new Faith Zanetti, the person I would perhaps have become if my father hadn't pretended (I mean, for God's sake) to be pumped full of bullets in a Belfast alleyway, was fully formed. The dress was a very pale grey, like a signet perhaps, or a spring sky. The shoes were high with an ankle strap that fastened with a tiny black bead. I blow-dried my hair (there is a first time for everything) and then used two diamante clips to push it off my face and let it frizz around my whole head. Then I opened the make-up box. This was a big challenge. I went for a tiny amount of lipstick and some pearly shit over my eyelids. I looked like a clown but it was, admittedly, more subtle than any other made-up face I'd ever seen. As I stood at the top of the stairs I remembered what Phoebe had said when her husband elected to hurl his full attention at me. 'Andi-fucking-amo.'

God knows how long I'd really been because there were voices from the basement, a floor lower than the sitting room where I'd spent the entire life-ending day. I crept down to find a very English-style lower ground floor kitchen where half the room is Agas and pans, garlic, onions and chillis hanging off the ceiling and pretty tiles and the other half is lavish blood-coloured rugs, a long table, expensive art, family photographs and French windows to the outside. These were open tonight on to a terrace that was lit by nightlights in coloured glass jars hung from Cypress trees. But inside. Inside my father sat at the table in a white shirt with the sleeves rolled up, younger in the candlelight, almost as I remembered him, though no memory could be as vivid as this, as sharp, as brutal. He was holding a martini up with a twist and telling the woman next to him a story so funny that she was crying. He was doing an impression of a Middle Eastern dictator, accent and all. The accent, I supposed, that he had used for his warning about the Cairnbridge flight. The warning that had been ignored. They all died. Including . . . Well. I would think about that later.

The girl was in her early twenties, Italian, wealthy. She wore two hundred and fifty pound jeans, a drapey silk top with bright patterns on it, huge pearl drops in her ears and an antique watch. She was young enough to be his daughter but, hell, weren't we all? There were three semi-blonde Italian boys who looked related to each other, all in pastel shirts with bright cashmere jumpers round their shoulders, an old man with the twinkle of enormous success in pin-stripes but no tie and a wife half his age – a blonde woman who smoked tiny cigars and eyed up all the men, including my father. Well, of course she did. An older woman with a grey bun and red lipstick and Walter, who didn't meet my eye. Yup. Walt Irving. He of the also faking his own death in the hotel fame. Christ, it is just all the rage. It was . . . there is a Russian word 'snogshibatelno' which means 'knocked-offyourfeet-ish' . . . so it was snogshibatelno to see someone I actually knew from real life in this dream world. Though I suppose meeting him was the beginning of this other mist-swirling universe in which the dead live and the orphans have huge families.

So. There they were. And Annarita, of course, who was in the kitchen coaxing the staff on. I appeared in a corner near (could it possibly be?) a tiny Vermeer lit by a candle in a brass wall-holder, at the bottom of the narrow stairs. And the whole table stood up and stared at me, breathless for a moment before erupting into applause, my dad with his fag between his lips, squinting to keep the smoke out of his eyes.

The old Faith said, 'What the fuck's your problem?' But she said it to herself. The new Faith was briefly stunned, and then she smiled slightly, held her dress up at both sides and sank to the floor in a huge mock-curtsey which sent them into a frenzy of clapping and laughing and talking in English and Italian. I moved forwards to the table and Annarita came up behind me, her hair loose and sweeping down her naked back (she had a white silk halter-neck top on over her very tight black jeans and black sling-back stilettos), leading me by the hand to the seat at the head of the table facing my father at the other end. He winked at me, as if that would somehow be comforting, and I sat down. When my arse was safe on my chair, the others sat down too. Okey dokey.

The staff, five middle-aged local women in black dresses with plain white aprons, put plates of sliced figs with mozzarella in front of us all. There were tall glasses of champagne already there on the white tablecloth. My father, who used to smear mustard on to chunks of cheddar cheese broken off from a supermarket packet, stood up. He shuffled around looking awkward, but really it was more of a show of awkwardness, like Hugh Grant playing geeky, and then bowed his head.

225

'Well,' he said. 'Benedictus benedicat.'

Everyone else, including me at this point, repeated what he'd said and then we all started eating and drinking. I couldn't help looking at Dad, for want of anything else to call him really, incredulously. Like, shalom? Aren't we atheists? Who are you? And he shrugged as if to say, 'Well, they like it and it isn't hurting anyone.'

Annarita reached out to hold my hand. If she spoke English, why the fuck hadn't she spoken it last night? Too tired, were you, sweetheart? 'I am so happy that you're here, Faith. He told me everything about you. Now the family is complete.'

She absolutely seemed to mean it. As though I'd had a shameful teenage pregnancy but now we'd talked about it I could be brought back into the fold. Everything? Like, you mean, what I was like before I hit double figures? Right then. But I didn't say it. I said, 'He's lucky to have found someone like you. How long have you been together?'

And then she answered. And, to my credit, I just patted the side of my hair like other women, perhaps, do. Instead of falling backwards off my chair or screaming or something.

'Twenty years now! Can you imagine!? It goes so fast.'

I clenched my teeth together and smiled. Doesn't it just.

And then one of the three boys got up. He had a belt on that was clasped with the intertwining letters 'D' and 'G'. It was gold. He raised his glass and looked at me, gesturing with his other hand that I should stand up.

'My whole life I know I have a beautiful sister. I know that our father's first child, the love of his life . . .'

The other diners whooped and cheered and Dad laughed. He said, 'Can we adios the fucking sincerity, Gabi? Uh?'

Gabi held his middle finger up to Dad. 'Fuck you. I am welcoming my sister. My whole life we wait for you. Me and

226

my brothers.' He made them stand up too and it dawned on me.

I leaned down to Annarita. 'Not triplets? Not seriously?'

'Ouch,' she said, laughing and looking down at where the scars must be. And you know what? At this, I laughed too. She'd got me. As a woman.

'And, Faith!' Gabi shouted. 'Here you are!'

And then he ran from his seat round the table to where I was, threw his arms round me and picked me up, kissing me on both cheeks, swinging me round and staring, smiling into my face. He tossed me to the other two who had joined us and were shouting and cheering and kissing me and throwing me in the air and we were all laughing, even me, if a spot hysterical, and the candlelight danced and the sea crashed against the rocks and . . .

I was home.

Someone had (when?) put Elvis on to some astonishing four-corners-hidden-in-the-walls sound system and 'I Just Can't Help Believin'' was blaring round the room as I yelled, red-cheeked and drunk to Walter. Who knew what he was doing here but I had now realised that a) he wouldn't tell me and b) if he did it might be some completely lunatic fantasy of his own.

'Walt, you dickhead! What the fuck is going on?!'

He met my eye, but wasn't laughing. He was serious. 'It's family, Faithy.'

'Not your family though.'

'No, Faith Zanetti. Yours.'

Dad had shoved Annarita out of the way and was sitting next to me, his arm round the back of my chair, arguing with the triplets about Israel. Every now and then one of them would get up and kiss me hard on the cheek and, drunk and relaxed, I'd take their hand and squeeze it. The old woman was Annarita's mum, flirting with the old guy who was a judge, trained at the English bar before doing Italian law in Rome and moving to Sicily 'for the sun' he said. The other stunning girl was, I realised as slowly as I could, Walter's date for the evening. It was the way he kept leaning down to kiss the top of her right breast that gave it away. And he talked into her ear absolutely non stop. Hmph.

Some time after the roast pork and baked fennel Dad went and got his guitar out. Sitting next to me by the flickering candle stubs he played 'Let It Be', 'Hey Jude' and 'I Wanna Hold Your Hand'. Laughing, I sang, twice making him change the key, and one of my brothers (what can I tell you?) harmonised. 'When I find myself in times of trouble . . .'

Dad's ash dropped on to the tablecloth and the women buzzed around pouring brandy. A bat flew into the room and Walter, whose beautiful attention was all – babbling, staring, joking, laughing – on his date, chased it out with his hands flailing. It was disturbing seeing him do it to someone else. I had believed it, after all. That it was for me.

But Gabi and I danced to a Flamenco-style thing Dad was playing and I almost fell with the whirling and the booze and the roomful of . . . love.

The new Faith didn't ask Walter what in the name of Christ he was doing here. Why he hadn't just told me or didn't he know? The new Faith didn't ask about the Bisacquino massacre and the blonde boys who, let's face it, bore a certain little family resemblance. Hell, the new Faith wasn't even thinking about that shit. This. This evening of wealth and safety and family I never knew I had, of love and singing and drinking and dancing. This was what I had been waiting for for twenty-five years. And I wasn't about to toss it away with some awkward questions and bitter snarking. No siree.

Not even when I saw a big framed wedding photo on a shelf. Dad and Annarita, not long ago maybe, the boys already in their teens. It was that, I think, that planted the seed I only acknowledged later. The seed that grew into the vast enormous oak tree of his not loving me. Not enough to be around. Not enough to miss me at his bloody wedding. I mourned and he got married to a lovely woman in an ivory shift and in a Sicilian lemon grove. But never mind that now.

I was barely in a state to take it in, but the eighteen-year-old triplets were called Gabriel (I leaned forwards asking for a repetition and laughing, the silk straps of my dress slipping forwards off my shoulders), Ruben and Davide. That's Davideh, not Daveeed. When I sang 'Love Me Tender' with Dad on guitar Annarita cried. And I refused to let any thought of Evie into my mind. So she had wrenched her heart out and lain on the sofa weeping silently, she had raised me as far as she could and she had built another life on a foundation of sadness and loss. But life is for the living, and Annarita was alive, with her triplets and her opulent home and her art collection and her staff and her new step daughter who wasn't much younger than her. Well, no more than a decade or so . . .
I spent all evening guessing which triplet was which, getting it wrong and sending everyone into a frenzy of happy laughter.

While Davide played guitar, Dad waltzed me all the way round the table, swirling and nearly falling and swooping out on to the black starry terrace and in again, diving and stumbling, both of us ridiculously drunk, and we spun and spun and he said, 'Do you hate your old Daddikins, Gleamer?' and I said, 'No more than I ever did.' Which was the ironic, non-emotional, we're not on *Jerry Springer* response required.

And I could hardly focus on Annarita when she told me. She leaned right in towards me and I leaned back, red-faced and beaming and she said, 'He's got lung cancer.'

And I was too far gone to make any distinction between my two personalities, so I said, 'Serves him right.' Or perhaps I didn't say it out loud. Perhaps not.

I think it can't have been too long after that that they came.

I had surrendered in every sense long before I was required to. Because suddenly, just as the sky was starting to pale at the edges and birds had begun to squawk far out to sea, gunfire erupted around the house. As perhaps I had been expecting it to.

The music stopped and the laughing and dancing, and it was all too quick to understand, shouting and yelling and twenty or so men in black with balaclavas on burst into the room via the stairs I'd come down and the French window to the terrace. Obviously, we had been protected (it turned out inadequately) from the outside because nobody in here was armed. The swift men took one person each while a few of them patrolled the entrances and exits. Given our drunkenness and euphoria, they seemed amazingly slick and well organised. We all had our hands tied behind our backs and were being hustled out on to the terrace before I regained focus. Before I had any idea what was happening.

We were separated in the darkness and Walter, who I couldn't see though I tried to spin round said, 'You started this, Zanetti. It's you who has to finish it, baby!'

I shouted back to him, 'Give me something, Irving! ANYthing! What the fuck is going on?'

I was being pushed now, round the outside of the house and down some steps. I could see that Dad was with me. Nobody else. I heard Walter's voice echoing.

'It's about you!'

Oh great. Thanks so much. Jolly helpful.

And as we staggered and slid down the steps, I heard Dad coughing and couldn't believe I hadn't taken it in properly before I felt my old self close in around me. The warmth of the family I couldn't do, not and feel real. This, being shoved around by masked blokes with guns – hell, it was my forte.

I spun round and kicked one of them in the face with my stiletto. A couple of the others laughed.

'E finito, Carlo. Capito?' the bleeding bloke said to Dad. And things began to dawn on me.

Chapter Twenty-one

And that's how we got into the cellar. I got punched in the jaw on the way and Dad, who had seemed so vivacious and so alive just minutes before, suddenly collapsed wheezing, semi-conscious. And I realised that, psychopath that I am, even in the middle of all this, I had fantasised him and had chosen not to notice the jaundice, which I'd decided to mistake for a tan, and the wheezing and coughing, how thin he was. But he was never fat and I hadn't seen him for some time, let's face it . . . But now, pushed down the stairs into the dark by God knows who – the CIA? Hardly? Some Cosa Nostra faction? Probably – I realised he was dying. Not only that but that there might not be long to go. And I'd felt his ribs dancing this evening and I hadn't wanted to wonder why they were so sharp under my fingertips.

I understood that that's why Sam Fischer had put me on this now, that that's why he'd let me find him despite the dangers, why he'd led me to him, in fact. That that's why Walter had helped rather than rebelling, only half-heartedly throwing me off the scent. And, for the Lord's sake, it may even have been why the Bisacquino massacre had happened.

Nobody really wanted to keep me from a dying man. And, for a lot of them, there were reasons for me to get in there before he went. So here I was. In the role of Butch Cassidy, for Christ's sake.

And he'd always hoped he might look a bit like Robert Redford which, of course, he didn't at all. I could hear gunfire getting closer and closer and the movement in the house getting more and more frantic when, at last, though my wrists were ragged and bleeding, my flex finally came free. It was cold, dark and damp and I had no idea where the others were. I stayed where I was for a while hoping that a plan would just come to me, that the answer would be blindingly obvious. But I was really on the point of just staying there in the cold until whoever they were came to do whatever they wanted. When . . . in Dad's shirt pocket, the phone rang. In Italian subtitles I notice that it always says, 'Squilla telefono.' Squilla seems like a good word for what they do. I was stunned by our luck. I leapt towards his pockets, patting and fumbling, knowing that our salvation lay in the feeling of the cold metal in my hand. Even with my manhandling him, Dad had barely roused himself and, in some kind of entirely misplaced reverence to his condition, I answered it in a whisper.

'Pronto?' I said, not being able to help with the languages even now. Because now, having nearly been sucked in by life's biggest lie, I was back. And I felt invincible. There were no fantasies left now. Nothing left to hope for.

'Hey, Faithy? It's me. Just checking in. You OK?'

I pulled the phone away from my ear and looked at it. Don's! Dad must have picked it up.

'Oh, Jesus! Eden! Thank God. Thank God. Thank God.'

'OK. Keep it together. What's going on? You said to call. I thought you said it was all fine.'

'Was. Isn't. Get the fuck here now. An hour or so out of Palermo into the hills. Huge villa alone on a hillside . . .'

I'd have carried on but Eden stopped me.

'Listen you imbecile. You didn't really think I wouldn't come, did you? Can you get down to the sea? I bought the patrol off. Three hundred bucks would you believe? I'm here with . . . sorry, what's your name? Ihsan El Sayed. That's right. Sorry. Al Jazeera guy. Met him at the hotel – insisted on coming. And Don, obviously. We can get quite near the shore . . . can we? Yes. So . . .'

I was laughing hysterically. 'We're under siege and I've got a cancer patient with me who can hardly move at the moment. And I might have a broken jaw. But I'll try. OK? I'll try.' And I would.

Eden didn't say anything for a bit, and then he shouted at me. 'Faith, you stupid bitch. We've got a son. We need to be surviving here.'

The first thing that occurred to me was a trailer for a TV show I never watched where the heroine is pointing a gun at someone and saying, 'If I liked being called a bitch I'd still be married.' But on this occasion it seemed almost justified. In fact, it was rousing. I wasn't allowed to give up yet, tempting though it was beginning to seem. I felt, from the sound of all the guns and the mounting hysteria upstairs (footsteps, stumbling and shouting), that our chances weren't superb.

'I know. I screwed up. I'll try,' I said, smiling. No really. Smiling. In bewilderment and regret. I really did spend a couple of hours hoping that the life some people have might be mine. That someone might be holding me. You know. Like the Biblical story when he says, 'Lord, where were you when I needed you most? I only saw one set of footprints in the sand.' And God says, 'I was carrying you.' Well. He wasn't. I'm carrying my bloody self. Oh. And the big guy too.

'OK,' I said. 'Come on, Sundance.' And I grabbed him under the shoulders and pulled. There were doors to the outside, rusting ones closed by a bar that was held on both sides of the wall by big hooks. Not sealed. Not even, by the sound of things, guarded. Nobody, apparently, was expecting us to get free of our bonds. Which seemed to me like a fairly major oversight given that one of us was totally conscious. Perhaps they didn't expect anything more than whimpering from a woman in an evening dress. Thought I'd wait and maybe faint or offer myself as a devoted slave. But, in fact, I was more conscious at that moment than I'd ever been before.

It seems weird now, but I was ready to be shot and killed. I felt then, in the instant, that I'd been through a billion lifetimes and wouldn't mind at all if they all ended in the squeeze of a trigger. So I was backing out of a cellar, arse first, in a dirty silk dress and no shoes, dragging a tall man who had been my father a quarter of a century ago and was now God knows who to whom but, to everyone who knew him, a dying man. A living corpse whose demise was compromising the future in some very unclear manner.

When we got out through the doors and into the light – it was probably not long after dawn – Dad seemed to come to again. It was impossible to believe that we'd been dancing round the tables only a couple of hours earlier. But maybe that's what cancer is like. The fighting seemed to be getting worse. It reminded me of El Salvador. There was always the sound of battle but there was a sharpness to it, a smell in the air when it was too near to keep on drinking tea and smoking fags.

'Get up,' I said. 'Please stand up. If we can get to the sea, we're OK.' It wasn't looking great.

It seemed hopeless. The sun so hot, the sea suddenly so

distant, the threat so real. I looked down at the cross I was having to bear. Dad – could it really be him? – smiled, if it can be called that, his face now as grey as his hair, his wheezing painful.

He said, 'Why didn't you tell me? There's a tunnel under the wine vats.'

Uh huh. OK then. I looked at him, incredulous, bent over, sweating, swearing.

'Well more of a staircase to be accurate, it's a sort of . . .'

'Whatever,' I said, bringing him back in as fast as I could, hauling his weight on my shoulders though he tried to walk, shutting the doors again and hoping that nobody had noticed our aborted escape plan.

Pretty much throwing Dad against a damp wall while I pulled the big green globes out of their places, I stopped worrying about snakes and guns and all the astonishing complications of whatever this story was. I just wanted to live. To get to Eden and to Ben.

I shook my elderly father (so strange to have one – mine had always been tall and dark-haired, potent and dependable in his way. I never got to experience the parental disintegration that turns most people into adults) until he came to enough to get down the hundreds of splintering wooden steps through the cold rock of the cliff to the beach. It was like something out of *Alice In Wonderland*. Half an hour's descent, at least, with Dad stopping constantly to cough and regulate his breathing in the pitch dark, me hoping he wouldn't fall, not certain that there was a bottom to this abyss. And in that dark hole I asked him.

'Why did all the boys at Bisacquino have our surname?'

And he stood very very still for a while in the blackness before he said, 'Faithy. It's a big family. I spent my whole youth trying to escape. Pretending they'd never come for me. But they got me in the end. They always do. Just when I thought I'd done it. There are a lot of people who want my job. My brother's kids. Ivano's boys.' Brother's kids? More family. There was just no stopping me with the new relations these past few days.

Yes. I imagine there are a fair number of people vying for the position. But he wasn't dead yet.

Not yet.

Eventually, when I had almost forgotten that there would be an end to this, my feet touched sand, and I could see the sea and the light of dawn at the end of a low tunnel that I would have to double over to get to the end of, by the looks of it. Dad, to my shame, crawled. And that was the end of anything I might ever have thought or hoped. A man who could barely breathe crawling along a tunnel for his life. This was not someone who, in any seriousness, could help me now. If there was going to be any salvation it was me doing the offering. Ah well. What can you do? The meek shall inherit the earth. Maybe. If we bequeath it to them.

As Dad emerged on hands and knees, like a mole blinking from his hole, Don McCaughrean took the pictures from his position lying in the sand with his elbows in a pool of sea water. I came out afterwards, bent double and straightened up with a stretch. Don assured me that I looked great in a clingy and wet silk dress with bare feet. Clearly, this was my chief concern. 'Ursula fucking Andress eat your fucking heart out,' he said, and I smiled, glad to be back with my real family.

'Fuck off, Don,' I said. 'Seriously. Can we leave now?'

On the beach below the cliff top where my father's house was, Eden and Don took my giant in a blue linen shirt under the shoulders and dragged him into the sea where, at waist depth, the boat was waiting. Ihsan, no honestly, had lowered in a tiny white ladder and I climbed up first, shivering now, as the men shoved my father into the speedboat, hauling themselves up behind him to sit on wet plastic bum-shaped seats as Ihsan drove us over to the mainland. Dad kept his head slumped to his chest. At one point, Eden's wool and cashmere (lovely) jacket wrapped round my shivering shoulders, I said, 'Don't worry. They'll be all right.'

Dad raised his eyes to mine and said, quietly, 'You idiot. Of course they will. It's us they want.'

I glanced up at Don but didn't say anything. He shrugged violently and took a couple of shots of me in a soaking cocktail dress against a dawn sky.

'How did you find me?' I asked Eden, and he made a face over at Ihsan who had the wheel, a fag trapped between his lips.

'I have always had a hunch about this place,' Ihsan said. 'And when Don described it to us, I realised immediately that I must have been right. It has been rumoured always that Carlo lives up there, completely freely with his family, that nobody would ever dare say anything. There is nothing anybody can make stick to him. Except perhaps . . .' and he flicked his cigarette butt into the sea, not finishing his thought.

Was there anyone who knew less about what was going on in my life than me? I reached out and took Dad's hand as a seagull swooped at our boat.

Without opening his eyes, he said, 'It won't stick. And who cares now anyway? I'll be dead in a week or two. That's what they say. The Grim Reaper's coming for me, Faithy. Bastard.'

'He's not ready for you yet,' I said, but I could see it wasn't true. The boat's engine roared and every time we went over a wave I got soaked, but the sun was warming up and there was blue all around. Beautiful really, circumstances aside.

We docked at the port in Messina, from where they'll never build the bridge to Sicily (if you believe my piece slapped together from cuts a couple of weeks ago), just as some of the fishing boats were coming in, their decks slithering with flopping, bucking silver fish struggling against the nets. Eden helped Dad up on to the pier, the sight of him, so similar looking of course, helping this man by whose memory I think he'd always felt crushed, was devastating, made my stomach tighten and eyes blink shut. There were men crouching on the quayside sewing nets and women squatting round baskets of fresh fish, the local restaurateurs poring over them.

Eden got a key out of his pocket and aimed it at a gleaming black four-by-four parked up in a blue-outlined pay-and-display bay outside a little café where the fish people were standing for an espresso and a cornetto. This means a croissant. Source of great confusion to English tourists countrywide.

'Thank Christ for that,' I said, having vaguely imagined driving for twelve hours in the Cinquecento with Dad, Don, Ihsan and God knows who else might be coming along for the ride.

Dad was pushed up into the front and came to enough to light a cigarette.

'Should you be smoking?' I asked, stupidly, leaning forward between the seats.

'Why not?' he said. This seemed like a good point. He pulled a strand of tobacco off his tongue.

Eden drove and Don, Ihsan and I got in the back.

'I don't mean to be rude,' I said, straightening the straps

of my evening dress. When I licked my lips they tasted of salt from the boat ride. Of course, not meaning to be rude is like saying you're being honest. If you need this preface then you're just about to be incredibly rude. 'But why are you people coming with us?'

Don burped.

'Oh, I see,' I said. Dad laughed, his hand on his chest.

'I am coming because I am hoping that in return for rescuing you, your father will let me interview him on camera before . . . while he is still able to . . . I have a crew on the way from Palermo where we shot Bisacquino,' Ihsan explained. Well, hey, it was honest.

'Me too,' Don said, not having listened to a word Ihsan said because he was trying to make his seatbelt stretch round his paunch – a hopeless endeavour.

'You're crazy,' I told them. 'I am not even discussing what story you might think you're on but, even if you're right, there's no way you're running it.'

'No,' Don said. 'You are, Zanetti, you dim cow.'

'In your dreams McCaughrean. In your tiny weeny little dreams. Not talking about it. Not doing it,' I said, lowering my voice to a hiss. 'He's ill for fuck's sake. Really ill.'

'I know,' Ihsan said. 'That is the story.'

I took a deep breath and made a decision that surprised me. I had felt duped by Dad and the house and the family, felt as though I'd been shown a dream and had it snatched away again. I'd been pleased to see these idiots out on the sand – people who really do give a shit about me and didn't fry me up with mushrooms and some crushed garlic for twenty-five years. But he was my Dad. And family is family.

'Pull over,' I shouted to Eden. 'Pull over now.'

Extremely unfortunately, we had just come out of a galleria, those long tunnels that run through mountains across

Italy and are connected by terrifying pieces of motorway raised above the landscape on concrete stilts hundreds of feet high. Eden, knowing my voice well enough to know when he needed to be obeying, pulled over, the cars behind us swerving and beeping, a bloke leaning right out of his window to tell Eden to go and fuck his mother.

'Get out,' I said to Ihsan. 'Get out of the car. Thank you for rescuing us but now get out of the car.'

Sitting next to him I could smell him and even here, on this journey, the smell made my head spin and my eyes close with desire. He looked at me with what was basically enormous disappointment. Disappointment in my journalistic ability. In my lack of ability to ignore my emotional involvement and break the story. But with this level of emotional involvement, hell, there was no question of objectivity. Not a jot. And, anyway, is there ever? Freud wouldn't have thought so. Ihsan, who I doubt had read much Freud and God be with him, leaned forward and I looked at the curve of his spine. He picked his small leather briefcase up off the floor and got out of the car, shutting the door gently behind him with a clunk. We had tinted windows.

'Let's go,' I said to Eden, and we pulled away, leaving him standing there, proud, by the side of the road, teetering above the fields of sunflowers below.

'Thanks Sneeden,' Dad said and then turned round to look at me. 'If we'd had the boys here I'd have got one of them to shoot him.'

I laughed. And then I stopped laughing. Not because my punched jaw still hurt. But because perhaps it was true.

It was a long drive during which Don McCaughrean slept, snoring loudly and occasionally shouting at dreamt people who were trying to get their hands on his apparatus. I organised a nurse to be at the house in Brandeglio when we arrived, using Eden's phone and Eden's Italian phrases, shouted at me while I tried to talk to someone at a hospice in Lucca. And Dad asked about me.

'How many O levels did you get?'

'Seven.'

'Who were your friends at school?'

'God. At what point, exactly? I can introduce you if you like.'

'What's Evie's new husband like?'

'He's not new. They've been together for twenty years.'

'I sent flowers to Mum's funeral, you know. Did you see them?'

'I really wasn't concentrating on the floral side of things.'

'They weren't cheap!' he said, and I remembered that he'd always left the prices on my presents, often ringing the figure in red felt tip. 'Seventeen ninety-nine that dolly, you know!'

'Cheapoid ones would hardly have been appropriate,' I said.

I told him about Russia, about getting married at eighteen, about being accused of murder last time I was there. 'I heard about that,' he said, as if I was talking about what had been Number One in 1993.

I suppose I had imagined that he'd be fascinated by me. But, obviously, if that had been the case he'd have given me a sodding call beforehand, now wouldn't he? When we passed Rome, an hour in ten lanes of stationary traffic, he said, 'How's Barleybonks?!'

Naomi Barley was my best friend when I was nine. I don't know really what he was trying to do, but it wasn't working.

'Dad. I have no idea.'

'Haven't you Googled her?'

It was things like this, things that a dead person wouldn't

know about, that hurt so much. That reminded me that he'd left us. And not died.

'Nope. No. I haven't. If you're so fucking interested why don't you do it?'

Not having a leg to stand on, he was quiet. Which was good.

When we got to Lucca, driving round the tall red walls, looking at the people cycling and calling to each other, I started thinking about the implications of what we were doing. How long, seriously, would it take whoever it was to find us? In Brandeglio, at Eden's house, I thought, not long. A few days maybe. I was at some point going to have to ask what we were escaping from and what whoever it was might want. So I leaned forward as we began to climb the hill to the village, the road strewn with chestnut cases.

'What do you think those people . . . in the balaclavas . . . what do you think they wanted?'

Dad laughed. 'Oh. They were going to kill us, Gleams. After trying to "make us talk".' He put on a German accent for this. 'I told you we were in trouble now.'

'What. Me too?'

'Oh. Especially you.'

'But I can't talk! I've got nothing to talk ABOUT!' I whined.

'Stop whingeing. Hey! Do you remember when I bought you that Bernard to make you stop whingeing in the back on the way to Poshington with Shirl? Where is Bernard?'

'He's in a box on the North Circular,' I said, but I had to bite my bottom lip if I was going to try not to cry. Do I remember? There is not a moment of the time I got to spend with you that I don't remember. Not a shred of your life, the shreds I managed to tear for myself, that I don't remember. How dare you ask me if I remember?

'God. The North Circular. Why hasn't somebody bombed it?' he sighed, genuinely baffled.

'They will,' I reassured him. 'Any time now.'

And I told him about the Highgate one-way system, though not about all the times that I'd tightened my hands on the wheel and held my breath with grief while I was driving through it, picturing him loping into a shop for some fags. Why I had ever imagined that this would be a thing he would care about I have no idea. He was barely listening. But it was just one of those tiny things that made me think, 'If my dad ever came back he'd lose his way here.' In fact, I don't know if I ever actually thought it. It just hovered there. The thought.

And as we pulled up at the house, the porch light on, Carolina, the woman who cleans for Eden, in there with Ben, my heart lurched towards it. And I was dying to get out of these ridiculous clothes.

Chapter Twenty-two

In the end it happened slowly. Not because I hadn't understood it the moment that thug called him Carlo, but because my brain, booze-addled as it by now is, was not able to cope with the amount of information that was being thrown at it. A bit like when Eden and I saw a porcupine on the road up here. I thought they only had them in Africa though I'd never seen one there. I suppose they probably avoid the landmined areas. And I'd never seen one in a zoo either. I've only seen pictures. So my brain scrolled and whirred and pieced things together until the word 'Porcupine!' arrived between my lips as my finger indicated the direction in which said spikey thing had just run.

And what is so weird about it is that after the initial madness of that evening with Annarita and the boys, my longing taking me over and making me see things that weren't there (like a healthy father, for example and, obviously, a healthy situation) I did ease into the fact that this guy was alive. Again, as with Ihsan's Cairnbridge film, linking the heroin to Cosa Nostra, once I had absorbed that it was true, it was just . . . well . . . true. I had thought I would be changed, that I

245

could have this strange fictional life with weddings in an olive grove and someone with my best interests at heart. But it was a brief dream and, reborn through a dark tunnel on a Sicilian beach, I realised who I belonged to. Yes, he was alive and I would look after him, but there wasn't going to be any salvation to be had.

So that night, when we got home, I found Carolina in front of the television in her Venus de Milo apron (you know the one) watching a game show where old men answer questions and a teenaged girl takes her clothes off. This show culminates with the girl having to smilingly open her legs so that these blokes who are probably too old to get it up any more can see her vagina. Yay. And there was the nurse setting up equipment in the little room on the ground floor behind the television, the room where Eden had put most of his Russian kitsch, including a bust of Lenin and a police hat that I, in fact, nicked off a policeman's head in Soviet times when I could probably have been sent to a gulag for ever and ever for it. Don went straight to the fridge and got himself – himself and nobody else – a beer, sitting down next to Carolina and draping his arm round her shoulders, exposing his sweat patches.

She leapt up.

'Oh. Sorry luv,' he said, arranging his camera bag at his feet.

Eden followed with Dad and laid him down in the bed he would probably die in. Wouldn't he? I didn't want to look at him lying down. I don't know why. Anyway, I had more important things to do. I ran upstairs and into Eden's room where Ben was fast asleep, rosy and hot in the enormous bed. I picked him up and hugged him until he woke up.

'Mama!' he said, smiling and pulling at a coil of my hair. 'Mama!'

'Baba!' I said back to him and kissed his cheeks until he pushed me away. When he noticed my dress he reached out and touched the material and laughed.

'I know, I know,' I told him. 'I'm going to change!'

I brought him down on my hip to hear Carolina talk me through the nappies and feeds and new words and how lovely he'd been. 'Farfalla,' he apparently understood. I smiled, pleased. She addressed none of this to Eden, of course. Of course. And when she lowered her voice to a mutter to ask who the ill man was Eden explained that he was my father. Since she'd never known he was dead she wasn't surprised he was alive and I rolled my eyes at how strange it all was and yet, already, how almost normal.

I stepped into the room where the nurse, a fat woman in her sixties with a gold tooth and bright blonde hair piled on top of her head, had put an oxygen mask to Dad's face and a morphine drip in his arm.

'Per ora,' she said. For now. I sat on the edge of the bed where my father was lying in his long long jeans and shabby trainers, his leather jacket draped on the back of a chair, his eyes laughing. I turned Ben to face him and said, 'This is Grandpa Karel. Carlo? Whatever. This is Grandpa.'

Dad reached out and shook Ben's tiny hand.

'I changed it when I thought I might get away from them, you know? When Dad kicked me out. I was fifteen and they always told me I looked Scandinavian. The Zanetti blondes. So I chose Karel. But when I went back. When they took me back I was Carlo again. Thirty-five years old. I hardly spoke a word of Italian any more. Just, you know, an espresso doppio per favore. That kind of thing.' Was this supposed to be funny, I wondered?

'Right,' I said, kissing the top of Ben's head and knowing

now that there was nothing flickering in the universe that could distract me from him any more.

But it was days later, days of baking (Delia Smith's shortbread biscuits) and watching DVDs (*Some Like It Hot*, *Groundhog Day*, *Curb Your Enthusiasm*), packing Don off back to Moscow (arrivaderci), sending emails and drinking the wine that Eden brought up from Non Solo Vino in Bagni di Lucca, walking Ben into the square to push his enormous plastic car around, watching Dad swim on the morphine and then be lucid and funny, eating in the kitchen and talking for hours on the phone to Annarita, a lot of which I understood and blanked out. I heard him mention names and huge amounts of money and I chose not to hear. It was strange to hear about election results and big business and know that it wasn't being talked about from a journalistic point of view, or even one of political concern.

When they'd realised we'd gone, Dad said without the smirk that nearly always turned the corners of his mouth up, they'd beaten the boys up quite badly, but they had apparently believed, in the end, that the triplets really didn't know where we were. Which they still didn't. Killing them would have been, Dad said, 'counterproductive.' Well, yeah. Yup. Killing very rarely productive. Unless you're trying to produce . . . I don't know. Organs for donation or something. Annarita had gone to her mum's in Sorrento and the boys had gone to New York. I wondered if she knew she'd seen him for the last time. I wondered if they dared talk about it. But even so, wouldn't it be better than not having known, like when me and Evie kissed him at the door and watched him drive up the road and wave from the corner, from the window of his taxi. And if we'd known we could have run and hugged him, kissed him, asked him to stay. But all that I had to do in his absence.

It still wasn't entirely clear to me who exactly our assassins were – though plainly not CIA or anything. Some rival faction if that was how it worked. I imagined Dad sitting behind a desk in a darkened room ordering murders and counting his money, life cheap and stakes high. But it didn't ring true. Not like that anyway. Asking properly, I supposed, would be asking the big question and I wouldn't be ready until I was ready. I'd told Tamsin I had food poisoning and was in hospital in Palermo. I had to say something.

'Well done on the Cairnbridge though. Sam's beside himself. How did you find that bloke? Such a weird story, isn't it?'

'Yuh huh,' I said, and hung up, pretending I felt sick. Well, to be fair, I did.

In the end it was Walter who made me do it. And I had the feeling that it was Walter who'd made me do most of this stuff. When it came down to it. We were sitting outside at the long wooden table that Eden had revarnished with his own fair hands; me, Dad, Eden and Ben. The nurse was only coming at nights now that everything was set up, to drain fluids and all sorts of other things that don't bear thinking about. I was down to about four a day. None of the terrifying raids I had been expecting had happened and we were almost relaxing into a routine, a routine that nobody was about to be admitting was just a death watch. And Walter pulled up in a Fiat that looked like a Lada with Phoebe at his side. They got out of the car as though we'd asked them up for sundowner and here they were, just on time, a bit exhausted by the drive but all ready for a good time. No mention of the raid on the villa in Sicily, the hostage taking, the escape, the aftermath.

'Ciao. Ciao. Buona Sera!' Phoebe cooed, a cigarillo in her

hand, a fuchsia kaftan sweeping the ground around her sandals and her hair scraped into a ponytail. She walked through
the gate as though the last time she'd been hadn't involved
tears, revelations and pain. I stood up and kissed her on both
cheeks as Walter swept in after her.

'Whaddyou live at the ends of the earth? What is this? A
mountain hideaway. I'm telling you, Lord Lucan's place in
Argentina is easier to find than this. You remember him?
Lord Lucan. Too pissed to kill his wife so he kills the nanny
instead? Easier to find Lord Lucan than find Faith Zanetti.
How are you the beautiful Faith Zanetti? You recovered yet?
From the news? Big big news. He lives! Hell, yes he does.
How are you doing, Karel, old chum? Good to know you got
out. They tossed us out by the roadside pretty immediately.
No need to worry about the small fry, right?' He leaned for-
wards to shake Dad's hand.

'And here IS Walt Irving,' Dad said. 'I'm not doing great
actually. As you know. Dying of cancer.'

'Ah! The big C. I heard. I heard. Annarita was breaking
the news to us all that night. Tragic. Tragic. Phoebs, you
remember Karel, right? From all that time ago? Faked his
own death. Very *Rising Damp*. Was it *Rising Damp*? No. That
other one with the same guy. Anyway, all the rage in the seventies, wasn't it?'

Phoebe, who had been warned, completely kept her composure. Except that when she had lost her composure, I
noticed, she stopped using her lavish English-accented
Italian.

She bent down and kissed my fading father on both
cheeks. 'So lovely to see you again, Karel. You haven't
changed a bit.'

Dad laughed. 'Liar!' he said. 'I've gone yellow and I
weigh five stone.'

'Well,' Phoebe said, sitting on a white wrought-iron chair just next to him. 'Apart from that.'

Speaking of yellow, there were yellowhammers in the bird feeder nailed on to the yew tree. I tried to concentrate on them. Was she going to tell him about Jessica? Did he already know? Did Walter? I shut my eyes and lifted my cowboy boots on to the table. It was time for one of my fags. Eden had gone in to fetch some alcohol. Hell, we'd be needing it. The lady next door walked past the fence and said, 'Buona Sera.' We chorused it back to her as though we were the most normal people in all the world. You know like the next-door neighbours always say, 'They were a lovely family. I never suspected a thing.' When in fact they've been dismembering corpses in there for twenty years and holding all night Satanic thingies and what have you. That was us.

Walter took his glasses off. He didn't seem remotely worried that someone might grass him up about his babe of a thirty-year-old girlfriend. But then again he never seemed remotely worried about anything much. And he was right. He needn't have been.

He touched my arm and, despite everything, I smiled and turned his way. Hey, he's good at what he does.

'So. Faith. Faith. Faith Zanetti. Are you going to do it? Are you going to step in, step up, take us where we need to go, guide us, protect us, be our shepherd. Are you? What do you say, Faith Zanetti? Is our cosa your cosa? Of course she will. She's a natural, right? Aren't you? I think so. I think you're a natural.'

I stared at him, with Ben on my knee sucking a rusk. Oh, holy shit, I thought. When I said it had dawned on me, well, not to THAT extent.

Dad turned in his chair, his back against the dusty pink wall, a lizard running to the gutter behind him.

'I haven't asked her yet, you prannet,' he said. 'We haven't discussed it.'

But now I think that Walter knew what he was up to. Because he winked at me. He was trying to tell me something. He was doing something I didn't understand, though, to be fair, I didn't understand much any more.

'Well, discuss it! Discuss it! What are you waiting for! She's great. She's a natural. She's exactly what we need. She's the answer, Karel. We've always known that. You know that. I know that. We all know that. Right? Right Faithy?'

He had never called me that before and it sent a shiver down my spine. Phoebe was quiet, drinking the Chianti that Eden had put in her hand, occasionally making funny faces at Ben, mostly looking out at the dusk creeping up the distant green mountains, listening to the village dogs bark.

And it was then that I let myself realise what I'd known since the balaclava men besieged the house. Nonno had in fact been my nonno. Carlo was my father, who'd tried to duck service and then tried to save me from mine. Or, at least, he'd tried to let me choose it, rather than it choosing me. But I'd been sent looking by Sam Fischer and Walter Irving, and now there was no escape. We all understood that. 'The people of Sicily welcome you,' the card on my flowers had said. It was a homecoming and I hadn't known it. The Bisacquino massacre had been about me. They were fighting each other for the right to get rid of me. I was Carlo's first born and I'd come home. A woman. A blonde, English woman with a baby and no husband. And a drink problem. 'Ciao, ragazzi.'

I don't even speak Italian.

So I looked at my dad's sunken face and hilarious eyes, the eyes that had always made everything funny, and I asked him. 'How did they make you come back? How did they make you leave me? You know I'd made you a welcome home card. At school. With glitter glue. I sat by the window and I counted the cars. And you didn't come.'

He reached out to take my hand as Umberto drove a tractor past loaded with logs. He waved. And we all waved back.

I didn't take his hand. I kept my hands clasped in my lap and it was Phoebe who put a hand on my shoulder.

'Cairnbridge. You must have worked it out?'

'Clever girl like you,' Walter added.

Eden put a shot of vodka in front of me and I drank it, squinting into the sun. 'Nope. Dad. I don't know any of the stuff that everyone thinks I know. From Gianluca Caprese's sister to Ihsan El Sayed. Even Evie knew you were a spy. I know NOTHING!' I shouted now and Ben started to cry. I handed him to Eden who walked him inside. The rest of us were frozen in our places like badly blocked actors on a plain black stage.

'Well. Nonno told me he'd have you killed if I didn't do the Cairnbridge job. A lot of our people in the States were at risk. A huge part of the business was going to be closed if that woofter and his friend got their information over. And we had to buy Boyd and Walter here – though you've been wonderful,' he smiled at Walter. 'And I bought the equipment off the Syrians in Malta, which was no problem. They were all planning to blow American planes up anyhow. I could have bought it anywhere. And there we were. Oh, and Sam, of course. We bought Sam Fischer. Though he's been a pain in the numbers hole ever since. Trying to get other people to break the story so he can salve his conscience. Without breaking his contract with us. But he chose you. Then he chose you. And it was all over.'

I stood up and walked over to the gate, taking hold of two of the iron spikes and leaning forwards, looking at the street

253

chapel and a plaster of Paris Mary holding her badly painted baby, so quiet and serene. I walked back, running my hands through my hair.

'You killed Captain MacDonald. He was alive when the cockpit hit the ground. Probably. The other people died when their lungs exploded after the roof was ripped off. One hostess lived. For an hour or so. There were . . .' I couldn't say it. I looked at Walter but he had his head bowed.

My father was crying. Tears were streaming into the deep crevices in his face. 'I saved a lot of other people. Our people, Faithy. You put Ihsan out of the car. You know family matters more than anything. Ben and . . .'

'Don't you fucking dare talk about Ben! Don't you talk about him! Don't you say anything about my son!' I screamed. I heard the shutters of Brandeglio being opened and closed.

'My grandson,' Dad said.

'Fuck you!' I screamed, and threw my shot glass at him. It bounced off the edge of his metal garden seat, but he had put his hands up to protect his face. To protect himself. Himself. Of course. All this to protect himself.

But then he stood up, so tall, and walked towards me. He took me in his arms and stroked my hair. And I let him. Not for my sake. Not one little bit.

'I did go to Reykjavik. Walter told me he had a friend on the flight. I must stop it. I promised I would stop it. I warned the embassies. I made the call. I did, Faithy.'

And I pulled away from him and ran towards the house, wanting to hold my baby.

'It wasn't a friend, Dad,' I said. But neither Walter nor Phoebe was looking at me. They were, however, holding hands.

*

254

I lay on the bed looking up at the beamed ceiling and I listened to Walter start yelling at my dad, words I could hardly have imagined him using. I heard Dad say, 'Put down the gun, Walter. This is a hopelessly pathetic gesture in the face of my mortality. Look at me. Would you kill me now? Think of your family.' And I heard Pheobe say, 'Pull the fucking trigger.' And I waited for the crack but it didn't come. I heard Walter's car drive away, and the nurse arrive, and Eden starting the washing up. I thought I even heard him typing. Was he really filing his column now? 'As the scent of chestnuts hangs on the late summer air, the clouds gathering round the verdant mountain, my ex-girlfriend's resurrected father avoids a half-hearted attempt on his life and admits that he murdered three hundred people a quarter of a century ago.' Hmm. That paper was going to sell like hot cakes. Ben was asleep in my arms but I felt as though I would never sleep again. Not until I went to sleep for eternity, that is. Dad, who I had heard coming slowly slowly up the stairs, pushed my door open. It was dark but I could see the shape of him. Could hear the appalling rattle.

'Fuck off,' I said, loud enough for Ben to flail his hands out.

Dad sat on the bed. 'They need you. They need guidance. You saw what Ivano's boys did. What the others are like. I'm not claiming that it has a good reputation. The films and all that crap. But it's changed since Nonno. I've changed it. We don't kill people. We've come on a lot, Faithy. Really. We run businesses and we help people out. Our people. Politics. The church.'

Our people? Hello? What? You put Berlusconi in power and get the Catholic priests to say what you want them to? Do you? Weren't Evie and I your people? How do you choose, Dad? How? I had less than zero interest in rowing about this. I just lay very very still and hoped it would soon be over.

I whispered. 'You just said you killed more than two hundred and twenty people. Personally. Seventeen were killed the other day. The businesses you're talking about are illegal. Dad. Karel. Whoever the shit you are. Prostitution, money laundering, drug trafficking and art theft are illegal. I remember when your Vermeer got snatched.'

He laughed. No. He did. And then coughed.

'You're talking about the Russians. We do property nowadays, mostly. I bought that painting at Christies in New York.'

'On one of the days when I was missing you.'

He didn't say anything. His lungs crackled horribly. 'Grim fucking reaper,' he said.

'You introduced him to a lot of people. Children.'

Your own daughter. Though I already knew he didn't care much about those. Not in a real sense. 'Family' to him meant something different from changing nappies and going to parents' evening, watching the school play and coming ice skating. It's like Communism. To Russians it means something totally different to what it means in English. To us it's the ultra left wing. To them it's theft, corruption, lies and murder. I could hear the old lady's television and wished I was anywhere but here.

'I didn't murder them, Faith. If I hadn't set it up he'd have had someone else do it.'

My throat was closing up.

'Yup. Lot of concentration camp commanders you could talk to about that,' I said.

'Faith,' he said. 'You go and live at the house, OK? Take Eden and the baby. You'll have a nice life. I'm leaving you everything. People call. They ask for advice on the businesses. You're a clever girl. You will stop the bloodshed. You will be able to keep the peace. Faith. I'm walking through the vale of the shadow of death. And I fear ill.'

Ah. Hymns. Yes. Well, I can see how they help. I'd always liked 'And then the night of weeping shall be a morn of song'.

Except the night of weeping just seemed to go on and on and on.

I suppose he must have left to reconnect himself to his machines and, when Eden came in hours later to tell me that Walter and Phoebe had died in a car crash at the bottom of our hill, it felt as though no time had passed at all.

Chapter Twenty-three

I think I had slept and in my sleep decisions were taken. Decisions that put Ben first. And perhaps even Eden. I tied the scared, precocious and dazzling little girl who had had the life knocked out of her to a chair bound and gagged. And she could stay there. I thought I'd grown up fast, but I realised that night that I hadn't grown up at all. Not until now.

Basically, what I did was I sent Eden and Ben to my flat in London. I felt like a human anvil now. Nothing could touch me. The death watch could be done by me alone. I wasn't even going to have any nightmares any more. The fears that had lurked in me had all been realised and it was liberating. Strange how having this pseudo family had freed me to bind so strongly to my real one. I didn't mind now that Eden wanted me to think of this house as mine too. I did, of course. Always had really. I mean, what did he think for goodness' sake?

And, naturally, for I was 'involved' now, it didn't cross my mind that Walter's death had been an accident. Though I had no clue what it was he'd done. Snuck out and clipped the brake cables? Made a call? But without proof or admission it could be written off as a tragedy for all those concerned. I didn't begin to understand this business, and all the films Dad obviously so despised and that I had thought were so ridiculous when Tamsin was on about using them for Bisacquino were, it turned out, genuinely my only source of reference. That and the televised funerals of the Bisacquino boys. They buried the two factions on the same day, some in Prizzi, some in Corleone, parading down the alleyways of the white baked graveyards flanked by black horses and women in black lace veils. Men with their hands clamped to their black hearts, or, at least, their fags.

I drove Ben and Eden to Pisa and watched them go through departures with all the normal people who held hands and bickered and sighed and complained about the speed of airport procedures in general.

'Excuse me, I think I was here first!' and 'God, you'd think they could manage to have more than one person on check-in!' and 'I told you to put the nappies in the rucksack!' All English, obviously. Italians complain differently. They're looking for results rather than just voicing discontent. The British are discontent masters. But I envied every single one of them. Did we look a bit like them maybe? Eden in his Italian get-up, holding the baby who wore stripy dungarees and shoes that we called sheepy padders – woolly slippers with a sheep on them. Me kissing Ben goodbye like mad, holding his little hands and putting them on my cheeks. And I probably had a tan from sitting out in front of the house with Dad, reading him Trollope. No, seriously. He asked me. *The Warden*. What can I tell you?

I think it was while I was reading to Dad, who smoked and drank dark coffee made on the stove with the Bialetti thing, that I first noticed my marine, walking past with a combat hat on like all the other mushroom pickers, carrying a basket with ferns on the top and a branch to beat the flies away. And when I was sure, when I knew I'd seen him, and he'd gone up the track and back down again and up again, without sitting to have lunch in the shade with a bottle of red wine, bread and salami, I started seeing others. There was someone on the roof of Piorina's house next door. At first I really thought he was working up there so high, carrying tiles. But he wasn't busy enough and he watched too much. And there was his not very well hidden gun, of course. And the blokes who were supposed to be building the house opposite. They were all heavily armed too.

And I waited, wondering, hanging sheets out, picking plums, looking out, but they didn't attack. And nor did anybody else. I made us gnocchi pesto with the basil from the garden, though Dad had stopped eating really. 'What's the bleeding point?' And I made damson jam (brava!), boiling the bright purple things in an enormous vat, decanting them into jars with greaseproof paper on top and labelling them with stickers. Eden would have been proud of me. Would have written a column about it. And I started to miss him. Not just Ben, whose absence was a constant ache, but Eden. And his strange calm presence not demanding anything, just offering.

I was sticking a label on to a pot of my home made jam (man alive) and finally allowing myself to notice that we were surrounded, when Dad began to really deteriorate. The fruit and vegetable van had done its weekly visit to the village, the man calling out the window on his megaphone, 'Apples! Mandarins!' as though he were advertising a bearded lady and flea circus, and Dad seemed to sort of sink. I wasn't going to walk at Kenwood with him again, or go for tea at Serendipity in New York and eat ice-cream sundaes as big as a dog. It is simply incredible that we don't let go of dead people. However incontrovertible the facts. Not really. And yet, we wouldn't do any of the things I finally admitted I'd longed to do. Partly because he was dying again, but partly because I wasn't the person who wanted to any longer. He wasn't the man I'd hoped in a tiny secret part of myself that I might one day by some bizarre miracle see again, and I wasn't the little girl he'd recognise if I did. He wasn't even interested really in the photo albums or videos. He just wanted to smoke and to listen to me read. And it was that day that the blood started coming up, the day I saw snow on top of the mountains at Abetone, and that I went to talk to them. I'd seen a fox by the apple tree.

I stopped my marine on the track near our car parking space under the hazelnut tree that's entwined with a bay.

'Hey! Scott!' I said.

'Buongiorno, Signora,' he said.

'Yeah. Seriously though. You know he's dying, don't you? You won't do anything? Please don't do anything. There's no point. He'll be dead by the weekend. The nurse says.'

She had said that, but I had ignored her. Now I knew it was true. He was pressing his morphine button more and more and was awake less and less. There was hardly any body left to live in anyway.

Scott, or whatever his name may have been, nodded.

'Thank you,' I said.

After that I kept hearing gunshots in the forest but it might have been the wild boar season starting. Or it might have been these Americans protecting us from the Italians. Because they must know where we were by now. Or perhaps, when they had us so briefly last time, they realised he really was toast and that I was hardly a realistic or, indeed, willing prospect.

There was a procession round the village the night my dad died. The church bells rang for half an hour, clanging and

261

echoing around the mountains, heard, they say, even an hour and a half away in the ski resort at Abetone. When the sky darkened there was a church service and then everyone held candles, protected by coloured paper and paraded, singing psalms, round all the little chapels in the village. Nightlights in red plastic cups were put out on all the window ledges and lamps put outside, their cords straining to reach. The crosses from church were carried, raised on a makeshift wooden altar, by Carolina's boys who wore white robes over their tight jeans. The last stop in the humming candlelit procession was our chapel, our virgin. Dad, who was sitting outside in his chair with his eyes closed, bats circling the porch light, crossed himself. I'm sure. I nodded and smiled and felt like they all looked at me with sympathy, even the really old people with thick ankles and sunken eyes, knowing that the time had come. Funny in a way, that one sees these things on television so often, relics of another world, a superstitious people who can't rely on harvests or social services, who throw themselves at the mercy of volatile gods – but this time, in this procession, I knew half of them personally. Bought honey and cheese off them, borrowed their strimmers and lent my (well, Eden's) pizza oven for parties when they'd all come into the garden to cook, our oven being the oldest and best in the village. I waved and nodded and then I took Dad inside.

And this time. This time I was holding his hand when he died. People often said to me that they thought it was better to go suddenly, shot in the chest in a Belfast alley and nothing to worry about. But I'd always felt cheated and I thought he'd been cheated too (silly me). I thought anyone would want to say goodbye, to see the adored faces and the shadow of the leaves on the hospital walls and to hear some poems and that last Ave Maria. So this time I said, 'I love you.' I think he smiled. And I meant it in some ways. At least, I was saying it to the man who'd died the last time, the time when I never got to say it. To the guy who'd bought me 'normous dolly and who'd played silly mountain and shown me how to crack lobster even though he'd had no idea himself. This here bloke? Well, I barely knew him. And perhaps he wasn't that nice. Charismatic. Funny. Sure. But there was evidence against him as fantasy dream man. Though maybe there always had been.

There was blood all over the floor where he'd vomited it up and it had been ages since he'd spoken, though I'd carried on reading. '"The roof is high-pitched, and of black old oak, and the three large beams which support it run down to the side walls, and terminate in grotesquely carved faces – two devils and an angel on one side, two angels and a devil on the other".' His chest had rattled and wheezed and he had been doubled up in pain as it came. But when it stopped he was still and peaceful and whatever it was that had been doing this to him had left. And he'd left too. The man who broke the filters off his cigarettes and loved HP Sauce and gin martinis. I took the drip out of his arm and climbed on to the bed, lying my head on his shoulder and holding his hand.

'Bye,' I whispered. 'Sleep well.'

I shut my eyes but they were hardly closed for a second before my marine and all his friends burst in, flashing their weapons and their ID cards. I say burst in. The door was open. It always is up here. The insurance company would only let Eden insure against forest fires, he said. There is no crime. Well, I thought, not yet.

'What did he tell you about Cairnbridge?' my marine asked, straight off, standing in a swagger by Dad's bedroom door, his gun reflecting in an old brass samovar, his mushrooming get-up tossed aside.

I thought about this. And I looked over at Dad, the shrivelled yellow shell of him. And I looked at the men who were all over the house like cockroaches and I thought about the triplets and Ben and what I'd decided and I said, 'Nothing. Why?'

I stuck to this story. I stuck to it for twenty-four gruelling hours while they sealed the house and wouldn't even let me call a funeral director or the embassy. The blood on the bedroom floor stank.

But eventually, when I'd sworn I had no new story to file and that I was on sick leave – about a billion times I said it, until I was hoarse – they disappeared as quickly as they'd arrived, just melting into the hills. Maybe they believed me. Maybe they were relieved that the agent who double-crossed them for the Mafia and murdered two of their best men was dead and gone. And maybe they couldn't have cared less.

I shipped the body back to London. It wasn't fun. The Italian 'systems' are very Soviet. Everything in triplicate, bribes for every Tomaso, Ricardo and Haroldo, all complicated by his lack of a passport and a total lack of proof that he was British. Hey, guess what I did in the end? I called Gabi in New York. A passport arrived at the British Embassy in Rome the next day. As did the corpse's official permission to travel. 'Why didn't you ask me, sister? You just needed to phone Gianni in Roma. Stupida!' I laughed. Che stupida. Of course. Gianni in Rome. How could I not have known? That old chestnut again. How could I not have known? Well, I just didn't, OK?

The funeral was at St Mary's in Hampstead. Again. No, seriously. But this time it was for Carlo Zanetti and nobody asked any questions so nobody got any answers. Different priest, and, in any case, it's not as if they check through the records to see if they've in fact performed this funeral before. It can't possibly crop up much. And this time the church was only half full. I didn't wear black. I wore jeans, a T-shirt and a new leather jacket I bought at Schott. I wasn't going to wear his any more. I also had my hair down with a diamante clip in it, my new locket on and a new pair of cowboy boots. But these ones are not black, they are brown. So there. I brought Ben in his pushchair and his dungarees and Eden came too, looking semi-normal in dark blue linen (I banned all those Italian pastels). We sang 'The Lord's My Shepherd' again. We sang 'Jerusalem' again. And we sang 'To Be a Pilgrim'. Again. But I didn't climb into the pulpit to read in a sad black dress and a small lost voice. And Evie wore a red silk cocktail dress and smoked throughout, occasionally humming to herself. I think it might have been 'Wake Me Up Before You Go Go'. She laughed when the priest entrusted Carlo Zanetti's soul to Heaven. It would have been funny were it not for Annarita at the front, in a black mini dress and a tiny hat with a veil. She shook with sobs from beginning to end, crossing herself increasingly frantically.

Even afterwards in Villa Bianca (Evie refused to come) where we all sat down for calves liver and spinach.

In church the triplets kept their arms round each other's besuited shoulders but didn't flinch. Well, they were the Zanetti boys. Pip had agreed to read on my behalf and he held the lectern so as not to shake too much, but in the end he just shook the lectern. He looked better though. Indeed, at the restaurant he started being quite a comfort to Annarita. He'd got to know her at the Irving double funeral in Grossetto while Dad was dying.

'There is a time to live and a time to die,' he read. Puh. This distinction seemed to have got a trifle blurred if you asked me.

265

I mean, what time? When? Don, who was at the back, kept calling out things like, 'Yes, Lord!' as though he was at some kind of Pentacostalist gig. He was very very drunk. Ira had kicked him out again and he'd been sitting in a chair at the Frontline Club for more than a week now. Still, he wouldn't miss a good funeral for the world. He'd even brought Ihsan along to make me feel uncomfortable. Well, to help get him in and out of the taxi, he claimed. It was true, he'd put a lot of weight on. But I thought he had other motives.

Last time it had been a tragedy. Last time the coffin was draped in flowers and women wept audibly, the church singing with their sobs. Last time we had a choir and had to open the balcony to contain everyone, like Midnight Mass. Last time I had known it was the end of the world and it was. Even when Ben was born my first thought had been how sad that Dad would never know him. But Dad had known him, briefly. And it was no great shakes. 'In pastures green he leadeth me, the quiet waters by.'

Well, I hoped He would lead him by them. However much of a bastard he might have been. He was my dad. I hugged the triplets tightly one by one, still not sure who was who. But who cared? Davide promised to grow a beard to help me out. Ruben said he'd slash his face but this seemed a tad excessive.

In Villa Bianca Ihsan sat on the other side of me from Annarita, elbowing people out of the way to get the seat. Flicking his starched napkin out over his thin knees. I looked at him, stunned.

'Why are you here? Why are you speaking to me? Sitting near me?'

He didn't raise his eyes from the olive crostini. 'Because I forgive you. I think you are being brainwashed and I want to help you,' he said.

'Right!' I laughed, throwing my head back.

He hissed at me. 'You are going to run this story, right? Seriously? Faith? You are going to run this?'

I was shocked. I'd thrown my phone away in the woods in Brandeglio and had pretty much forgotten that I'd ever worked for a newspaper. I lit a cigarette and drank my champagne in one gulp. I mean, I'd been through a lot here.

'What?' I said, refusing Eden's offer of Ben for my lap because of my fag. He rolled his eyes, exasperated. Don was shooting as though we were a wedding party, always entirely sober the second the camera viewer came into contact with the surrounds of his eyes.

'What you found out? What he told you? You are going to run with it? Put it in the twenty-fifth anniversary edition? You know Sam Fischer's disappeared?'

He looked almost pleased with himself. He touched my hand and it made me think about sex. But that was just so that I didn't have to digest what he'd said.

'You're joking?' I said, though I knew Ihsan had never knowingly joked.

'Ha ha,' he said, blankly.

'Oh God,' I sighed, putting my head in my hands. 'Oh God. Has Tamsin gone too?'

'No. She's acting editor. By the way, you look good in lipstick.'

'Whole new me,' I said, and got out of my seat. I suppose I was on my way to call Tamsin. Annarita was still crying but Pip was being a tower of strength. I winked at him and he raised his middle finger at me. His other hand was on Annarita's knee. Well, let's face it. Upper thigh.

I walked towards the door, holding my refilled glass and my cigarette, thinking how pretty the flowers looked cascading down from the balcony when Ruben, or was it Gabi, got up and took me round the waist. A pianist played 'O Sole Mio' from the corner and Ruben, I'm sure it was, started to dance me round the tables. 'It's now or never, Faithy,' he said. I realised that Elvis's 'Now or Never' is to the tune of 'O Sole Mio'.

'What is, half-brother, dear?' I said, looking into his green eyes as he looked into mine. We both laughed at the strange trans-gender mirror.

'Come back with us, Faith. You're the eldest. You've got to help us keep the peace. Otherwise the killing will never end. Only you can do it. Come back with us! Sorella bella.'

I stopped dancing and put my glass down on Don's table. I took a deep drag of my cigarette and looked over at Ben.

'Ruben . . .'

'Gabi!'

'Gabi. I have a son. I'm a reporter from London. This is your world, it's not mine.'

'It's yours now, Faithy. We need you. We always knew you'd come. Ordinary Sicilians need you. We all do.'

I laughed. This was just unbelievable. Or, it would have been if he hadn't then said, 'Nobody wants to do what Nonno did to Carlo to bring him home. But we can. If we have to. You're family, Faithy. Come home.'

And I didn't go outside to call Tamsin. I went back and sat next to Ihsan. 'And if I don't?' I asked him, glancing down at the burnt hands that had touched me as a waiter bent to fill my glass again. 'If I don't run the story?'

'Then you are a coward and a traitor,' he said. Al Jazeera talking. So high-minded this lot.

'Well, we always knew that,' I smiled, but he didn't smile back. People with morals don't have much of a sense of humour. Is that true? I think so.

'If you don't run it, I will,' he said, letting his smoke slide out of his mouth before sucking it back in again. Oooh. I am a fool for that.

'You don't have it, El Sayed. You don't have it. And anyway,' I added, turning nasty, 'nobody will take any notice.'

He stood up and I stood with him, glowering into his eyes. 'Nobody, meaning the English and the Americans? You arrogant bitch,' he said and he spat in my face. Pip, Don, Eden, Ruben, Gabi and Davide all stood up to defend me and attack Ihsan, dotted about in the restaurant's dappled light, coiled, poised, all willing to do violence on my behalf. And it felt powerful. I felt powerful. I held my hand up to stop them and they obeyed, sitting back down. I picked up a napkin and wiped the spit off my cheek. I gestured Ihsan to the door and he obeyed, leaving. So, it was true.

I sat down and Annarita, feeling that a decision had been made, kissed me on the cheek. The pianist carried on playing 'O Sole Mio' and all the mourners, such as they were, clapped. The old man and his young wife from the Sicily dinner were there, and some loud New Yorkers who kept shaking my hand vigorously and calling me Donna Vera. Oh please. Maybe, I thought. Maybe it is all about family, however disparate and broken, whether it's wrong or right. I mean, isn't it?

Chapter Twenty-four

It was hard to find. They have built new houses where the old ones once were. A little estate with clusters of little homes, two cars in the drive, net curtains in the windows. And it was cold up here, raining sharply, lashing our faces as we traipsed round the tiny village. We'd booked into the pub, The White Bear, where we got a room opposite the bathroom that had a photo of Los Angeles framed on the wall, though the view out of the windows was of green hills shrouded in cloud. It was one of those places where there's nothing to eat that wasn't packed up and frozen years ago. Strange, when lambs gambol deliciously about the fields and the whole of nature seems so lush, to be served a Findus crispy pancake. But a lot of Britain is like that, I suppose.

I had a cranberry juice and fizzy water at the bar (I needed my wits about me now, avoiding getting murdered and all – though it was easier than it seemed in the end, once I'd settled things down), sitting on a round, high red leather stool, chewing on my Nicorette and rapping my fingers on the table just like my dad used to, until Eden told me to stop.

'Sorry,' I said.

'We should ask someone.'

'No. I don't want to,' I said. 'They probably don't like talking about it. Anyway, I want to find it by myself.'

'Shall we call Kristy before we go?' he worried.

'No. They're fine. We'll be back tomorrow anyway. In any case, it's not as if Annarita and Pip aren't there to help. They're not idiots, you know.'

'They are.'

'Well. OK, they are. But he's nearly two. Not a baby any more.'

'You have not a shred of maternal instinct in you, Mrs Jones,' he said.

Oooh. He'd got nasty.

'I didn't take your scabby name. OK? Didn't want it, won't have it. Fuck off.'

'God doesn't share your view,' Eden smiled, slooshing his brandy around in its not very clean-looking glass.

'God does not give a toss what name I chose to take. Anyway, shalom? It was a register office so fuck off more.'

'Whatever,' Eden shrugged.

Oh, all right, all right. I did it. On the Farringdon Road. I'd had that grey silk dress from the house in Palermo cleaned and it came up OK. Not the shoes though. I wore my boots. No, it didn't look as bad as it sounds because my hair balances it out. My brothers all brought dates. Two of them were from Sicily, girls they'd been seeing for ages. Davide brought Angelica whom he'd met at the Camden Palace and whose Mum played some minor part in *The Archers*. She was studying psychoanalysis at the Tavistock Clinic. I avoided talking to her but I imagined her 'finding out' like that film where Hugh Grant is trying to marry some New York Mafioso. But that's a film and I know now that it's nothing like that. Well, apart from the 'finding out' process because people always panic and think about the films.

Eden took my hand and looked me in the eyes. For a bit too long.

'Look, Jones. I told you before. I didn't get the job. OK? Trust me. I was interviewed, I'm not denying it. But I didn't get the job. It's just the house. And a bit of consulting for the family. Don't worry. I think it's one of Ivano's boys . . .' I said vaguely. 'We've gone straight. OK. Don't worry about it. Stop already.' For the billionth time he nodded, accepting. Needing constant reassurance.

We were about to leave and pootle about in the dark when we got distracted by the television. There were a couple of blokes drinking pints listlessly by a fruit machine and a TV on one of those strange corner brackets. The news had already been on for ages but they were showing a photo on the full screen in the kind of way they only do when the person is dead. It was Ihsan.

'Hey! Could you turn that up?' Eden shouted to Mrs MacIntyre, who shrugged and aimed her weapon at the box, scratching at the area in her bra underwiring that was clearly bothering her.

'The head, found by the roadside about five kilometres outside Kandahar, has been positively identified as that of Ihsan El Sayed, the Al Jazeera correspondent kidnapped from his hotel room three weeks ago . . .'

Mrs MacIntyre screwed up her face in distaste, not at the horrors of the world but at the revoltingness of having the ways of these barbarians thrust upon her, and Eden bowed his head as though in great appreciation of his ability to do so.

'Did you sleep with him that time?' he asked, not looking at me. Something had changed in Eden. Something that asked and minded rather than making a barbed little scratch of a joke.

I sucked an ice cube out of my glass and crunched it between my back teeth.

'Yes,' I said. 'Dad didn't like him.'

Eden finished his brandy. 'Apparently not,' he muttered. I wasn't sure if he was joking or not, but I didn't chase it. And then he said, louder, 'Christ. I wonder how his wife's feeling.'

At this I looked up, though not into his face, more at the banks of upside-down spirit bottles behind the bar.

'He said he didn't have a wife,' I wondered, quietly, knowing perfectly well that this was yet a fucking nother thing that people would be unable to believe I didn't know.

'Huh. Well, he would've. In Damascus. Kids too.'

It figured. Of course it did. And who was I to judge him? I mean, especially now.

We were somber on our shadowy walk, arm in arm, the only people on the wet streets, the orange street lamps reflected in the splash of grey pavement.

'Maybe here?' I said, seeing some kind of memorial, an obelisk thing in the middle of a small deserted roundabout. But it was a war memorial it turned out. 'To the Cairnbridge men and women who gave their lives . . .'

Eventually, we turned a corner into a street with an old church at the end of it. A grey Norman thing, it looked like, incongruous in these surroundings, the churchyard scattered with lopsided gravestones but the huge black arched door open, candlelight inside.

'Oh come on. It's better than nothing,' I said, and tugged Eden in where it was colder than out in the elements. The cross on the altar glowed gold and the tiny stubs of candles flickered in the gust of air we had perhaps brought in with us.

'If not me, who?' I said, quietly.

'What?' Eden whispered, as we sat down in the back pew, still holding on to each other.

'If not me, who? If not me, you.'

I wanted to kneel down but I felt a fraud, with only my child's secret prayer as a credential.

'Is that Talmudic? Wrong venue, Faith. If not now, when? Right?'

'Yes,' I said. 'If not now, when?'

And so I left Eden staring towards the front of the church, his arms wrapped round himself against the cold and I went towards the banks of candle ends, put my pound clunking into the black box and took a new one out, lighting it and positioning it, somehow ostentatiously long against the ones placed earlier in the day, on the stand under a slightly lurid painting of Christ. And then I put my hand in my jacket pocket and took my note out, unfolding it for a last read.

'To the beautiful dimply little girl in the stripy jumper. From her big sister! Wait for me, Jessie! I won't be long now. With so many hugs and kisses from Faith. You'll know me by my silly hair. XXXXX.'

I folded it back up and put it behind the criss-crossed elastic of the noticeboard by the candles, with the other messages. I had meant to put it under a rock or by the memorial I'd hoped was here for them all, but we hadn't been able to find anything in Cairnbridge. It's probably something they'd all rather forget. And anyway, it's twenty-five years ago now. My piece ran last week. About finding the Reykjavik warning. But nobody's yet found Sam Fischer. And, to be honest as poor old Walt would hate me to be, I don't think anybody ever will. Tamsin Godwin – Britain's first female broadsheet editor. And, hell, she deserves it. What with Camillagate and what have you.

I sat down again next to Eden and leaned against his shoulder.

'I've got you, Faithy,' he said, trying to be reassuring and manly.

I elbowed him in the ribs. 'Don't be ludicrous, Jones. I've got YOU. Come on, let's go home.'

'Yes,' he said. 'What time's our flight?'

'We'll get to Heathrow by midnight and I think we're connecting straight to Pisa. But there's no way I'm going back to Sicily until the weekend. Pip and Annarita claim to be staying in Brandeglio until Feragosto. The boys can manage until then, don't you think?'

'I would say so,' Eden nodded, kissing me on the cheek. 'I would say so.'

And as we were about to walk out into the rain and back to the pub for our bags, I turned and looked back at the altar, thinking about Captain MacDonald and his thumb, about Perry Boyd, poor heroin dealing Gianluca Caprese, Walter, Phoebe, my mum and dad and now Ihsan too and his smell of lemons and his sweet kisses. And I started muttering to myself, 'Dear God, please keep everyone perfectly perfectly safe, in the whole of this evening, the whole of tonight and the whole of tomorrow . . .' Because after all, it's all any of us can do in the end. Pray.